SAPPHIRE

A Murder for Your Thoughts

A Josh Decker Novel
by

Paul Jannereth

Edited by
Cassidy Fitzpatrick

Cover Art by
Sarah Simmons

by the sea

TM

Publications

For more information about the author visit
www.facebook.com/bytheseapublications

By the sea Publications
Copyright ©2018 by Paul Jannereth

Two friends, Parker and Philip, were lost during the writing of this book. They are gently remembered within these pages...

"Go in peace and do no harm."

SAPPHIRE
A Murder for Your Thoughts

1 – Vienna (30 years ago)

He placed the little girl on his lap. He then gently poured an array of gemstones from a small silk bag onto a black cloth.

"Oh Daddy! This one is so pretty!" she said as her eyes immediately fixated on one of the stones near the center. She reached out and gently touched it.

"Some say stones like these can manipulate energy. Control moods. Bring good fortune, or ruin." She touched and turned various stones, amazed at their sparkle, color, and shape, as he continued – talking more to himself than to her.

"The ancients believed in magic to explain the inexplicable. Cuneiform tablets tell of stones they believed facilitated conception, birth, even love and hate. Can you imagine the power to fall in love, captured within the glittering stone? What is more powerful than love? Perhaps envy. Envy of another who has love can drive someone to hate, and destroy."

"Like this one!" the little girl innocently held a stone up to his face. She wasn't really listening, too young to understand all he was saying. He smiled as she placed it in his hand.

"No, no. That's topaz. Topaz is said to calm the soul, and ease the troubled mind."

"This one?" she again held a stone to him.

"Emerald. A new beginning, green and living like springtime."

"And this one?" she asked.

"Amber. They believed these are the crystalized tears of those who grieve from loss."

"What does the white one do?" she asked, pointing to a large, sparkling gem.

"That's diamond. The strongest stone in the world. Strength, power, and longevity. A rulers' stone. Complete dominance and power over others. But a few diamonds are said to be cursed. Some say they are the source of sin and sorrow. The 'Hope' diamond brought fear and misery to those who possessed it. They are bought and sold, stolen, and the source of countless bouts of jealousy and rage – like an heirloom that tears families apart. It's cold, emotionless. And yet so much emotion has been projected onto them by humans. For what?

"Daddy, this one is my real favorite," she said pointing to the one she had first fixated upon.

"That's my girl! That one is a very special stone. It brings clarity to our thoughts. It is said to tap the power of the 'Third Eye', the mind. From this clarity of thought comes the influence of spirit and soul – and harmony in life." He took the stone and held it up and slowly turned it into the light. A kaleidoscope of light fell onto their eyes as it passed through its rich blue color and elegant oval shape.

"The stone itself holds no power. But powerful people possess them. Affixed into the crown of a ruler, upon his scepter, or hanging around a woman's neck as an emblem to the power she commands over others. It is the stone of destiny. It was said to be able to interpret ancient oracles, and attract wealth and protection. It is the gemstone that can facilitate the untapped potential of the most personal, private, secret world of all – the mind."

"What is it called?" she asked.

"They say, 'If on your hand this stone you bind, you in Taurus born will find, 'twill cure diseases of the mind.' It's called the Sapphire."

2 – Chicago

A tall, gaunt looking man rose and took his place at the podium in front of an audience of industry professionals, financial hopefuls, and potential investors. They were a proverbial who's who of the national and international medical industry led by pharmaceutical companies, tech companies, medical associations, hospital conglomerates, and military officials. Twelve years prior, the man at the podium, Dr. Eugene Sullivan, had become a noted Neuroscientist working with several pharmaceutical companies on new drug combinations that would ease various sleeping disorders. The conference featured a number of speakers and workshops, but everyone was most interested in Dr. Sullivan and his over thirty years of research and acquired expertise. For not only was his work controversial, he was also known for being a mysterious recluse.

"Thirty seconds!" Dr. Sullivan shouted into the microphone, stunning the audience. The image of the man hardly suggested such a strong and determined voice. The room shuttered with a buzz of anxiousness before settling quickly down into silence. Sullivan waited. Starring off into space, with beads of sweat beginning to form on his large forehead above his slightly quivering lips. The silence soon became uncomfortable. It was a purposeful demonstration of just how long thirty seconds was. He placed a pair of thin gold wire rimmed glasses far down on his nose. Finally, he broke the silence in a calming, yet authoritative tone – his voice rather sharp and nasal. Looking intensely down at his notes he went on.

"Thirty seconds," he said. "A man named Languille had just had his head removed by the razor sharp blade of the Guillotine. It was June 28, 1905. He was woken early and moved into position at precisely 5:30." He looked up at the audience and continued in a softer, light-hearted tone, "There is no account of how well Mr. Languille slept the night prior." The audience chuckled. He looked back down and continued.

"Languille was a murderer whose death now became an experiment for Dr. Gabriel Beaurieux who wanted to learn how long a severed head was aware of its plight. Blood had spilled like a large bucket of hot, dark red water, causing steam to rise from the cold concrete floor where the head had toppled and sat upright. His shoes stepped through the warm, steamy blood and he bent down onto his hands and knees to observe Languille ever so closely." The audience, especially the more sophisticated women, began to feel sick. Several caught themselves looking down onto their recently consumed desert, cherry pie, the remnants of which produced pools and streaks of dark red filling on their desert plates and forks. Several covered them with napkins as others held their stomachs due to queasiness.

"The doctor carefully observed the executed man's face," Sullivan continued. "The nerves having been severed, Languille's facial muscles contorted here and there for several seconds until finally they relaxed and his eyelids gently came to rest." Then very loudly and sharply Dr. Beaurieux shouted, "Languille!" The audience once again shuttered at the unexpected volume, the microphone projecting a bit of feedback in the form of a short piercing tone. "And after he had called to him, those seemingly dead eyes slowly opened and gazed toward the scientist. Languille's pupils dilated and fixed themselves upon him. *There was life!* Lingering life, looking back onto our world if only for a moment longer. Then slowly they relaxed and closed again."

"Twenty seconds had passed and, 'Languille!'" the doctor shouted once more. "And once again, the man's eye lids slowly opened. And he gazed alive! Alive but hopeless. His pupils fixed themselves and looked into the Doctor's own living eyes. It was one last glance at the world – of life. A world where every breath is taken for granted. Every heart beat ignored until one day when it can no longer cope. This is the science of life, and science is cold, it is hard, and it is unyielding.

"My friends, we have such little time to live. Such little time to be inspired. Such little time to waste. And yet waste it we do. Until that everlasting sleep finally touches us all. No one escapes this predator. Elude him you may, but escape has never been successful before. That is, until now."

The members of the audience seemed spell bound.

"Until now we have accepted the concept of a single life. And humans have been torturous creatures in order to rob others from that precious state of existence. From Dark Age trials by ordeal where a man's hand was thrusted into boiling water to determine guilt or innocence, to a myriad of horrendous executions such as drawing and quartering, impaling, or even nailing him to a cross! Or severing his head from his body and giving him only thirty more seconds of utter terror and hopelessness. But then reason was rediscovered. Science and reason, applied to save lives and enhance the quality of life for all. This reason was used to determine our sense of justice, and our sense of morality and push the boundaries of new frontiers! Medically speaking we now routinely transplant the human heart, allowing thousands of people a second chance. Now we transplant many vital organs and look to do even more. Liver transplants, lung transplants, hair transplants, even face transplants! And yet they laugh at the idea of head transplants. They also once laughed at Columbus, and the man on the moon. But today is different. A new frontier has been reached. Already my research has made significant progress in restoring memories in Alzheimer's patients. But why settle for baby steps when our time calls for giant leaps!"

"We are the product of that age of humanism. And the torch is now passed to us. Ladies and gentlemen, we need no longer confine ourselves to blind faith. We have the tools and the power to transpose the human mind into an entirely new existence. To overcome the last of nature's hurdles and live forever in tandem with our own minds transplanted into a system that allows us to be young, to be healthy, and live life again and again and again. Death will become a welcome exchange, like trading in a new vehicle. My friends, we are at the beginning of the end of humanism and barbarism! As I introduce to you the idea of the world's first ever transplant of the human mind. The storage of memories similar to saving a file on a computer will preserve the human mind and create a blueprint of everlasting life. And I now announce to you here tonight, that through my research this vision of a more perfect existence is finally within our grasp."

"What a bunch of bullshit," Paul Thomas exclaimed to the others seated at his table as Dr. Sullivan continued to present his theories about advanced cybernetic technology. "Sounds more to me like some fascist science fiction than anything close to real science." He stood up and left the table. Kristina had been unable to take her eyes off of Paul throughout the evening. She worked as a receptionist for Nexus Pharmaceutical, a global company with offices in downtown Chicago. Paul worked there as well and was one of their top sales representatives. He was on the fast track, climbing the corporate ladder and Kristina had been infatuated with him since her first day on the job. She arrived every day to work with him on her mind, with the hope of one day wearing his ring on her finger.

Twenty two years old and very attractive, she was what every office would desire as their company's first visual impression. Her main interest in the convention was not science, or neurology, but rather getting Paul's attention. They had flirted in the office many times and over the past several weeks had begun a promising and, so far, innocent relationship. A few weeks prior he had stopped by the receptionist desk and asked her if she'd be attending the conference, looking forward to the opportunity to mix business with pleasure.

"Well, I don't think they take along the receptionists to those things, do they?" she had asked.

"No, but what if I took you as my guest?" Paul answered with a flirtatiously raised eyebrow and smile. He had just turned thirty, knew his business well, and it showed, especially when it came to a beautiful young woman.

"In that case," Kristina smiled adoringly, looking up at him from her desk with her deep blue eyes, "I wouldn't miss it." They had been talking and walking the convention all day and had made their seat at the same table as Anita Reynolds.

A beautiful, slim blonde in her mid-thirties, Anita turned heads whenever she walked into a room, or down the street. She was a competitor of Paul's and had a reputation for being aggressive and cut throat when it came to sales. Paul was an excellent salesman and as such she viewed him with great disdain. Moreover, she had grown increasingly annoyed at how he was, in her mind, working over Kristina. 'He'll do whatever it takes to get into her pants, like he would to secure a sale' she thought. A practice she knew all too well, although Anita's flirting typically stopped short of much more than drinks, attentive petting, and allowing her clients to imagine more was always possible. She seemed acutely aware of this power in herself, and had practiced focusing her most lavish attention onto those who could help her advance her career the most. Otherwise, looks alone were as much as she'd allow men to access. But to see it from the outside looking in it seemed so obvious to her, and she disliked Paul's arrogance and cunning in any event. Once he left, she quickly turned her attention back to Dr. Sullivan. And as she gazed up at the good doctor delivering his morbid monologue, her face gleamed with opportunity.

"'To sleep, per chance to dream,' such as the poet once said," Dr. Sullivan concluded. "We dream with our eyes wide open, and yet never see what is right there in front of us. An opportunity. A revolution. A brave new world meant for only those daring enough to see it! Let us not waste another moment, another heartbeat, another breath! Let us not gaze sadly back onto this world as it slowly slips away. For the awareness lingers for only thirty... little... seconds. Thirty seconds to ponder that we had so much more for which to live."

The room fell silent, then into thunderous applause. Anita was first to her feet, and the last to stop clapping.

3 – Highland

The "Dream Catcher" gently pulled up anchor and slipped quietly out into the channel, making her way into Lake Michigan. A bit of fog had kept her at bay for hours on the cool, crisp autumn day. Another summer season had come and gone and one by one the short term residents of means began making their way out of the small coastal town of Highland, Michigan, to return home. The town of Highland was sleepy in the winter and restful in the summer, despite the visitors from nearby cities. For almost a hundred years it has served as a welcome escape from the stifling summer heat of Chicago and St. Louis. Some drove, others took the Pier Marquette line out of Chicago's Union Station. But most vacationers made the trip by boat, a time honored tradition. The downtown was typical Midwest in style and friendliness. A small village square lined with strips of one and two story buildings with brick facades; mainly seasonal shops and a couple of bars. Most residents enjoyed the relative isolation while still living within walking distance of the town center. The thickly forested hills around town ran south along the lakeshore furnishing hiking and biking trails for miles.

It was a long and winding gravel road that took Josh Decker up to his cottage. It was late and he was craving his sanctuary and a drink after a long drive and a less than satisfying day. It had been almost four months since he was home, but he wasn't sorry to have missed the busy tourist season. He had been working in the Philippines as a security consultant for a large contractor who had just opened a plant there as part of a government contract. It was hardly adventurous, but it paid well and Josh wasn't a thrill seeker. Before heading home, he planned to stop by The Chance, a bar in town, to pick up his mail and buy a bottle of whiskey.

Charlie Webber owned The Chance bar and knew Josh well. He was 68 years old and kept tabs on his friend by collecting his mail when he was out of town for such long periods and allowing him to stay in one of his two cottages atop a large wooded dune just south of town. Josh hoped to talk with him before heading back home. Charlie was a confidant, and even though Josh was not a talker by nature, he felt the need to bend Charlie's ear a bit tonight.

Just as Josh arrived and before he could take a seat at the bar Charlie plopped a stack of mail on the bar in front of him.

"How'd you know it was me?" Josh said.

"A good bartender knows when his best customers are nearby," Charlie answered with a smirk.

"Bullshit," Josh said.

"Yep," was his reply.

Charlie went over to help a couple other customers, and Josh opened a piece of mail that had caught his eye. It was from an old friend he worked with when he was on the Chicago Police force. As he began to read the letter his eyes glazed over, sighed, and allowed his hand to fall down onto the bar, partially crumpling the letter. It was bad news. He looked more angry than sad and though Josh usually was able to cloak his emotions, it was clear that he was feeling a deep sense of loss. Charlie was busy. No need to bend his ear tonight, especially now. He just wanted to get home. He reached over, left some cash, took a fifth of whiskey off the shelf, then quietly left unnoticed.

As long as the thirty-hour trip had been, it was the last few miles that seemed the longest. It was actually quicker and easier to walk to town from his cottage – the only road wound for several miles through the woods and around a deep ravine before completing almost a circle back to the cottage. But he had his travel bag with him and he preferred to keep his car nearby. Nestled in the woods, the glow of the sunset would still manage to seep through the trees, especially after the leaves had fallen. He was tired and wanted nothing more than to sit out on the front porch, alone, with a drink and the sun setting over the lake in the distance.

Josh Decker stood about six foot one. He had a solid, yet slim build, medium length dark brown hair, and brown eyes. He was 38 years old and had spent almost fifteen years with the Chicago Police Department, retiring early as a decorated detective. Yet in recent years he seemed more like a drifter, working various consulting and private detective jobs all over the world, with his only anchor being the little cottage in Highland.

Finally, he drove up, parked, and shut off the engine. The feeling of needing a drink suddenly became overwhelming. Still in the car, he opened the bottle of whiskey, poured a few shots into his empty paper coffee mug and took a large sip. He sat there for a long while, just looking at the cottage from across the ravine. He sighed and took a deep breath as if to let out a lifetime of stress and anxiety that had built up in him. He had nothing else to do now, not until his next job was slated to begin in another month. By then winter would be closing in and Highland would see its few remaining tourists off.

It seemed like a long hike from where he could park, down the path around the edge of the ravine, and finally up to his front porch. Josh refilled his cup with whiskey and placed the bottle into his travel bag. He took another large sip and reached to open his car door. It was then that he noticed it. Ever observant, he stopped and waited. Across the ravine he observed one of the curtains in the cottage was closed. He didn't remember closing them before. In fact, he never closed them. Privacy was not a problem being so isolated. The nearest cottage was Charlie's just up the hill behind his and that was a few minutes' walk. He also preferred open windows allowing the sight and sounds of the deep woods and the waves breaking on the lakeshore to permeate into the bungalow. Patiently, he finished his whiskey and took out a 9mm from his bag. He pulled back the slide and released it, snapping the first bullet of a fully loaded magazine into the chamber. He stepped out of the car, placed the pistol in his belt behind his back, and grabbed his bag.

4 – Chicago

"Great minds think alike, my dear," his nasal voice softly pierced the silence as the good doctor leaned over a large book and a few empty beakers. A few weeks prior to the conference and speech Anita had called on Dr. Sullivan at his office. She had been his leading pharmaceutical sales representative for a year or so and he had grown to trust her.

"My, my, my. What are you up to?" Anita asked as she strolled in wearing her usual sales call attire, a low cut blouse and short skirt.

"Great minds. It is how all the trouble in the world began," he began rather obtusely. Then he looked up at her and continued. "You know, when I was a child I used to keep a notebook by my bedside and set my alarm for various times throughout the night. I'd wake up and still half asleep, I'd quickly write down as much as I could remember of the dream I had been having. Then go back to sleep for more. I did this over and over again. I only wanted to remember my dreams. I wished I could have recorded them on a VCR and played them back. Not the same as living the experience though. Did you ever have a flying dream?"

"Yes! Oh Sully, it was so amazing," Anita said in a manner which would have come off as pandering to any outside observer, but to Dr. Sullivan it was received as the gentle tone of grand admiration that Anita had mastered. She knew just how to stroke him, and his ego.

"Yes indeed!" he continued. "I wanted to capture that *feeling*! It was only a child's fantasy but it was then that I became fascinated with dreams, convinced that they held within them some secret to life itself. Years later I re-read those childish notebooks cataloging my dreams. I never took them seriously before, but when I read them I noticed something incredible."

"What?" Anita asked as her eyes continued to roam around his laboratory. It was a plain and simple office consisting of a desk, a table with glass beakers, a few bottles of chemicals, and a nice leather recliner next to an I.V. stand. She decided to make herself at home and took a seat in the soft recliner, pulling on the lever until fully reclined.

"It was a pattern. A genuine, distinctive pattern. The dreams formed a complicated structure, as if it were a quilt. Patches of information that individually made no sense at all yet when placed together in the right order, conveyed a particular message. Did you know we forget most of our dreams?"

"I forget those that I don't want to remember!" Anita said with a seductive smile.

"You may have a hundred dreams a night. I would wake myself up seven, even eight times a night, but it wasn't enough. And my ability to accurately write every detail was certainly not sufficient. And yet, despite the significant missing chunks of data, I was able to discern a definite pattern!"

Anita was now confused. Dr. Sullivan seemed to be talking to himself as if she hadn't been there at all. She became slightly annoyed and decided to take advantage of the diatribe to rest her eyes. Sullivan noticed and rolled his chair so that he was sitting beside her, like a doctor to his patient. Anita opened her eyes, looked up and smiled.

"You know the FBI director just announced that there really is no such thing as privacy," he said.

"No, I didn't hear that."

"Every communication you make on your phone, every text, every social media post, every single word uttered over a telephone, is being stored now in massive data bases – some over a million square feet large. They've removed all the copper telephone wire from people's homes. It's now all one large computer matrix using fiber optics."

"Scary, isn't it?" Anita asked.

"Do you know who Rene Descartes was?" Sullivan asked her, as he began to stroke her forehead.

"No, who was he?" Anita asked, smiling and enjoying the attention she had been desiring.

"He was the philosopher who said, 'I think therefore I am.' He doubted, actually. *HE* doubted the entire material world around him until he was left with only one thing, the one thing he could not doubt: that he was doing the doubting," Dr. Sullivan's beady eyes widened. "His mind was the only place of refuge from the world. Alone there, with his thoughts, he was secure."

"Interesting," Anita said. She began to see where Sully was going with the conversation. He wandered off toward the window and proceeded to talk to himself more than to her.

"It is a case of Singularity. The transferring of consciousness from one being to another. Or from one being, to a machine." He pondered his words carefully as he gazed out onto the city and the people below. "They are so tiny. Insignificant little ants all working to forge something greater than themselves. This city! What a monument it is to human achievement! Mounds of steel and brick, pulsing away with energy! The life blood of our new frontier! The essence of humanity's destiny. A god we created ourselves!" He turned back to Anita saying, "The 'Big Bang' was nothing more than pure energy. And from it came all life, all existence."

"It seems impossible, doesn't it?" Anita said.

"No. Nothing is impossible. Just how to do something eludes us." He sat back down, picked up a thick needle that was attached to the other end of the I.V. and held it up to Anita's eyes. "What if I told you that I found a way to reach your inner most thoughts?" Sullivan inquired.

"You can read my mind?" Anita asked, in a calm but amazed voice that was almost a whisper.

Sullivan gently placed the needle back down onto the table beside her and then rolled his chair rapidly back toward the counter. He quickly reached up to a shelf and took down a dark brown colored bottle. He rolled slowly and carefully back.

"The secret is in this bottle. Sleep disorders are curious things. You have to understand the mind, not just the chemistry. But the ultimate answer is not psychological, it is chemical. I've developed a chemical compound that acts as a conduit to the brain and can recover memories from the pre-frontal cortex via the parietal lobe. That's where your brain makes sense of all the sensory information it receives. There is a distinct pattern associated with short term, and long term memories. It's easier to decode the short-term memories, especially when they are vivid, and powerful: emotional."

Anita's eyes were now transfixed on Dr. Sullivan. She had always felt physically stimulated by his vast intellect. But now, she was positively tingling with excitement.

"In this bottle is the chemical compound I call, Sapphire. It contains a derivative form of aluminum oxide. The same compound that makes up your lovely gemstones." He smiled and touched Anita's necklace. Although she wasn't wearing sapphires, he slowly ran his bony fingers down her long necklace toward her chest and allowed his fingers to keep moving down once the limits of the chain had been reached. She did nothing to stop him. He ran his fingers down inside her blouse and stroked her cleavage just under the center of her bra. He smiled at her as he gazed onto her through his thin rimmed glasses, and she returned the seductive smile, took a long, slow breath, and slightly licked her lips before offering a gentle moan as she continued to relax in the leather chair.

"The secret is actually not in the conducting, but in the insulating properties. My particular mixture creates just the right balance of resistivity to be able to read and interpret brain patterns. Every thought leaves a specific pattern on the brain, a neuropathway of sorts. My chemical process allows it to be read using this computer and this electrode." He held up a large needle that was paired with an even larger metal probe. The total diameter was about five millimeters.

"It must be carefully implanted. From behind the ear." He touched Anita behind and just under her right ear, behind her jaw bone. "The needle and probe are inserted into just the right spot, directly into the cerebellum. It has only motor skill functions but acts as a key conduit for all brain processing. It stimulates the brain and makes it fire along its neuropathways. The needle injects just the right amount of my Sapphire and the probe both stimulates the brain with just the right electrical frequency, and maps the results. The computer records the data, and once a pattern is established, the software I've written can translate, and even save memories forever!" He smiled as he moved his fingers from around Anita and stroked the bottle as if it were the glorious curves of a beautiful young woman.

"It sounds dangerous," Anita said, sitting up and vying for his attention.

"Oh, you might say that. The chemical is also self-destructive, and dissipates on its own after a few hours, leaving no side effects, or traces. Well, except for one rather serious side effect that I'm working to overcome. So far, it only works on someone who is recently dead."

"Dead?" Anita repeated.

Sullivan leaned over her nearly touching his lips to hers and whispered, "Do you still wish to volunteer?"

Anita was suddenly disturbed and answered a defiant, "No!"

Sullivan laughed. "Of course not! But I am ready to test it on a living human. I'm confident that the results of such testing will quickly lead me to being able to use it successfully on the living as well as the dead. And in the short-term, it could be an entirely undetectable way to transmit massive amounts of data from one place to another by using the human brain as a storage vessel: avoiding the world wide electronic grid entirely!"

"To what end?" Anita asked.

"A complete mind transplant! As well as the ultimate encryption. The ability to pass vast amounts of technical information, sensitive information, without any detection. Such information is worth a lot of money. That money I will need to develop my process for eventually mapping the entire brain of an individual and saving it into a computer. Eventually, that knowledge could be transplanted into another. My goal is to transplant the human soul! The essence of life and awareness! And I can do it, Anita. I know I can!"

Once again Anita was stimulated. "I want to help," she said.

"I need a test subject. Someone I don't know, and who has recently had a memory for which I can distinctively search. Someone who is highly emotional. When you fall in love, for example, you cannot stop thinking about the other person, no?" he asked.

"No, your mind constantly dwells on them," Anita answered, reaching up and stroking Sully's cheek. He took off his glasses, leaned over and kissed her.

"Perhaps you can find someone who is romantically inclined? Talk with them about something. It can be anything! But make sure the idea, or object is vivid, and clear. Don't tell me what it is you plant into their conscious mind. Just let me know as soon as you have finished the task. I'll handle..." he stopped and kissed her again, "everything else."

His hands quickly lifted Anita's loose fitting blouse up out of her tight black skirt, and he almost tore off its three loose fitting buttons before standing up and loosening his tie and belt. By the time he was finished with his shirt buttons, she was already at work down below.

5 – Highland

The cottage was a small single story bungalow built in the late 1890s. The roof extended over a large decked porch where two chairs sat facing west. He walked into the main living space that held a sofa, couple of chairs, and a dining table. In the back to the left was the kitchen, and to the right two small bedrooms with old cloth curtains serving as bedroom doors. As soon as Josh stepped inside, he noticed the distinct smell of vegetable soup. He had moved his arm around to his back, keeping a grip on the butt of his pistol. Quickly looking around he spied a cloth tote bag hanging off the back of a chair near the adjacent bedroom doorways.

"You can come out," Josh said in a flat, low tone. There was no reply. "I know you're here. I'm not mad. I'm not dangerous. Come out," he said softly, in a normal speaking voice, his hand still on the butt of his gun.

"I can't do that," came a young woman's voice from the bathroom.

"I won't hurt you. I live here and I'm not leaving," he said.

"Well then, would you turn around for a second?" she asked.

Josh thought about this request and as much as he now believed the situation to be less than dangerous, he had learned long ago not to assume anything when it came to his livelihood. He answered directly, "No."

After a moment of silence, a girl walked meekly out of the bathroom, breezing swiftly into the living room. She was nearly naked, her hair still slightly damp, wearing only bikini style panties, and doing her best to cover herself as she walked over and reached for her bag.

"Would be nice if you had a towel in this place," she mumbled as she quickly made her way to one of the bedrooms, drawing the curtain behind her and proceeded to dress.

Josh took his hand away from his pistol and began to walk toward the kitchen.

A minute later the girl came out from the bedroom, her bag tossed over her shoulder, and proceeded to make her way toward the front door to leave.

"What's for supper?" Josh asked as he stood over the pot of warm soup. The girl stopped at the door but didn't answer. "Smells good," he added.

"It's vegetable soup," she answered, still rattled by his unanticipated arrival.

"Well, I'm hungry. I bet you are too." Josh walked to the cabinet and took out a couple of bowls and began to serve the meal. The girl slowly made her way from the door back into the living room and put her bag down. "Do you have a name?" Josh asked.

"Abby." she answered.

"Josh," he replied. "Well Abby, looks like you already made yourself at home, so why don't you sit down?" he said.

She hesitated but once Josh sat down and began to eat, her hunger persuaded her and she joined him. She sat across from him at a small round table in the kitchen. It was a very quiet place, the only sound was the antique clock ticking in the background.

"You wound the clock," Josh observed.

"It was too quiet."

"So, Abby, how long has it been?"

"Only a few days."

"I mean since you ran away," he said confidently. Abby was caught off guard by his correct presumption.

"I didn't run away," she corrected and took another sip. "A few months," she answered.

"That's a while," he said.

"Yeah, where the hell have you been?" Abby asked with a touch of humor and a smile. "I mean, you're never home, are you?"

Josh smiled, "Different places. I'm sorry to have been neglecting you so," the banter continued.

"Oh, that's ok. I mean, I'm low maintenance anyway. But seriously, you need to get some groceries."

"Yes, I do. But you have to admit, I wasn't exactly expecting company."

Abby looked up from her meal, for the first time looked Josh in the eyes. "I'm sorry about this. I really am."

"That's alright," Josh said. "Seventeen?" he asked.

Abby looked up surprised. "How do you know?" she asked.

"Well, you look at least sixteen and if you were eighteen or older you wouldn't be a runaway, so that leaves seventeen."

"I didn't run away."

"Sure you did."

"How do you know?"

"That's why you're hiding out here, of all places. In the middle of nowhere."

She smiled, shook her head back and forth a bit then said, "Wow. You're clued in. I'll be eighteen in a couple months."

"Who might be looking for you?" he asked.

"No one," she replied, taking another sip of soup.

"Let me ask it another way. From whom are you running?" he asked in deliberately proper English.

"My story? You want the story right? You've probably heard it before so what difference does it make?" She asked.

"Well you're hiding in my cottage, in a very isolated corner of the woods outside of a small town. You've been here a few days and on the run a few months. That tells me that either you're making your way to some destination, or you're running away from someone who might want to hurt you. I just want to know if I should expect any more company. You know, before I go grocery shopping," he explained.

"I see," she replied. She looked across the table at him in a manner that scanned his face and his eyes. He was handsome. He looked tired, but very alert and not condescending in the least. He didn't appear to be judgmental and after some intuitive consideration, she believed him to be honest.

"I never knew my Dad. My mother died four years ago and I've been living with my alcoholic, doped up uncle and his wife ever since. They've let me know what a fucking burden I am over the years. They never abused me or anything, but I end up always cleaning up after them and dodging their shady friends. A few months ago one of them, this fat guy, broke my bedroom door while the folks were passed out. But the asshole tripped on his own drunken two feet and hit his head on the footboard of my bed!" she laughed. "What an ass. Anyway, I left, right then. That was three months ago. Believe me, no one is even looking for me. They're probably glad I'm gone, if they've even noticed. Which I'm sure they will once the trash piles up like Silvia Stout!"

"Who wouldn't take the garbage out," Josh answered.

Abby laughed, "Yeah, you know about her, huh?"

"Shel Silverstein," Josh answered. "Where the sidewalk ends."

"Yeah. I loved reading that as a kid. I read a lot. Still do," Abby answered.

"May I ask you one more question?"

"Was I dropped much as a child? Did my mother neglect me?"

"Which bedroom are you using?"

"The one on the left. It's all made up and I didn't take anything I promise." she added.

"I know. I just wanted to know where I should sleep."

He stood up and made his way toward the living room. He picked up his bag and continued to the front bedroom. He laid his gun down on the night stand, took off his jacket and pants, and got into bed. He was asleep in no time.

Abby was perplexed by his behavior. It was unexpected, and in its own way, welcoming. As she cleared the table she noticed he had left a piece of mail on the counter. Hoping to obtain his full name, she looked at it. 'Josh Decker' was hand written on the front. Then curiosity took over and she removed the slightly crumpled letter from inside and read it. It was a short letter, one that left her with a tear in her eye.

She walked over to his room to check on him.

"Josh?" she whispered, but there was no response. She pulled back the curtain and peeked into his room. There was enough moonlight to make out his face and that he was asleep.

She just watched him sleep for a few minutes and wondered about a great many things. He looked sad but her gut told her he was a kind soul, and she suddenly felt very safe, for the first time in a long time.

Then she went back to the living room and took a book off the shelf. She settled into a chair under the soft glow of a reading lamp. She turned to the title page which read, 'Great Expectations'. Somehow it seemed quite appropriate.

6 – Chicago

The German chef had really outdone himself. The thick aroma of Sauerbraten, potato dumplings and Swabian pancakes dripping with apple sauce and raisins still hung in the air as VIPs mingled during a private reception with Dr. Sullivan. After a night full of conversation, laughter, and the latest gossip, one by one the guests began to hint of their departure leaving all the signs of a successful dinner party: crumb-filled plates, slightly crusted wine glasses, crinkled napkins, and the best of jokes – all dirty. Everyone appeared satisfied and complimented the Doctor on his speech and cutting edge research. The good doctor seemed to relish the attention, and Anita stood proudly by his side, shaking their hands and nodding in agreement as if to share in his discovery.

Among other things, Anita had seen Kristina and Paul flirting all evening. Following Dr. Sullivan's speech she began tracking their movements around the ballroom before arriving upstairs in the Maple Room, a more intimate setting for the private reception. The couple had settled into a quiet archway leading toward one of the exits, a place once occupied by pay phones. She had watched as Paul placed his arm around her waist and pulled her gently closer toward him. Her flirtatious smile beamed as she gazed up into his eyes and the two kissed. A few more words were exchanged and Paul slowly departed by stepping backward toward the hallway doors, their hands reaching toward one another until the bond was, at last, broken. Anita moved in as soon as he was out of sight.

"Oh there you are! I was wondering where you had gone," Anita feigned sincerity.

"Oh I've been just wandering around," Kristina blushed, almost giggling with excitement.

"Yeah, I've noticed," Anita smiled. "He's quite the catch, I'm so happy for you."

"Thank you," Kristina said. "The first time I met him, when he came into the office, I knew..."

"Of course I've seen him with several young women recently," Anita interrupted.

"You have?" Kristina asked, dejected. "I mean... How many?"

"Oh, I don't know," Anita teased, her voice projecting some concern. "There was Sharon last week at Dr. Russell's office. And Mellissa who gave him a..." she stopped herself, pretending to just notice how hurt Kristina was feeling. "Oh, but listen to me, none of those encounters were anything like what I just saw!" Anita reassured.

"Really? What were they then?"

"More like, innocent flirting. I wouldn't think too much about it. It's part of the job, you know. It's not just the young ladies who bat their eyes at the handsome doctors, no matter how hideous they are!" Anita laughed.

"Ha, ha," Kristina tried to laugh along, "Well, I suppose you're right."

"Oh, but I'm sure you're different," Anita reassured, this time with more conviction.

"Really? I just felt like he, I mean... I felt like I would just feel... I know that I would..." she struggled to get her words out.

"Sapphires!" Anita interrupted.

"What?" Kristina asked.

"Sapphires, my dear!" Anita clarified. "That's perfect!"

"What is?" Kristina asked.

"My dear, tell him about how you noticed my sapphire necklace." Anita touched her beautiful necklace which was lined with several of the elegant blue gemstones. "And tell him how sapphires have always been your favorite. How your father had given your mother sapphires one time for Valentine's Day, just to show her how much he cared for and loved her." As she spoke, Kristina's eyes brightened and her beautiful young smile grew. "Yes, you must mention it to him. Sapphires. Do not forget it. Repeat it over and over in your mind. Sapphires, and Paul. Sapphires, from Paul." Anita smiled, her sexy eyes peering down into Kristina's in a way that projected her most seductive techniques onto her.

"Sapphires," Kristina repeated, almost hypnotized. "Yeah, why not, right?"

"You see these?" Anita touched those strung around her neck by a glistening silver necklace. They were set in a 'V' shape with the largest gemstone in the middle and two slightly smaller ones on either side. Her hand moved over them like a model showcasing a prize on a game show. "A doctor friend of mine gave me these. It shows his affection of course, but much more than that. You will know for sure how he feels. But men are foolishly naive. So you must also learn how to ask for such things. And a man likes a woman who is a little demanding from the start. It shows him you're worth the effort and no girl worth having comes cheap."

"Of course not."

"But you also need to let him know of the payoff for treating you right," Anita smirked and raised her eyebrow, giving a slight wink. She moved close to Kristina and whispered, "Then behind closed doors you treat him like your master, doing anything and everything he desires."

"Oh, that's not a problem," Kristina laughed and blushed. "But is it too forward to..."

"Forward?" Anita interrupted. "Are you kidding me? Paul is a top salesman, he needs to know exactly where things stand. Why, you can lead him right to where he can close the deal."

"Right," Kristina said.

"Just remember, to be unique. It must be sapphires." Anita lowered her voice just enough to emphasize its significance. "It's all about *sapphires*."

"Sapphires!" Kristina said, excitedly.

"Here he comes. Go make him a very happy man, my dear," Anita smiled.

"Thank you, Anita!" Kristina clasped Anita's hands in gratitude.

"No thanks necessary," Anita said. Kristina left to meet up with Paul and the two almost immediately left the ballroom together.

"That should do it," Anita whispered to herself.

Dr. Sullivan thanked and said farewell to his last guest before turning to his wife, Marsha. "You're looking rather tired my dear. Go on up to the room. I'm afraid I have quite a few more people to meet and business to attend to."

"You never stop working, do you?" Marsha mumbled irritably.

"Go upstairs," he said calmly but with a stern undertone. His wife gazed over toward Anita with her beautiful blond hair and stunning figure, then turned and walked out. Anita instantly sidled up to Dr. Sullivan.

"I suppose I'd be too obvious to use her for our little experiment, wouldn't it?" Sullivan remarked.

"Well, perhaps she'd sign a waiver," Anita smirked. Sullivan giggled, a rare moment of humor that he'd allow himself.

"Ah yes, the lawyers would have much fun with that one," he said. "But do you have someone else in mind, my dear?" he asked, placing his hands down along Anita's hips, just below the little black belt that wrapped around her thin waist. Her dress was low cut and revealing, as usual. The dress ran down to just above her knees so as to show off her smooth long legs. And the deep blue color of the dress matched her silver and sapphire necklace.

"I do," she replied, bringing her hands up to touch his cheek. "I have a name, and a message." She began to run her fingers through his thinning, graying hair.

"I'll take the name."

"I'm afraid you'll have to earn it, doctor," she said, pouting her lips and moving them ever closer to his. He stood stone faced, and straight.

"Tell me," he gently ordered.

Anita smiled, and brushed her cheek onto his and whispered into his ear, "Kristina Hanson."

"Who is she?"

"Oh, you can't miss her. She's been throwing herself at your man Paul all evening."

"In love with the spy?" Sullivan thought for a moment. "That may be, just fine. Yes, I think that could really work well. An excellent choice, my sweet," Sully smiled, his beady eyes twinkling at the prospects the night held. "Meet me upstairs. I'll order a little more wine."

"Don't keep me waiting, Sully."

Anita slowly moved away, stroking his tie as she let it fall from her fingers. Sullivan couldn't help but watch her tight ass walking so elegantly toward the door. As she left, she turned back and shot him a seductive gaze.

He took out his phone, pressed a button, and said, "Go. And the girl too. Kristina Hanson. Make sure it's her and that she isn't harmed." He tapped the phone, ending the call, and placed it back in his jacket pocket. He then walked to a hotel courtesy phone and ordered a dozen roses, and a bottle of DOM PÉRIGNON.

7 – Chicago

A cold wind whipped around him as he pushed open a heavy metal door that led to an ally. It was two in the morning, the only light bleeding from the main street a couple hundred feet away. Several large trash bins lined the smelly brick lane between two skyscrapers. The sounds of the city loomed as careless echoes bouncing off and around the buildings like a pinball. It was colder than he expected. His bare hand began to feel painfully chilly as he held a closed portfolio pad and a large brown envelope. He buttoned his suit jacket and took out an open pack of cigarettes. He smelled the fresh tobacco as he lifted it toward his mouth, his lips securing one before replacing the pack in his coat pocket. With the same hand he reached for his lighter, took it out and used the envelope and pad to shield the flame from the wind. He lit the cigarette. A puff or two, then began to pace the area. He was waiting, but not patiently.

"Oy there!" an angry voice shouted down the ally. He turned, but saw that it was not directed at him. A homeless stranger was barking at another over his claim to a warmer corner near the street. "Get the fuck out of my spot!" the shouting continued and a distant argument erupted.

He had stopped pacing. Looked up from the arguing men toward the sky, which was clearing. Stars were slightly visible through the rapidly moving night clouds, brightened with a gold hue from the city lights below. He began to think about how insignificant our little world must be, even within the confines of this great city. He took a long drag on his smoke, breathing it in deep.

A soft, yet sharp whisk of air was heard, like a chord whipping through it, simultaneously with an immense, yet tightly focused punch in his chest knocking the wind and smoke out of him. A small tingling sound followed as if an aluminum can had been tossed down the road. Instantly he couldn't breathe. It was as if he was under water, struggling to rise to the surface as his lungs quickly filled. He began to gurgle, convulsing and spitting up the liquid. It was dark red, made darker still by the shadows surrounding him. He became aware, but almost immediately also became dizzy and fell to his knees. The envelope and portfolio fell beside him to the ground. Another major convulsion as his body struggled to clear his blood filled lungs. Blood filled his nose and mouth as if he had vomited, yet there was no relief. His collapse continued as he fell onto his hands and knees.

"Aye mate," a voice from behind came suddenly, "let me help you there." He felt the man pulling him up by his left arm. He was strong and leveraged his own body to force him back to his feet. Together, they walked forward toward the closest garbage bin which was angled out from the building and had several bags of garbage sitting behind it, between the bin and the wall of the building. Strangely, one of his final thoughts was of the man's English accent.

"Come on now," the voice said. "A bit too much time at the pub I see." He felt his feet moving but he was basically being carried by the man. He was unable to talk, still coughing up pools of blood and he seemed no longer able to stand straight. The entire world was now spinning violently and he soon could go no further. He felt the fall. It was hard, and cold. The thought of '30 seconds...' flashed in his mind. The man helping him along had shoved him in between the trash bin and the building, and let him fall as if he was a drunkard on the binge of a lifetime. He felt the bitter, frozen coldness quickly cover him like a blanket, from his feet and hands to his core. And then everything stopped. No noise. No feeling. No light.

The man adjusted his thick dark winter coat and made his way back toward where his prey had dropped the envelope and pad. He picked up the envelope, opened it and looked carefully in the dim light to inspect it. Then he resealed the flap, tucked it under his arm, walked down the ally opposite the arguing homeless men, and disappeared.

8 – Chicago

"Ey Jimmy, sorry I'm late mate. A little business to attend to," Robert Gordon "Gordie" Chase announced in his thick cockney accent as he entered an exclusive penthouse suite at the Essex.

"Business at this hour? It's almost two! Sun will be up soon! Must still be on London time my friend," Jimmy said with a smile as he showed Gordie to the party. The room was flooded with a rich perfumed aroma, hard core Jazz, free flowing liquor, and dozens of hauntingly alluring young women.

"Not unlike you," Gordie said. "You're workin' it all hours of the night I see." He smiled as Jimmy handed him his first drink.

"That's my job! Making sure our guests enjoy themselves thoroughly." Jimmy proceeded to walk Gordie over to the center of the suit toward the windows that overlooked Grant Park and Lake Michigan. The lights of the city below quickly gave way to the dark horizon of the great lake, where only the tiny lamps of boats cruising along pierced the thick darkness.

"Ladies, ladies!" Jimmy announced. "Here he is, fresh off the boat from London, England, and needing to spend some quality time with us for a couple of days. Make him feel at home, will you?"

Smiles and laughter instantly surged Gordie's way. He was 30, tall, slender, and powerfully built. His hair was cut short, almost a true buzz cut, and he dressed in a black suit and white shirt, no tie.

"Hello ladies," he said as three of them led him to a couch and sat him down.

"Tell us about England," Jessica asked. She was dressed in a sparkling white, skin tight dress that accented her perfect 'Sports Illustrated' shape, dark hair, and immaculate blue eyes. The other two ladies began to fawn over him as well. A stunningly beautiful Asian woman named Sue, with a pixie haircut, took her position on his right tucking her silky legs up onto the sofa. She wore an extremely thin and short brown dress and rested her hands on his shoulder placing her mouth near his ear. The third, Mindy, a blond bombshell wearing a smooth long dark red dress made her presence instantly known by taking her place on the floor at his feet resting her arms on his left thigh. Gordie took it all in stride, pleased with the pampering while sipping his drink as if just having returned home after a long day at work.

"England is bloody England. Who gives a fuck?" he said as the ladies all giggled.

"I love your accent!" Mandy said.

"I'd rather learn a bit about you lovely ladies." He placed his right hand on Sue's knee and moved it up until it was snuggly in between her soft little legs, a move that only prompted her to adjust her position in order to make herself more accessible to his fondling.

"Hold this for me love," he said to Jessica and handed her his drink. She complied with an adoring smile as he said, "That's a lovely dress you've got on there, isn't it?" he said as he ran his now free hand down her right strap to her breast. He then traced her curves all the way around to her left side. She followed his tracing with her eyes, then looked up at him and took a sip from his drink.

"Do you like it?" Jessica asked ostensibly referring to the drink, yet her raised eyebrows and seductive smile suggested otherwise.

"Hell yeah! Not bad at all, love." He quickly turned his hand so his palm faced her chest and ran it down inside her bra to cop a complete feel. He squeezed and slowly lifted his hand back up and took his drink.

"You have such strong hands," Jessica admired as she stroked his leg.

"Strong hands? I don't know," he turned back to Sue on his right, removing his hand from her crotch and wrapping it around her waist. He grabbed her small, tight ass with significant power and asked, "Do you think they're strong?"

"Oh yes! I do," she answered as she moved and caught her breath, fighting to hold back the pain he was causing by his squeeze. "Good! Ya want to know about England? Well, some of us can be a bit on the rough side, you know." He unclenched his hand and gave her a healthy slap on the ass. She smiled, exhaled, and resumed her position on his shoulder.

"I'm sure you can show us what you mean," she said. The other two girls quickly agreed as the drinks and petting continued.

At the far end of the room stood a bar. Sitting in the last seat was Dr. Sullivan who seemed to be watching Gordie nervously. He sat next to Valery Zhukov, a native Russian who spoke English with a thick accent.

"The job is done," he said to Dr. Sullivan.

"You sure?"

"He's here. That's enough," he said.

"For both?" Dr. Sullivan asked.

"As discussed. We're agreed on the price?"

"Yes," said Sullivan. "Where is the girl?"

"She's being delivered as we speak."

"Unharmed?"

"Alive," he said. "Disposal is your concern. I want the results."

"I'll get them." Dr. Sullivan assured. "And when I do I want the money and papers. No delay."

The man nodded, finished the last of his drink, and stood up. He had left a tan envelope on the bar and said, "Make sure he gets this in the morning. He'll not leave without it." He signaled the barkeep for another shot of vodka. "We're giving you three more weeks."

"What? That may not be enough time, Mr. Zhukov."

"It is all you have. We've invested enough with nothing to show for it. Someone better be in Moscow by the 30th, with the proper encryption we provided."

"It works now. I just need to perfect the implantation and extraction process. It takes time," Dr. Sullivan wheezed.

"Well, you have three weeks time," Zhukov said as he downed the shot. He was an older, heavy set man who resembled an old fashion Mob boss without the accoutrements. He stood up and walked toward the door – his walk looked as if it took a lot of effort, slightly limping on his right.

"Jimmy!" He shouted. Jimmy waved his hand from across the room. "One for the road tonight, yes?"

"Oh, you got it Val!" he answered, then took a young blonde girl by the arm, whispered in her ear and walked her over to him. "She's brand new Val, keep her company."

"Good man," Zhukov said as he handed Jimmy a few hundred dollar bills. The two left the lounge.

Dr. Sullivan inspected the envelope and its contents. In it was a series of codes and account numbers arranging for several financial transactions. He pocketed two of the sheets of paper, then licked and sealed the rest into the envelope and placed it onto the bar. Having noticed Zhukov had left, Jessica excused herself and made her way over to Dr. Sullivan.

She ran her fingers through his thinning hair saying, "You're looking a bit lonely tonight."

"I am. So very lonely my dear," he said methodically, as if he were poorly rehearsing a script. He then tapped the bar and picked up his drink. Jessica discreetly took the envelope, placed it in her purse, and walked back to Gordie and the other girls.

A few drinks and an hour later Gordie strolled out of the party to his hotel room accompanied by all three women. The intense romp that ensued was accompanied by loud and frequent moans until nearly dawn.

As the sun began to peak through the curtains, the three ladies began getting dressed. Jessica removed the tan envelope from her purse, unfolded it, and placed it on Gordie's chest as he snoozed in bed.

"We're leaving sweetie," Jessica said as she kissed him. "Here you go."

9 – Highland

'That wasn't so bad, was it?' a soft woman's voice echoed through a hazy mist. Her long brown hair and warm arms wrapped around him as he pushed back the tears.

'Someone should have been there. Someone should've known!' a frantic woman said crying, her voice broken down into echoes.

'I didn't know' he thought, 'how could I?'

'Don't give me that bullshit! I want answers!' a stern voice yelled.

'But I didn't...' he thought again. Was it true?

'Don't pay attention to him...' a man's voice dropped in, his face unseen.

'I promise it won't hurt...' the soft woman's voice softly emerged from the right.

'It's here somewhere...' he thought as he reached down to his feet, his hand sinking into the water that rose up to his knees. 'I know it's here...'

'I want answers!' the stern voice commanded.

'Don't pay attention to him...' a man's voice dropped in, 'he's under the gun and doesn't mean it. You did your job.'

'My job?' he thought. 'Gun?'

'He's under the gun,' the man repeated.

"Under the gun, how?' he thought. The water was getting very warm. He lifted his hand back up and placed it over his ears. 'No more voices!' Then he rubbed his eyes, the wetness on his hands was thick and hot now. He pulled his hands away and looked at them. They were covered in blood.

'That wasn't so bad...'

'I want answers!'

'He's under the gun and doesn't...'

Josh woke suddenly with a deep gasp for air. He quickly sat up in bed and looked around. He was sweating and huffing out of breath. He looked at his hands, they were clean. The clock – it was 5:30, a couple hours before sunrise. He calmed down, dressed, and walked out of his bedroom to the kitchen where he poured a shot of bourbon into a glass and drank it. Then he poured another and walked out onto the deck. Through the trees he could hear the softness of waves rolling into the shore of the great lake. He sat down in the chilly morning air and stared off toward the sound, slowly nursing the bourbon.

As the sun began to fill the sky with beautiful purple and red hues, Josh made his way back to his bedroom. He tried to fall back to sleep, but it was no use. Having been so preoccupied, it was only then he remembered he had a guest. Or did he? Wagering in his mind that the girl had probably just snuck out during the night, he rose and walked out to the nook which led from the bedrooms to the living room. The curtain to the second bedroom was only drawn half way so Josh was able to easily see Abby laid out on her bed sound asleep. The room was bright with morning sunbeams, made a few tones darker by the partially closed red-orange drapes hanging in the window.

She was sleeping on her side, half curled into almost a fetal position, her legs edging out from under the blanket. The instant he saw her he heard the voices in his head again and flashes from the nightmare returned with one image in particular that his mind, for some reason, was unable to ignore.

'I didn't know' he thought, 'how could I?'

'Don't give me that bullshit! I want answers!' a stern voice yelled.

The nagging image was of a girl, lying similar to Abby, but in a pool of blood.

'But I didn't...' he thought again.

'I want answers!'

'I didn't... How could I...' His voice and the others, in his mind, trailed off. Was it true? He thought.

'Stop!' he yelled through to his thoughts, forcing the voices and the image to vanish. The nightmare needed to end, but he knew it was only a break. It would be back. They would all be back - it had never faded since it began. He shook his head and took a deep breath. He looked once more, quickly into Abby's room. She hadn't moved. She looked fine and healthy. Josh closed his eyes to concentrate, took another deep breath and made his way to the kitchen.

He made a pot of coffee and prepared some toast. He picked up the letter from the counter that he had received the night before, then sat down to eat. He took a bite of toast and began to read it once more. As he finished reading, his hand holding the letter dropped to the table.

"Damn," he sighed.

"What's that?" Abby said yawning as she entered the kitchen from the living room.

"You're up," Josh said.

"Smell of coffee woke me. May I?"

"Sure." He folded up the letter and placed it in his shirt pocket.

Abby poured herself a cup of coffee and sat down across from Josh at the kitchen table. There were few lights in the cottage, but well placed windows allowed for an ample amount of light. It was a very quiet, rustic retreat. No television or telephone, only a few shelves of books, left by several previous owners over the generations. A couch and a set of chairs made up the living room, and two more comfortable wooden chairs sat out on the deck in front with Lake Michigan in the distance. Fall was in full bloom and it would only be a matter of days now before the lake could be spied from the cottage. Abby had observed him carefully and waited patiently for Josh to begin a conversation. But since one didn't seem to be forthcoming, she took the lead.

"Are you happy?" she asked. The question took Josh by surprise. It wasn't the usual conversation starter.

"I suppose." he answered dryly.

"Happy to be here? At home? Or happy, like as a person?"

"Are you asking me or asking yourself?" Josh said trying to turn the tables.

"What do you mean?

"I mean you are the one who is apparently not happy, otherwise you'd be home."

"No, I'm actually happy because I'm not home," Abby answered. "I couldn't wait to get out on my own."

"But you're not on your own."

"Well I was, until you came home." Abby laughed and took a sip of coffee. He noticed how when she spoke she had a tone and manner of maturity about her. She was certainly independent, and naive, but she spoke well and with great confidence. She continued, "You're avoiding my question. Are you happy?"

"Are you a shrink now?"

"No."

"Then why?" Josh asked.

"Why what?" Abby answered.

"Why don't you go home?" he asked.

She paused. "I told you, I hate it there," she paused. "I just got so sick of dealing with them. It's like I'm the adult and they're the kids."

"That can be rough."

"I did have a dog for a while. I loved that dog. She was..." Abby began to choke up but caught herself and took a sip of coffee. "She was my best friend. Pretty much my only friend," she smiled. "But I'm happier now," she nodded confidently. "I hope to make it out of the country someday. I just want to go somewhere, you know? Somewhere far away. Either some place where no one else lives, or in a huge city where no one would notice me. Either way, I'd disappear and do what I want to do. I thought about Paris!" Her eyes lit up. "The city of light! Full of life, and art, and energy! Maybe not forever. But if I were to just fade away somewhere, Paris would be so incredible."

"You should temper your expectations," Josh cautioned after listening carefully.

"I have," Abby answered. "You know, just when you're at the edge, something grabs ahold and pulls you back to reality." They sat in silence for a moment, the phrase struck Josh who thought about the letter, and his nightmare. Then she continued, "To believe that someone cares about you in ways that you can't imagine only to let you down." It grew quiet again. Abby believed he would say something. When he didn't, she continued, "Believe me, I have no false illusions. I don't plan on letting anyone dictate to me what I can and can't do though. I will make it to Paris someday, that's for sure. I have dreams. I have lots of dreams."

"Me too," Josh said, referring to his nightmares more than life dreams. He took a sip of his coffee and finished his toast.

"Maybe what I should've asked is, do you ever get lonely?" She said. Josh took a moment to think about it.

"No," he answered.

"No wonder! You're a wonderful conversationalist," she said sarcastically and smiled.

Josh stood up and walked out to the deck. It was a beautiful clear morning and the birds were lively filling the air with their songs. Abby followed him out and stood to his side. They both looked out toward the lake as the morning sun began to filter out brighter and brighter.

"The fact is, right here I have everything I want," he began. "The woods, the lake, and solitude. People will always disappoint you. Dreams? They are a cruel fiction that just vanishes with the dawn's early light. Keep your dreams simple and you'll never be troubled by them. For every dream there's a nightmare."

"At least you're not cynical" said Abby, continuing the sarcasm.

"Just a realist I guess. It's experience talking. You're better to just be completely happy with yourself. You're the only one who'll never leave and the only person in the world you can actually count on," Josh said as he took another sip.

"Well, Mr. Decker, looks like we have a lot in common," she said with a smile.

Josh raised his eyebrows and turned his head toward her. He was aware that he had not given his last name and yet somehow she had found it out. He was impressed.

"Why did you stay?" he asked.

"You mean last night?"

"Yeah. You could've left."

"I don't know. I got this feeling, you know. That you were... a good guy. This place is kinda like a museum. I expected you to be a lot older actually."

"You're perceptive. The guy who owns it is an old fart." Josh said. She laughed.

"I guess I just... felt safe," she said.

It was a sincere compliment. It had been years since he had heard one. He even managed to crack a smile.

Abby continued, looking straight ahead, "Can't run away from yourself, I guess. But you need to take your chances. You need your dreams. Especially when they take you far away from here. I mean, even right now, they can take you anywhere. And you don't need anyone's help. Paris from the top of the Eiffel Tower."

She paused, and allowed herself to get lost in the thought for a moment. Soon, she began to smile as she stared off toward the lake. Josh watched her with pleasure. "You see," she continued, "Dreams are so liberating. Every moment matters and this one is completely up to me." She sat down in a chair, fully satisfied and confident. Josh sat down in the chair next to her and glanced toward her every so often. The two pondered for a long while until finally he looked back toward the lake.

"Well, I'm never getting a dog." he said.

Abby laughed adding, "Ok then, no dog."

10 – London

It was one of Molly Wheeler's earliest, most vivid memories. She was only five years old when her auntie took her to St. Paul's cathedral in London. She didn't remember much about the visit except for the amazing array of colours that seemed to rain down from the sky above onto the floor and walls around her. She spent time counting the red pieces, then the blue ones. To her they were a kaleidoscope of imagination. With her tiny finger in the air she'd trace patterns and discover new shapes and figures. Colours from the bright glass canvas's tucked under majestic arches and within quiet nooks produced beams of light that seemed to dance as she moved about them. She remembered feeling regal. Royal. Bathed in its radiance.

Her auntie took her often to church, but only to St. Paul's on special occasions. The flash of memories broke her concentration and brought a brief half smile to her face. Now, twenty-three years later, the simplicity of red and blue had given way to the sophistication of crimson and cobalt. Molly was working in the spare bedroom of her second floor flat in Corydon, a southeastern London suburb. The window was open, overlooking an ally – not much of a view. But it had been her own place for the past two years, thanks to her boyfriend who put down the deposit and paid the rent. Soon she hoped to be self-sufficient. She had a few opportunities lined up that would allow her to work full time on what had become her passion ever since that childhood stroll through St. Paul's.

Molly was an artist who, among other things, created and restored stained glass windows. While the world outside her flat was often dreary and gray, inside her studio the lights beamed through various filters of vibrant colour arranged in random patterns along tabletops, in drawers, and hanging works. Glass cutters, pliers, and a soldering iron juxtaposed with paints, brushes, and sketches which more or less were strewn all around the room in a bit of organized chaos.

Perhaps it was the music that first diverted her attention from her work into the daydream walk through St. Paul's. Her mp3 player had randomly landed on the orchestral song 'Earthlight', by Tony Banks, and the mood it created seemed entirely appropriate. She had taped a sketch of her current project over her desktop. Now it was nearly finished. Three by two meters, it lay on her large work space as she put the finishing touches of paint onto the delicate sections of her mainly cobalt and gray glass canvas. She still had no idea where it would eventually be displayed. This particular window was not part of a commission – but personal. It was inspired by a dream she had one night several weeks before – one of hope against all odds, strength, perseverance, and gentleness. An acute description of Molly herself.

'I should give auntie a call,' she thought. It had been too long. Her aunt had raised her after her parents were killed in a car accident. Molly had no memory of them and had no other family locally. She had a slender build and her long dark brown hair was pulled back to keep it out of her way as she continued to paint the detail of a small pane of stained glass. She had, as her auntie described, 'the most beautiful and expressive eyes she had ever seen'.

She held a piece up to the light – the colours softly caressing her when suddenly the door slammed, jerking her out of her relaxed trance.

"Moll! You here love?" Gordie announced powerfully and with a sense of urgency. The sudden disturbance nearly caused Molly drop the glass pane, but she was able to catch it before any damage had been done and lay it down on her desk. Impatient as ever, Gordie quickly burst into the studio and condescendingly bellowed, "Hey! I been calling you!"

Molly took her ear buds out and still slightly shaking babbled, "Oh, I'm sorry. I couldn't hear you with..."

"Stop it!" Gordie interrupted. "I have something important for you and I don't want it fucked up." Molly's eyes had strayed from Gordie back to the pane of glass. She wanted badly to make sure it was securely on her desk, she seemed concerned for its safety and her own at the same time. Gordie snapped his fingers directly in front of Molly's nose. "Hey!" he shouted sternly. "Pay me some attention will ya?"

"I am. I'm listening." She could barely get the words out before he cut her off and continued. This time he pounded his fist on the edge of her desk, causing many pieces of glass to bounce and rattle. But Molly knew the routine. She never diverted her eyes from his until he had finished.

"You got to get this right, love." Gordie bent down, placed his right hand behind Molly's neck and pulled her close with a jerk of her head. His breath smelled of cigarettes and booze. He reached into his pocket, took out the tan envelope he received in Chicago, and held it out toward her saying sternly but in a very low voice, "Take this down to the bank tomorrow morning. It's a wire. Bring this to Mr. Stephens, he sits at the second desk. You are only to work with Mr. Stephens, you understand?" Molly nodded.

"Say it."

"Mr. Stephens," she answered.

"Right. Don't forget your ID, and sign the paperwork in your name. Give him your account number and this envelope, sealed!" He held it up in front of her. "Don't you fucking open it! If anyone else there asks, the money is going to your friend who is on holiday in Russia. Stephens will handle the rest. You have to be there at 9:30. What time?" he asked quizzing her.

"9:30," Molly quickly answered.

"9:30," Gordie continued. "Don't be late! It will not be a good thing. I will be very upset if anything goes wrong."

Now that he had finished he sighed as if a load was off his mind. He plopped the envelope down on the glass pane that she had been carefully painting. She opened her mouth out of concern for her work, but said nothing.

She was still sitting on her stool when his hand returned, landing softly on her knee, moving swiftly up her left thigh.

"There, there..." He said, as he stroked Molly's right ear. He then moved his hand down over her shoulder and beneath her arm, around her waist. Feeling his way around her back, he began to move her closer to him as his other hand continued its way up her right thigh. He pulled her in forcing a kiss onto her. Molly quickly broke off the kiss and pushed him away.

"No don't," she said.

"Yeah?" Gordie responded. Then suddenly his powerful arms grabbed her by her blouse and pulled her to her feet. He attempted another kiss but this time Molly turned her head.

"No!" she cried softly. Her arms up against his chest and shoulders, but she knew it would be in vain.

"Fuck you!" he yelled and slapped her across her right cheek. As she fell from the blow, his left hand reached out and grabbed her blouse, attempting to pull her back to him with much more force than before. Instead, her shirt tore open, ripping the buttons clean off. Molly fell to the floor in front of her desk, her stool rolling backward from her fall. She began to cry, holding her sore cheek.

"What the fuck's the matter with you?" Gordie yelled. He was about to kick her when he stopped short, remembering that he needed her to deliver the instructions he gave her to the bank in the morning. He composed himself, looked down at her said arrogantly, "You know I could have it if I wanted." When there was no answer he insisted on a response. "Huh? Yeah?" he said calmly. "You know it."

He walked over to a mirror on the wall, ran his fingers over his short dark hair and straightened his cheap old tie a bit. He gave a sniff of approval to himself, then headed back to Molly.

"Got to go love. Sorry I can't stay for supper." He took the tan envelope again and placed it in front of her face. Bending down over her he grabbed her by the chin and lifted her head up so he could look her in the eyes. "Don't you dare forget anything tomorrow."

He slapped the top of her head with the envelope sharply, causing her to blink as a reflex. Then and placed it back on her desk, atop her project. Then, without standing up, and to drive home his point, he made a fist with his large right hand and slammed it down upon the envelope. She heard the horrific sound of glass shattering beneath his fist. Other pieces fell onto the floor breaking into countless fragments. He stood up, then walked out with the sound of grinding and crackling broken glass under his feet – the slamming door knocking one final piece of glass to the floor.

11 – Highland

The sound was unusual and puzzled her initially. It was an irregular snapping sound coming from the main room, but she couldn't quite place it. Abby yawned and stretched her way out of bed, her loose t-shirt pulling up exposing her midriff as she wrapped the blanket around her. It was a bit chilly and she had only a few articles of clothing with her. She got up and walked out to the living room with the blanket serving as a robe. Josh was seated at the desk on the far side of the room, his back toward her and the kitchen off to his right.

"Good morning," he said, without looking as he continued to type.

"What are you doing?" Abby asked, still a little groggy.

"Finishing some work," he answered. Abby walked over and looked over his shoulder.

"I know you're not really into computers, or technology in general, but don't you think this is a bit primitive?" she asked with a sly smile, gesturing to their surroundings where the most modern piece of technology seemed to be a small twenty year old radio. The entire place seemed like a throwback by at least twenty years or more.

He stopped and looked up at her. "I happen to enjoy things from a simpler time." He smiled and resumed. "Besides, Charlie has yet to upgrade the place."

"Who's Charlie?" she asked.

"A friend." He noticed by the look on her face that such a simple answer was not going satisfy. "He owns this cottage and the one up the hill a bit. That's where he lives."

"And he's the old fart?" she asked.

"That would be him."

"Well, this is more like primitive," she said. "I mean really, do you have to go that far back to find a simpler time? You know you can still type on a computer even without WIFI. You don't need that... contraption."

"This is a 1951 Royal Deluxe," he said as he typed. "They don't make these anymore."

"Well, I can see you're quite a proficient typist. Perhaps you missed your calling," Abby teased.

He stopped and pulled the remaining paper out of the typewriter and held it in front of him. "The truth?" he asked.

"Certainly." She was on the verge of laughing at him and his use of an antique typewriter.

"Actually, I am quite proficient with computers and technology. Which is exactly why I'm typing. Everything you do on a computer can be tracked somehow. The cloud, a hard drive, email, keylogger, even encrypted files can be hacked. But you can't hack the old fashioned typewriter."

"Sounds a bit paranoid."

"I am a security consultant. By typing my reports I assure my clients that only one copy exists. And that copy cannot be hacked."

"Couldn't someone just make a photocopy?" she asked.

"Of course, well, it's surprising how often people overlook the obvious. But once I place the report in their hands, my job's done. I don't transmit anything electronically. And you can't hack a human brain!"

"Not yet," Abby chuckled. "Okay, I'm impressed."

"Do you know how to work this, contraption?" he asked.

"Well, kind of... Not really." He gestured for her to try typing. She reached over and attempted to type her name but pressed the keys as opposed to striking them with a degree of force. The result was a tiny smudge of ink where a letter should have been.

"Snap it! Like this." He struck a key and it snapped onto the page.

Abby followed suit and typed her name precariously.

"There! Wow, my fingers are sore."

"You have muscles you never knew you had."

Josh got up, went to the kitchen and poured himself a cup of coffee.

"You must have strong hands," she said as she began to have a look around. The bookshelf had about a hundred books, each at least twenty years old, most in a worn hard cover binding.

Classic novels along with history and science books made it a virtual academic library from the 1960s. Crowded into a corner was a small sideboard table, a couple of antique wooden folding chairs, and several boxes. Between the bookshelf and this corner of storage she noticed what looked like an old, worn, hard paneled suitcase – tan with a black handle.

"What's this?" She said, out loud but to herself. Noticing a few records stacked on the table next to it, she realized it must be an old record player. She released the buckles and opened the lid revealing a vintage phonograph in excellent condition. She bent over it for a closer look, slowly closed her eyes and took a deep breath. It smelled old, like the pages of an old book but more metallic. She smiled taking several more breaths.

Josh took his coffee, proceeded to the porch and sat down. His eyes looked tired. It was as though he wanted to just float away from every care and concern, every action and responsibility. The dry reports he had been working on for his most recent client were almost finished, but further procrastination didn't bother him in the least. None of it seemed to matter, he thought. The good deeds go unnoticed and the criminals get all the attention and even praise. It was as if the more you learned about life, the more meaningless it all became. He had hoped the work would distract him, but his contemplative thoughts only led to another deep breath and sigh, followed by another long sip of his coffee. He secretly wished it was whiskey.

Abby took the top record off the pile and placed it on the player. She searched for the chord, which was also packed down into the case. Pulling it out she found an outlet and plugged it in. The player came to life immediately, having been left on prior to being stowed. She took the needle and rested it on the revolving vinyl record. She adjusted the volume as the song played, then stepped back staring at the magnificent machine which to her, seemed to light up the entire room with its crackling monotone melody.

"This is so incredible!" She said loudly and with excitement. "I mean, I've always loved old things like this. Just think of how many records, sounds, and people listening..." She paused, thinking, and then slowly became more serious and sullen as she said, "All those people… Everyone has a story, a secret world only they know…" her thoughts seemed to drift. "How many lives this must have touched, gossip overheard." She turned toward Josh with a teasing glow in her eye, "How many romantic nights this would have partnered in! The love it might have created! The joy of finding someone!"

Josh was listening to every word but made no sound, or motion to show it. He was a world apart from her in thought. Finally, as the music played the words began, *"It's only a paper moon, hanging over a cardboard scene. But it wouldn't be make-believe if you believed in me."*

Upon listening, her mood shifted once again from happiness to a slight sorrow as she continued, "Or keeping you company when the loneliness of missing them became too much."

There was a long moment of contemplation for both of them. Abby broke her trance and slowly walked over to the doorway where Josh was seated. Standing slightly behind him, she looked out through the trees to the lake in the distance. The cool breezes shook the branches and the soft muffled sound of the waves on the shore seemed to float into the air like a graceful mist.

"Is there someone you miss?" Josh asked.

"No," Abby answered quickly. "You?"

"No," Josh answered. Then took another sip.

"But I can imagine," Abby continued. "I can imagine what it must feel like to be left all alone. Especially when you were counting on someone."

"You can't count on anyone, kiddo."

The music continued, *"It's a Barnum and Bailey world, just as phony as it can be. But it wouldn't be make-believe, if you believed in me."*

Abby noticed a heart shape had been carved into the side of one of the old trees near the bottom of the porch steps. It looked as if was done ages ago and she tried to imagine what it must have looked like the day the couple decided to engrave it. It led her to greater thoughts which she finally expressed, "I always wanted to do something I would be remembered for. You know, to have someone want to remember you."

"That's not in your control," Josh answered, dryly.

"Of course it is," she said looking down toward him. "What do you mean?"

Josh paused, then looked up at her hopeful brown eyes. "You don't get to choose who remembers you or what for. And you're not around anyway once they do, so what's the point of it?"

"Have you always been such a pessimist?" she asked, disappointed and somewhat aloof.

Josh didn't say anything. He wasn't ignoring her. He actually thought about it. Was he really that negative? To him, it was simply experience – that the nature of life was cold and heartless. But the more he thought the more he realized it was his answer that seemed to bother him the most.

"Look," he started, "It's good that you can see the good side of people and life. And I hope that never changes for you. But the higher you set your expectations the greater the fall you can expect. Just be careful. You have to be realistic."

"I prefer to be idealistic first. Reality has already screwed me enough. I'm not letting it fuck me around anymore." She took a seat on the chair next to his.

Josh started to laugh under his breath which soon emerged more vocally.

"Something funny?" she asked, slightly upset.

"It's like a clown," Josh said.

"You're calling me a clown?" Abby said, wanting to be angry but instead finding herself smiling and starting to laugh with him.

"No, no. I mean, there was this time on the force when we arrested a clown," Josh began.

"Wait, what force?" Abby asked.

"Chicago Police" he answered. "I was a detective. And one time when the circus was in town, we were called in to investigate a missing person. A midget. Not that that's funny, but we were looking for this guy that had supposedly met with some sort of foul play, and we ended up finding him locked up in the base of the human cannon."

Abby's eyes were wide and bright, both of them fighting back the urge to laugh at the situation he was describing.

"Apparently, he pissed off one of the female clowns in some sort of lovers quarrel. So much so she tied him up and locked him inside this cannon. And she was planning on launching him across the arena during the next show. The cannon used air pressure to shoot the guy out, but it was set for a full grown man, not a midget. So the idea was that the midget would be fired across the whole place and overshoot the netting. It would look like an accident, right? I mean, can you imagine what that might have looked like?" They both found themselves laughing hysterically.

"It's not funny!" Abby managed to say.

"No, of course not," Josh replied. "But when we finally caught up to the clown, she was in full dress, you know. Big woman too. I mean, big! She took off and started throwing animal shit at us, spraying water from those stupid seltzer bottles, and you name it. It was ridiculous!" he said, the laughter continuing.

"Finally, I almost had her when she ran into the elephant pen and I slipped on a huge piece of elephant shit! Straight onto my back! I was left looking up at this ten ton elephant as I laid in his shit!" Abby grew hysterical, grabbing her stomach and lifting her legs off the ground into a fetal position in her chair.

Finally, she asked, "Did you collar your clown?" and laughed.

"Yes!" Josh said with excited determination. "I did. She was wearing those big red shoes, you know, and finally one of them tripped her up. As for me, I made it to my feet and was slipping and sliding all over with elephant shit on my shoes. God, it smelled awful. Don't know what the hell they fed that animal, but let me tell you..." They both continued to laugh. "Well, I finally caught up to her after she tripped and her little red nose fell off!" They laughed again.

"By that time, all the other cops there were now laughing

at me. They just let us run around the big top guarding the exits so she couldn't leave, but none of them helping me. They were enjoying the show! I tell you, it wasn't so damn funny at the time that's for sure," he added. "So I refused to change and went in to the station smelling like elephant crap all day, just to make them suffer."

"Sounds, really disgusting," Abby said, composing herself.

"Yeah. That was a long day," he answered. "But that is exactly how I was remembered, for a very long time. The detective who fell into a pile of elephant crap trying to collar a clown."

Abby laughed again at the vision in her head of Josh running around a three ring circus, chasing a clown. "Ok, so you may not be entirely in control of your own destiny," she admitted.

"We're all clowns, kiddo." he said, now composed. "And life makes fools of us all. None of it makes much sense in the long run. My guess is that we'll be remembered for who we were, not what we've done."

The record, having ended, continued to crackle as it bumped up against the center label. After a few moments of quiet she asked him, "So why did you leave the force?"

Josh gave a fast, well prepared answer, "For the money."

"The money?" she asked with surprise. "Are you kidding me? You live in someone else's cottage, have no family to support, drive an average car," she said teasingly, "I don't buy it."

Getting no further response from him she pressed, "Was it a woman?"

"That's enough," he said.

"It was a woman! Wasn't it?" she said with excitement. But Josh was not amused.

"I said, that's enough," he replied calmly, but sternly. He stood up, walked inside, and was about to pour another cup of coffee. Instead, he poured a shot of whiskey into his coffee cup and took a long sip. Then he made his way back to his desk and sat down to finish typing his report.

"I'm sorry," Abby said after a while.

"I know." He said and gave her a reassuring smile.

12 – London

Molly did as she was instructed. The 9:30 appointment at the bank would still allow her time to make her meeting at the Holy Trinity Church. She was interviewing for a commission to lead their stained glass window restoration project. She switched trains at Victoria station, and again at Green Park where she picked up the Piccadilly line to Leicester Square. She walked a quarter mile to the bank and asked for Mr. Stephens, all per Gordie's precise instructions. The time was exactly 9:30 AM.

Simon Stephens was quick to spot her and rose from his desk to invite her back to a vacant office where they sat down.

"You have something for me," he stated factually. He was about thirty, short, heavy, round man who appeared to have a severe authoritative personality.

"Yes," Molly said as she reached into her bag and took out the folded manila envelope. She placed it on his desk.

"You didn't open it," Simon said, again as a statement not a question.

"It's sealed," she answered.

"Doesn't mean you didn't open it and reseal it now, does it?" he snarled. He peered at Molly practically accusing her of some treacherous action.

"No," she answered forcefully.

"Huh. Let's take a look," he said, suspiciously.

Simon inspected the envelope carefully, feeling its surface so as to determine its contents before opening it. He took a sharp letter opener and slowly slid it across the flap. The sound of the ripping paper added to Molly's anxiety. He opened the envelope and took out the contents. His breathing was labored and slow as he inspected each page carefully before placing it face down away from Molly. He'd look up at her from time to time, almost accusing her of something with his eyes. Every once in a while his breathing would be exceptionally long as he studied the pages. Then he'd gaze across at her as if she was a contemptuous suspect.

"Identification," he said bluntly.

Molly reached into her bag and placed her ID on the desk. He took the last sheet of paper along with her ID and walked out of the office. Molly watched him carefully as he disappeared around the corner. She figured he had gone to the manager's office, probably for some sort of approval for the transaction. Still puzzled, Molly had now grown even more curious. After all, it was her account, her name which was on this transaction and she didn't have a clue what it was all about.

She turned to see where Mr. Stevens had gone. He was out of sight. She then looked at the papers which were still face down on the desk. Without hesitation she reached over and lifted the top one. It was a document written in a foreign language. If she had to guess, she'd say it was Russian. She flipped through a few more of the pages until she saw what had been the top page in the envelope. It was in English with the precise instructions Gordie gave to her, but more. It included the name of the person to whom money was being sent, account numbers, and amounts. Her eyes widened when she saw the amount of the transfer and her mouth spontaneously opened. £23,500 was transferred from an account in Moscow, to her account in London, and then to an account in Zurich.

Molly felt as if she was being violated. 'What is going on?' she thought. But time was of the essence. She pulled out her phone and quickly took photos of the papers. She captured the first three pages, including the one in English and two in Russian. There were more in English but she didn't have time to snap them before she heard Simon's labored breathing and congestive cough coming around the corner. She quickly placed the documents back under the stack, and as smoothly as a magician, dropped her phone into her bag on her lap.

"Here," he said as he tossed her ID back to her and sat down. He placed two documents in front of her, covering up the top portions of each with his fat hands. "Sign here, press hard," he ordered.

"May I see this?" Molly asked.

"No." he said. "Just sign," he demanded, looking her straight in the eyes. She thought about protesting, but then she considered the price she'd pay later with Gordie. She signed the documents.

Simon counter signed them and said, "You're all set. Tell your boyfriend I said hi."

"I will," she answered. "Thank you." There was no reply.

She stood up and walked out of the office. Once in the lobby she turned around, pretending to be completing a deposit ticket. She was partially obscured by a pole but could clearly see Simon stack the papers, fold them and place them into his suit jacket pocket. He then stamped the documents she had signed and walked out heading back to the manager's office. She couldn't see anything at that point so she turned to go.

Once outside, she used her ATM card to check the balance of the account. It was a bank account she had never used but one that Gordie insisted she open as a vacation savings account and that he would fund it. When the balance appeared on the screen, she was shocked. She immediately ended the transaction and removed her card. She quickly looked around her to see if anyone had been watching. But there were only businessmen and pedestrians going about their busy day. She took a deep breath, replaced her card in her bag, and walked down the road to catch a bus to Holy Trinity. The amount in her account was £402,775.

13 – Highland

'That wasn't so bad, was it?' a woman's soft voice echoed through a hazy mist. Her long brown hair and warm arms wrapped around him as he pushed back the tears.

'That's my big man,' she said as she hugged him tightly.

'Someone should have been there. Someone should've known,' said a man's voice, deep and stern. 'I want answers!'

'But I didn't know,' he wanted to say in reply. He tried to speak, but couldn't. He knew he didn't know, and that he should've known. It was his fault.

'Don't pay attention to him, he's got people to deal with...' a new voice came and then trailed off like a song fading out.

'I want answers!' the stern voice returned.

'I promise it won't hurt you,' came the soft comforting woman's voice. 'As gentle as a butterfly...'

Bang! A deafening gunshot rang out.

Bang. The short echoes again, and again, and again, eventually trailing off.

He frantically looked around the room. 'My gun. Where's my gun?' he thought. Frantically he began to search the bed. The floor. But there was only water, a few inches deep. His hands moved back and forth searching and searching, but in vain. The room was empty now, only the sloshing of water could be heard as he threw himself down onto his hands and knees, still searching. It was futile. The water was incessant. As soon as it moved it was replaced and he was growing more and more frantic.

Footsteps could be heard approaching, like a gunfighter in a television Western slowly pounding on the boardwalk, coming toward the door.

'I want answers!' said the stern voice.

'That wasn't so bad,' said the soft woman's voice.

'But I can't get away! Something's got me... let me go!' the panic began.

Another shot? No, an echo. Then it was over – was it too late? The footsteps – getting closer! He stopped. The water was still. He was breathing terribly hard. A door creaked from the other room. More footsteps. Closer now. Closer…

'My gun!' he screamed in his mind as the frantic search began again. The sloshing of the water grew deeper as the water level rose. He stopped long enough to notice that it was no longer water, but blood. He lifted his hand, dripping with bright, thick red blood. He felt its warmth silkily sliding down around and between his fingers.

'That wasn't so bad, now…' but the voice faded and the footsteps were getting much louder.

'I want answers!'

BANG! a shot fired and echoed.

'Fly away little thing… I didn't mean it!

'A gentle butterfly…' the woman's voice comforted

'Fly away… please… please now…'

'That didn't just happen.' he thought. 'No, that did not happen.' It was lifeless. 'I should've known…'

He stopped the searching as the blood had filled the room up to his face. Still on his hands and knees, he felt something. It seemed like a piece of metal. A gun! He reached for it, but it was stuck to the floor below and he couldn't see it. The footsteps stopped and the small brass door knob jiggled. He pulled harder, again and again, but the pool of blood all around him now rose above his face. He couldn't breathe. The door knob continued to rattle. He began to panic! 'I can't let go! I can't let go! I didn't know!'

'I want answers!'

'Harder!' she yelled! 'Pull harder, you can do it!' the voice began to fade.

'I can't reach it… I can't… hopeless!' he thought. 'No!'

Suddenly the door flung open and the gun came loose. He instantly swung his body around to face the doorway, and fired!

BANG! the shot rang out.

Josh sat up quickly in bed. He was covered in a heavy sweat and breathing excessively hard. Instinctively, he reached over to his left and picked up his gun and aimed it back over to his right, toward the curtained doorway as fast as a reflex.

A moment later he had composed himself and placed the gun down on the bed.

"No," he said out loud, to himself.

14 – Chicago

Anita walked off the elevator onto the nineteenth floor and entered her office through a sleek glass door. She barely acknowledge the secretary, who greeted her politely, anticipating a stack of papers sitting on her desk, a slew of emails in her inbox, and the voicemail light on her desk phone to be blinking incessantly.

"Good day today?" a coworker asked sardonically, knowing of her reputation for pleasing her best clients.

"It's called hard work and hustling, Brad," she replied with her usual confident arrogance.

"Is that what it is?" Brad retorted. As Anita headed toward her office she walked out of her way in order to pass Brad's desk. She leaned over exposing him to a scenic view of her cleavage.

"Maybe someday you'll figure out how to be number one," she said to him sarcastically. She stood back up, exaggeratedly looked him up and down before adding, "Then again, maybe not." She smiled and walked proudly off to her office saying, "You can stop starring at my ass now honey. It's just me leaving you behind once again." Brad caught himself, shook his head, and went back to his work.

Before she even sat down she noticed an envelope from Dr. Sullivan's office. It had been hand delivered earlier in the day as there was no stamp and had the secretary's initials and time written on it. She reached for her gold plated letter opener, an award given for being the top producer of new business for five consecutive years. It was one of many such awards. Her office was practically a shrine to her sales prowess. She had the corner office, the best book of business in the city, and the attention of her company's top executives. She not only knew how the game was played, but how to win.

The opener swiftly sliced across the seal of the envelope with ease. Inside was a single sheet of paper, folded into thirds. She opened it revealing a single word: 'Sapphires.'

"AH!" she shouted out with extreme excitement before immediately catching herself and placing the paper up to her lips, not wanting to draw undo attention from her coworkers. She began to laugh quietly to herself, but pretty soon she simply lost control. She kicked off her heels and began pounding her feet in excitement. She stood up, walked over to the window still giddy and laughing as she pressed the note up against the glass – as if to show the entire city below.

"We have a winner!" she exclaimed.

15 – London

"The committee will be happy to entertain your proposal Ms. Wheeler," said Mr. Fischer, Chairman of the Holy Trinity Church finance committee. "How long do you believe the project will take?"

"The removal of the panels and restoration work should take around ten to twelve months," Molly answered.

"That seems a bit long, doesn't it? We have proposals that complete the work in only six months."

"Yes, but it was requested that new ideas be a part of the bidding process, not simply cleaning and restoration of the existing windows. That is why I'm here actually. I am proposing replacing the lower band of stained glass with new artistic panes. The result will be an eclectic combination of the older collage around the parameter of the arched windows with a more modern and detailed painted stained glass in the centre, it will enhance the window's themes. I have several samples to show you."

"Ah, that won't be necessary, Ms. Wheeler. This is the finance committee not the design committee. We are more interested in the bottom line. The real reason you're here is because your initial proposal fit within, albeit barely, our budget. But now you wish to replace several more as part of your artistic vision?"

"I understand..." she began before being cut off.

"Indeed, it looks as though your proposal is more in line with someone that has a great deal more experience," the aloof Chairman Fischer stated dryly.

"Yes, but I feel that the design will help justify the figures. If I may..."

"There is little room for any cost overruns..."

"Sir, I only ask to have my proposal considered within the context of my ideas," Molly answered, sensing her chances of securing the commission slipping away. It would be her first major project and the career break she desperately wanted.

"We do not have extra money for embellishments or extravagance, Ms. Wheeler."

Mr. Stewart Langley interjected, "But sir, the other proposals are not that far off and we shouldn't expect that Ms. Wheeler's work be economical simply due to her youth."

"Our funds are limited. And we must obtain the best quality those funds can afford," Fischer barked.

"Surely we're not only interested in time and money Mr. Fischer," Langley chimed in. "If I may, the windows are not just old and in need of a facelift, but they lack a certain artistic refinement as well. An issue only Ms. Wheeler seems to have addressed."

"What exactly do you mean, Mr. Langley?" Fischer asked.

"Well... would *you* like to say it Ms. Wheeler?" he smiled at Molly reassuringly.

Molly smiled in return of his eye contact, "I defer to you of course, Mr. Langley."

"Well then, as the one and only member of the design committee, how do I say it... the windows are bland."

"Bland sir?" Fischer retorted.

"Bland," he reiterated.

"Bland? I would hardly suggest they were any such thing, my goodness sir," Fischer said as he removed his reading glasses to gaze upward and around at the various windows of the church.

"Yes, bland!" said Langley, a forty-eight-year old man with graying hair, thin at the top and a slowly expanding bald spot toward the back of his head. A bit lanky, he was an architect and had been placed in charge of approving the artistic designs for the windows. "The windows cry out for something new and bold. Something that does not detract from the original artistry, but rather will expand on their glory. Let us not choose a contractor, but an artist! New life with new light," he ended, poetically. He looked back toward Molly hoping to see her agreement. The two made eye contact. Molly couldn't help but revel in the compliment. She smiled, then looked down meekly.

The other men murmured for a moment before Fischer continued, "Well, I shall leave the artistic facets to you Mr.

Langley. I confess my wife is in agreement with your assessment. I have never had an eye for the arts, but a keen one for the numbers. And I'm not entirely sure your proposal makes enough financial sense Ms. Wheeler."

Before Molly could speak, Mr. Langley interjected, "Perhaps Ms. Wheeler and I could meet to discuss her ideas in detail and work on a way to also ease your concerns Mr. Fischer?"

"But sir," Molly began, "I know of no other way to accomplish the..."

"Ms. Wheeler." Langley interrupted urgently, "Why don't the two of us discuss things first and then the finance committee can reconvene, say next week, with a proposal that fully accounts for your artistic talent as well as the general costs."

"We do not need another delay Mr. Langley," Fischer stated.

"Of course, sir. But are we not interested in a high quality standard both in longevity and in craftsmanship?" Langley argued.

After a moment's thought Fischer conceded, "Well then, if you both could discuss the details I see no reason we cannot postpone a decision until next week's meeting."

The group of five men disbanded and walked out of the church. Molly began to pack her papers into her portfolio as Mr. Langley approached.

"I hope you weren't overwhelmed by Mr. Fischer," he started.

"I was afraid I'd blown it. But the numbers I proposed were quite reasonable and I just want them to see..."

"No need to explain, Ms. Wheeler," he interrupted.

"It's Molly." She said.

"Molly," he answered with a smile. "Let's meet tomorrow afternoon at my office to discuss it. I assure you we will work something out," he kindly rubbed her shoulder.

"That sounds great. Thank you for coming to my rescue, Mr. Langley."

"It's Stewart," he said.

"Thank you, Stewart," she said as the two exchanged another glance and smile.

16 – Highland

"Decker!" a call echoed through the woods from behind the cottage.

Abby carefully peaked out her bedroom window, the red and golden colors of the curtains bleeding onto her face as the mid-morning sun was still rising. She saw an older man with thick black glasses walking briskly toward the back of the cottage down a pathway out from the woods. The man's haste caused her some concern. The same path led up to the second cottage about a quarter mile before veering downward through the woods toward the edge of town a mile or so away.

"Decker!" the man called again once he reached the back the cottage and he proceeded toward the front. Josh was sitting on the front deck with a cup of coffee. Abby ran nervously out to the living room, being careful to stay out of sight. She could see Josh sitting quietly, sipping his coffee as the man rounded the corner.

"There you are, damn it! It's too cold to be running up here this early," he said, brisling and a bit out of breath.

"Good morning to you too, Charlie," Josh responded.

"The kid needs you. Something's up on the north side of the channel."

"Did he say what?"

"No, but I've never seen like this before. He came barging in this morning white as a ghost. Now I know he can get a little excited and overreact, but this just…" he paused then added soberly, "It's bad Josh, whatever it is."

Josh stood up and walked to the end of the deck, threw out the rest of his coffee and turned to go inside when they both noticed Abby had appeared in the doorway. He stopped, not knowing exactly how to explain this to Charlie.

"Well, well," Charlie said with a slight smirk. "I see why you've been hiding out more so than usual."

Josh opened his mouth to speak, then in a somewhat exasperated tone, he said, "Abby, this is Charlie. Charlie, Abby," he gestured to her.

"Nice to meet you Abby." Charlie said gently, his voice a bit husky from age but very kind.

"And you," Abby said, then turned to Josh, "Are you going into town?"

"I am."

"May I come with you?"

"Maybe you better just stay here."

"Well, I was asking more out of courtesy," she smiled. "I need to go into town for a few things."

"Fine. Only until we get to town, then you're on your own," Josh said.

"Great. I'll get my bag."

"She's pretty," Charlie said.

"She is," said Josh. Charlie looked at Josh for a moment before Josh looked back at him. "What?" he asked.

"Nothing!" Charlie smiled. "We better go. The kid's gonna have a nervous breakdown if we're not back in a jiffy."

Josh stepped into the living room and picked up a pistol from inside a drawer of his desk. He quickly checked the magazine and snapped the loaded cartridge back into place. He pulled the slide back and released it, instantly readying the first round as it sat in the chamber. Then he tucked it inside his belt around his back, leaving his thick hunter green jacket to conceal it. He turned and was out the door when Abby came rapidly through the living room and out the front to catch up with the men who were already walking briskly along the side of the cottage toward the path.

17 – Chicago

Dr. Sullivan walked purposefully into the Palmer House hotel lobby paying no attention to the golden chandeliers and ornate ceiling. He crossed the lobby and ascended the stairs to the second floor overlook. He moved into a nook where there was a white house phone. He picked up the receiver.

"Valery Zhukov," he said and waited.

"I need one more... I know what I said... Well, I consider the first few to have been damaged goods... Fine... Younger the better, female, and someone who has not had a lot of drama..." he ordered. "No she doesn't need to speak English... A nurse? Why?... A witness?... I know it's been going on for a while but..." he was interrupted. "Fine, but she cannot get in the way... No, I will accompany the girl back to Moscow when we're finished. Then you will have the code and I will have my cash... I'm very close, but there's no guarantee... You'll know when I do... I had it, I found the code in the last one!... No, it was working! She was already sick, that's not my fault!... Just make sure this one is healthy... No disabilities... Good. Where?... London? You're going to dispatch him from there? That means another week?... Fine... I suppose I can keep a lookout for someone closer as well... But they may need to give me more time... I promise it will pay for itself... I look forward to it."

Dr. Sullivan hung up the phone and proceeded toward the elevator. He took it to the seventh floor and walked the hallway to room 704. A 'Do Not Disturb' sign hung from the door handle. He knocked five slow, distinctive knocks. The door opened. Anita stood seductively in a transparent red negligee, holding a glass of wine.

"Have you brought me anything?" she smiled and stepped aside, inviting him in.

"I have." He placed his briefcase on the desk and pulled out a small, long white box. "For you my dear. Your help has been immeasurable."

"Ooh! I have tingles up and down my whole body!" she said excitedly. Sullivan's eyes probed every curve of that body as she opened the box and pulled out a beautiful sapphire necklace. She immediately held it up to her neck and gazed at herself in the mirror. The sapphires seemed to illuminate under the lights culminating in a large pendent that resembled an elegant letter "A" with the gemstone seemingly floating between the two downward curved silver edges. It was a stunning and remarkable piece, one that was clearly of custom design.

"Look how they glisten in the light! So elegant and graceful!"

She starred pointedly as if she had been momentarily hypnotized. She didn't immediately take notice of Sullivan's hands as they stroked up and down her soft, bare arms or his warm breath as he slowly worked his way to kissing her shoulder. He took off his thin wire glasses and placed them on the desk in front of the mirror. Then he gently moved her long blond hair to the side as he began kissing her neck, all the while she stood admiring the jewel laced necklace resting upon her bosom.

"It's all I ever wanted."

18 – London

"Do you think I know how to be happy?" Molly asked her friend Anne as they sat next to each other outside a café in Knightsbridge.

"Of course you do, Moll. You just need to get that break, you know?" Anne said.

"It just seems like..." Molly hesitated, "seems like I'm lonely. I mean, I've always valued my solitude. I like spending time on my own. My creations are what brings me the most happiness, but they are static and lifeless."

"Oh no, Moll, they are so beautiful! You're an amazing artist! You bring things to life like I never could!" Anne tried to reassure. Molly smiled at the compliment.

"Thank you. It means a lot, really. I mean I try. I've always been inspired by the colours and light! I try to bring life not just to images, but to ideas! But I guess no one else really sees it."

"I see it." Anne answered.

"Well, you look for it. Most people don't appreciate things the way you and I do. You're a great artist as well!"

"Musician, not artist." Anne corrected.

"Music is art." Molly insisted. "Maybe that's why we get along so well. We see each other like we apparently cannot see ourselves!" they laughed.

"So what's really the matter?" Anne asked. "Is it Gordie? He's up to it again?"

"I don't know," Molly answered. "It's complicated, I suppose." It seemed an easy cover but her friend persisted.

"We've known each other for over a year now but you never told me how you met him." Anne inquired.

"It was a couple years ago at the pub. One night he came in with his mates and were laughing, drinking, having fun. Seemed nice enough."

"Nice enough?" Anne asked skeptically.

"Well, that's not it really. That night I had a difficult table. Couple of rude young blokes on a business trip and they wouldn't leave me alone," she explained.

"Pinching your ass and shit?" Anne said as she lit a cigarette.

"Oh yeah, and they're drunk as can be, asking me out, slapping my ass every time I walk over."

"Why the hell do you put up with that shit?" Anne asked.

"I need the money. And the American's usually leave good tips. Especially the drunk ones!" Molly laughed.

"Ah, them Yanks!" Anne said as she exhaled a cloud of smoke.

"Well, it went over the top when one of them asked me how much I'd want in order to come to their hotel room. I said, 'No thank you' and he insisted by grabbing my arm and practically pulling me over. 'Let go!' I said. 'Come on sweetie, I learned never to take no for an answer!' and he laughed and pulled me over trying to kiss me."

"Jesus! What happened?" Anne asked.

"Gordie," Molly answered. "He stepped in, grabbed the guy and practically lifted him out of his chair!"

"No shit!" Anne said, impressed and smiling.

"Yeah, he forced him outside and walked him down the street and around the corner. His mate followed him, and I never saw the guy again." Molly and Anne both laughed. "I didn't see a tip either!" They laughed again.

"So Gordie came back and asked me my number. And I guess I'm impressed or something, so I give it to him. I don't know. Maybe I have a thing for the knight in shining armor," Molly finished, turning serious and disappointed.

"Yeah, well, he's no knight that's for sure," Anne said trying to reassure.

"No," she said. "He was for a while. I mean, he can be very charming. I wasn't sure about him, you know. Something just didn't feel right. But then he told me that a window I had designed for a church chapel should never hang there. He said it was too good to be relegated to a church. That it belonged in the Queen's parlor."

"Really? I didn't know he could be so sophisticated." Anne remarked.

"Well, he seemed sincere, but now that I think about it he may not have even realized how nice a compliment he was offering. A lot has changed now. He's gone a lot more and he drinks a lot more. We just had our second anniversary and he didn't mention it at all."

"He's still hitting you around, is he?" Anne asked, knowing the answer. "Why do you stay, Moll?"

"At first it was only when he'd be drinking," she explained. "And he put me up in my flat. Skipped the entire wait list. Still don't know how that happened. And I liked that I had some free time when he was gone on his trips. He works for a logistics company and travels all over the place, you know. Makes good money. Apparently much more than I thought actually."

"Money's nice!" Anne said.

"It's not happiness," Molly answered. "Oh Anne, I wish I could run away. I don't know where, just some place far away from here. I dream all the time about living without..." Molly paused holding back and tearing up a little. "Without the fear of hearing that door open and slam shut. Ah, he's home again. Fuck! You're supposed to love it when your man comes home! You're supposed to miss him when he's gone! Right?" Anne just listened as Molly sniffled and composed herself. "But he set me up in my flat, my studio... Oh, all I need is one good commission! Then I could afford to get my own place and take care of my Aunt. But for now... I just feel trapped."

"You're not trapped love, you're stronger than you think!" Anne said. "Want me to talk with him? I can get you out of it. You can stay with me," Anne offered as Molly shook her head.

"You don't understand, it's not that simple. He's..." Molly spotted Gordie walking over to meet her as arranged, so she changed her mood instantly and forced a smile saying, "He's walking over now actually."

"Hey love!" Gordie said in his normal, arrogant tone. "Ready?"

"Let me use the loo, I'll be right out," Molly smiled and walked inside. Gordie didn't sit down. He walked away a bit and reached for a cigarette and leaned back against the building. Anne stood up and followed him.

"Hey!" Anne began. "You know, you shouldn't be fucking around with my girl," she said confronting him.

"What's that?" Gordie answered coolly.

"You're such a fucking bastard – hitting her around! You don't deserve a girl like that. I don't know why she puts up with your shit but I can tell you I'd kick you in the balls so hard they'd be rolling around on the floor. And I'd laugh watching you laying there trying to scoop them up again."

"Would you now?" Gordie said. He took a puff on his cigarette and stood up straight. He spread his legs and said, "Well then, go for it little bitch."

Anne smirked. As much as she would have enjoyed actually doing it, she couldn't bring herself to make a scene and grew concerned over Molly. "Just stop hurting her."

"Maybe you should mind your own business," Gordie said. "Either that, or take your best shot!" Gordie pretended to brace himself by stiffening his body in the posed position and squinting his eyes. Just then Molly walked out.

"What's going on?" she asked somewhat amused by the scene.

"Nothing," Anne said. She walked by Molly quickly saying, "See you tomorrow." She picked up her purse from the table and walked off.

"What was that all about?" Molly asked curiously.

"What, that girl's a real rough one! Gonna give me a whipping if I didn't straighten up I'd say!" This made Molly very nervous. Anne had said something to him and now Molly didn't know what to expect. He walked over and put his arm around Molly and the two began walking in the opposite direction from Anne.

"What do you mean? What did she say?" Molly asked, this time trying to hide her concern.

"Oh, nothing, no worries," he added. "I heard you were at the bank this morning, did a proper job for me. That's a good girl."

"I did what you asked."

"Yeah. Now let's just get you home, have a little fun before I head out," he said patting her ass. "There's always a pay-off when you do things right."

Unimpressed knowing what the implication meant, Molly asked "You're going somewhere?"

"Yeah, you know, something just came up. Got to take care of," he answered.

19 – Highland

Josh and Charlie approached Dean "Dino" Slater, who, along with the Chief, made up the town's police force. He was standing with another man and his dog along a small dirt trail. The pathway was often used by hikers and four-wheelers in the summer and cross-country skiers and snowmobilers in the winter. The only one who didn't look freaked out was the dog.

"What've you got Dino?" Josh asked.

"A body," he replied, his hands visible shaking. "It's a young woman. Um, she's ah, I think she's only been here a short time."

"You found her?" Josh asked the man who was with Dino.

"Technically, my dog found her," he began. "He went racing up there. I always let him play in the woods, you know. But he wouldn't come down. I yelled over and over but he wouldn't come. Just barked a little and kept sniffing around. So I went up to take a look and saw this woman." He struggled to compose himself, his breath visible in the cool air. "Well, I ran into town for the Sherriff, but you know he's in Florida for the winter, so I called Dino and here we are."

"When I got here and realized it was for real, I went and found Charlie and had him find you," Dino finished.

Josh began walking up through the woods carefully, Dino and Charlie following behind. Josh was looking around the scene as he walked, noticing every broken branch, disrupted leaf, or any sign of a body being dragged. But the woods were as they always were and nothing obvious stood out.

"Did you touch anything Dino?" Josh asked.

"No. I was… No," he answered, his voice trembling.

"First time you've seen a body?"

"Yeah. And I hope it's the last."

"Take it easy kid," Charlie said as the three continued to make their way slowly up the wooded hillside. "It's never easy to see a body up close."

"I'll never think of your war stories the same way again." Dino commented, trying not to throw up.

"You get used to it kid, when you've seen enough." Charlie added.

"Oh God, I don't ever want to reach that point." Dino finished as they approached a very small clearing.

Dino instructed them to turn left. It was a rough fifty yards or so down the side of the hill facing the lake in the distance. The body was still half buried, nearly nude, only a small undershirt and panties. She was lying aside a large tree, half covered in dirt and leaves.

"Sloppy. This doesn't look professional," Josh commented. Then he knelt down next to the body for a closer look.

"Out this far, I don't think they wanted her found," Charlie added.

"No. They didn't think she'd be found until spring. If then," said Josh. He bent down over her to get a closer look. Using his gloves he carefully removed some dirt around her hands and feet. He inspected her fingernails but they were clean. He examined her legs and torso as best he could, but they too were free from significant bruising.

"I agree Dino, she hasn't been here long," Josh said.

"No?" Charlie asked.

"But I'd be surprised if she died here. She was placed and I don't think it was an easy job for whoever did it."

"She's got a lot of marks on her arm. Her face has some marks as well. Think she was beat up?" Charlie asked.

"I don't know. Most of these marks look post-mortem," Josh answered. Then he noticed something peculiar on her neck, below her right ear.

"What's this?" he asked himself, but out loud. He moved her hair back a bit further to get a better look. A strange mark which looked like a faded bruise ran down the side of her neck about an inch or two. At the top was a clear small puncture in the skin. The area was clean, no sign of blood, but a bright blue color seemed to ring the puncture site, as if it were some leftover residue. "Wonder what the hell that is?" he asked again to no one but himself.

"What do we do?" Dino asked from several feet away, not wanting to look at the body again.

"We call the coroner," Josh added, and stood up. "Dino, I think the State Police are the ones who should handle the crime scene. And everything else. Probably just a Jane Doe who was dumped here. They'll check the missing persons and see if there is a match."

But even as he spoke Josh had a feeling that there was something more to it than a simple missing person, or murder. While there were no obvious signs of foul play, the blue mark was intriguing to say the least. He bent down to take a second look at the mark.

"Is that all?" Dino asked. "I thought you could figure out how she got here, or how she died, you know?"

"I don't do that anymore," Josh answered stoically.

"Isn't there anything else you can do?" Dino insisted.

But Josh was already taking a long look around asking that same thing to himself. If he were to dispose of a body here, he thought, it would need to be done at night. He'd need to know exactly where he was going, or else he could get lost or injured out in this area of the woods. A body is heavy, even a small woman like this represents a lot of dead weight. 'If I was alone, I'd need to drive her up here somehow.' he thought. The pathway wrapped around the hills and the side opposite from which they had just climbed was even more remote. Without answering Dino he walked up to the top of the hillside, about fifty more yards. It was there he noticed fresh tire tracks.

"Stay here," Charlie said to Dino and followed Josh.

"Four wheelers," Josh said to Charlie who had followed him up. "They came up here," he said pointing to the left, "and stopped over there." It was a point just shy of the top of the hill. "From there, he'd be moving her mostly downhill. Easier to carry, and not be spotted or heard."

"Aren't too many tourists left this time of year. Someone local perhaps?" Charlie asked.

Josh was caught up in thought. A moment passed before he answered, "Perhaps. Hell, what do I know?" he said.

They left Dino to watch over the body and meet the State Police. After giving Dino his statement, the owner of the dog went back home. Josh and Charlie went back into town to the Sherriff's office and called the State Police. Then they both headed over to The Chance bar for a drink before meeting up with Abby.

20 – London

"These are the windows of Sainte Chapelle in Paris," Molly said showing Stewart Langley examples of restoration work and inspirational pieces from her portfolio. The final interview would determine whether or not she would obtain the commission to lead the church's window restoration project. Mr. Langley, a fifty-year-old man who served on the church's architectural committee, sat alone with Molly, side by side on a sofa outside the church office – her portfolio spread out on the coffee table.

"I would love to see them!" he said enthusiastically.

"Here." She flipped the page to a close up view of one window pane. "It's so complex, and yet so elegant and beautiful. The colours just dance."

"These inspire you?"

"Yes. So much so. I've always wanted to go there and see them in person."

"You should indeed," Stewart said, his eyes fixed on Molly's aspect and expression. She was positively glowing as she spoke about her passion.

"You're quite young, I'm sure you will someday."

"Perhaps, but I don't know."

"Now, now, I would say that without a doubt you will be walking the streets of Paris, at night, turning every head and making the entire city envious."

"You're very kind Mr. Langley," she smiled.

"It's Stewart," he returned the smile and touched her hand. "Show me more. Please."

Molly happily turned the page revealing more windows from Sainte Chapelle. "They were recently restored," she added as she continued to discuss meaning and significance of the detailed photographs of the various windows. It was clear that Molly knew her stuff.

Then she looked up at Stewart and added, "Oh how I wish I'd been a part of that!" she smiled, and noticed that he had been resting his chin on his hand staring not at the pictures, but at her. She blushed and smiled shyly. "I'm sorry, I don't wish to bore you."

"Not at all, please go on!" he said.

"Well..." she paused glancing between his face and her portfolio. "You see just how detailed these are? So remarkable to imagine putting them together with every shape and colour in mind, and with a purpose. Reaching so high up above, like arms to Heaven, glowing with richness, stories, and life. They move as the light rises and falls, just like life itself." Molly had placed herself almost in a trance as she pondered her words and the window panes.

"Absolutely beautiful," he said.

"Yes, they are."

"The word doesn't say enough, does it?" he added, referring to her.

"No. And there are few who take the time to admire them," she said referring to the windows.

"There is such beauty in the world which man has made, and yet nothing will ever compare to the beauty that lives in the eyes of a woman he loves."

Molly looked up at him and gazed at his thoughtful comment as it dawned on her at last that his comments were directed to her. Momentarily speechless, he moved closer to her and attempted a kiss. At first she was willing to receive it, even closing her eyes in anticipation as he neared within a breath. But at the last possible moment, she inhaled suddenly in and moved away. She felt confused. While he was much older than her and traditionally not the most handsome of men, the attention and support he had given her regarding her work and talent had formed a bond that she didn't expect or wish to ignore.

"I'm sorry..." she began.

"No, no. It's fine." He interrupted apologetically. After a moment composing himself he added, "Show me your favorite original work."

Molly smiled and turned the pages of her portfolio to the back, revealing a sketch of the project she'd been working on, the one Gordie had smashed. The sight of it forced her to contemplate more than the art alone. Her relationship was miserable, and Stewart so kind and supportive.

Stewart managed to take his eyes off of her and study the sketch. Then he turned to her and said, "Simple. Yet remarkable!"

"Thank you," she smiled.

"There's a much deeper meaning to it, isn't there?" he asked almost rhetorically. "She's a beautiful butterfly, delicate, and yet strong. Struggling to be free." He stopped and looked back at Molly who was gazing deeply at her work, pondering much more than the lines scratched onto the page.

Stewart broke the silence, "You must design a new work for us here at Holy Trinity."

Molly giggled, "I've not gotten very far with the committee I'm afraid!"

"Well, I'm a member of said committee, aren't I? Certainly I will be your champion," he smiled and smirked.

Molly looked into his eyes, smiled and playfully said, "I don't think I've ever had a real champion before."

"Never?"

"No."

"Never to have had someone rescue you from the mouth of the monster?" he teased. Molly smiled and laughed. "Never a brave knight to rescue you from the clutches of some vile creature?"

She shook her head, wishing that just such a hero existed to take her away from all her troubles.

"Never to have had anyone shield you from the cold of winter, or the beating rain of the storm?" he finished poetically.

"No, never!" she said playing along. They both laughed a bit before he turned more serious.

"Come now, Molly, surely you have found your champion!" He placed his arm around her shoulder and moved in to kiss her. Perhaps it was loneliness but this time she allowed it, closing her eyes as he wrapped her in a firm yet gentle embrace. They kissed a few more times before she finally broke it off.

"I'm sorry... Stewart. But I can't."

"Oh Molly, my dear I don't want you to think this has anything to do with the appointment."

"No, no, I um... I have someone. You know... a boyfriend," she said afraid to look him in the eye.

"I see," he said doubting her sincerity. "No chance then, is there?"

"I... Well... ah, no... not really," she said, trying to sort through both her emotions and the practical situation of her relationship with Gordie.

"Well then, perhaps it is best that none of this... ever happened," he insinuated.

"Yes, right," she agreed. "Did you still wish to see my ideas for the chapel panels? I did several sketches that I think you'll find interesting..."

"No, no. That's fine. I'll present the ideas we've discussed to the committee next week and be in touch with you soon after." He stood up and walked over to his office door as if business had suddenly called him away. He projected no emotion whatsoever, his words cold and detached. "I really have much to do today."

"But you haven't seen them yet?"

"No, but I'm sure they will be fine. Good day Ms. Wheeler." He went into his office, closing the door behind him.

Molly felt completely dejected. It was clear to her that her new hero turned out to be a fraud. All the hard work and persistence seemed now to have been for a lost cause. As she packed up her portfolio she couldn't help but believe the entire interview lacked sincerity. As she walked the damp streets to the Underground it was dusk. The hurt she felt was soon followed by anger and resentment toward Gordie. 'If only...' she thought to herself, over and over again. 'If only...'

21 – Highland

Charlie went behind the bar, picked up a bottle of whiskey and poured a shot for Josh and one for himself. The two downed the drink.

"So, who's the girl?" Charlie asked, referring to Abby.

"A runaway," Josh answered.

"Where from?"

"I don't know."

"You don't know?" Charlie probed.

"No. I don't ask too many questions."

"The hell you don't. All I ever hear you do is ask questions," Charlie joked.

"She's just hanging out for a while. I don't think she's in any serious trouble," Josh reassured.

"She's very cute," Charlie added.

"She's very seventeen," Josh said.

"Seventeen doesn't last that long," Charlie smiled.

"What the hell is that supposed to mean?" Josh was getting slightly defensive, but both men knew each other well enough to make their points through humor.

"Nothing. Just that I'm sure it gets lonely up in that cottage," Charlie said.

"Are you really insinuating what I think you are?" Josh asked.

Charlie smiled and laughed. "No. Not for a second."

"But it bothers you?"

"No. Not at all," Charlie answered. "In fact, I think it's really good that you have some company. I don't like you being alone for too long."

"I'm always alone."

With that they heard a commotion outside the bar. A woman screamed and several loud male voices were heard shouting and scrambling just a couple store fronts down from the bar.

"That's Abby," Josh said and rushed out the door. Charlie followed behind.

Once outside Josh caught a glimpse of a man running, having just turned the corner ahead of him into a quiet intersection next to the bar. He heard Abby scream again.

"Leave me alone asshole!"

As Josh rounded the corner he saw three young men. Two laughing and looking on at the largest one who was holding Abby's arms behind her back.

"You think that was fucking funny, bitch?" The big guy said and pulled her arms tightly until she writhed in pain. "I'll show you what it feels like," he said, and began to pull her toward the rear of the row of buildings, behind the bar.

Josh walked steadily and calmly up to the guys and before they noticed he said in a loud, distinctly cold tone, "*I wouldn't do that.*"

The young men stopped and turned back toward Josh who kept walking directly toward them.

"Who the fuck are you?" the big one shouted. It was clear that he was their leader. He was tall, muscular, and more than one scar visible on his face and thick arms. Almost immediately Charlie turned the corner as the two smaller guys moved in on Josh. Within just a few feet of the first guy, whose intention was to intimidate, Josh lunged without any warning or hesitation, jabbing him in the throat with his right palm. He fell instantly to the ground struggling to catch his breath. The second guy immediately stopped and retreated several steps. The big guy just held on to Abby who was breathing hard and seemed stunned by what she had just seen. Josh continued walking toward them when the man pushed Abby away, preparing to take Decker on. It clearly would not be his first fight.

The big guy ran a couple steps toward Josh and swung his right fist toward him. Anticipating this, Josh ducked it and quickly jammed his leg under the man's gut while extending his right arm up over the back of his neck. With his left he pushed him swiftly over his knee, spinning him head first into the concrete parking lot. In a flash, Josh had him face down on the asphalt, his knee on the big guy's neck, drew his gun and placed it point blank in his face. It was over almost before it began. Charlie quickly moved toward Abby intending to keep her safe. He put his arm around her shoulders and moved her toward the back of the building. They looked on from there.

"Name," Josh commanded.

"Derrick," he said. Blood began to seep out from under his head from where he was scrapped during the take down.

"Now Derrick, I'll answer your question. I'm someone you don't want to fuck with," Josh said calmly as Derrick lay still, looking intently at the gun pointed at his forehead. Josh's knee kept a firm and intense pressure on his neck.

"You a cop?" Derrick asked.

"No. That's what makes all this more interesting. I don't have to follow the rules." As Josh said this he looked up at the other young men, the first now staggering to his feet and the second obviously scared to death having just pissed his pants. Josh also noticed a couple of four-wheelers parked behind the building, where they were taking Abby.

"I see you enjoy the four wheeler," Josh started again. "I've been thinking about taking it up myself. Tell me, where's your favorite place to ride around here?"

"I, I don't know," Derrick stuttered.

"I was thinking up on the north ridge. On the north side of the river. You know the place – up in the woods just beyond the town limit near the north shore?"

"I guess so," Derrick answered, his voice sounding squished against the pavement.

"You been up there recently?"

"No."

"Really? It's funny because we found something up there that was very interesting. A young woman. A dead young woman," said Josh.

"Oh shit," said the kid who had just pissed his pants.

"Shut up!" the second one said having recovered just enough of his voice.

"Now gentlemen, didn't you hear me? I'm not a cop. Just a curious type. Tell me about her," he demanded. But Derrick didn't move or say a word. Josh pointed the gun toward the younger kid. "You. Tell me. Now!" The intimidation worked.

"We just delivered her, nothing else," he said, tripping over his words and pissed his pants some more. He was visibly shaking, nearly falling down.

"Shut the fuck up Johnny!" the second kid yelled.

Josh stood up from Derrick and lowered his gun. He walked over to the first guy who quickly backed away fearing another blow. Josh stopped and turned toward the younger one and asked, "Delivered?"

"Yeah, we just got the deal. Derrick does the deals, I was just there you know, helping. I swear we didn't kill her or nothin'" he finished in a panicked voice.

Derrick had moved onto his hands and knees and gave an evil look at the kid who instantly went quiet. Josh returned to the leader. "Get up," he said as he put his gun back into his belt. Derrick stood up and waited. "Where did this delivery come from?" Josh asked.

"I don't know. They don't tell me anything," Derrick answered.

"Tell me what you do know," Josh said looking at him coldly in the eyes. His look was intimidating and Derrick began to soften up.

"I get a call. It's always a different number, always a different person. Usually I just take an envelope, or package, and deliver it some place. A house, a trash can, you know, stupid things. And they pay me for it. That's all."

"When?"

"Whenever they call. A few times a season."

"Who delivers this to you?"

"It's just left somewhere. I don't see anyone most of the time."

"But not this time. You killed her."

"No!" Derrick said. "No way."

"Well, we got some evidence at the scene that I'm guessing will link to those four wheelers. And blunt force trauma to the body. That happened before she was killed. And we caught you trying to assault another young woman. I think you're in some pretty deep shit unless you start talking," Josh said.

"We picked her up from a boat. It comes and goes all the time. Different people, they come and go all season," he answered. "We didn't kill her. We didn't even know what it was until they got here and made us take her."

"Who dropped her off?"

"I don't know. Honestly. I never saw him before and I doubt he knew what he was delivering. He was just like us you know. Said he was told to take the boat and come here with it."

"With her," Josh corrected.

"Whatever," Derrick replied.

"What's the name of the boat?"

"I don't know, man."

"Dream Catcher," the younger kid answered again.

"Damn it Johnny! I'm gonna whip your sorry ass!" Derrick screamed.

"No you won't," Josh said quietly as he stared Derrick down. He stood silent yet defiantly.

"How do you know this, Johnny," Josh asked.

"I saw it on the back. Dream Catcher, Chicago."

"Ok," Josh said. "Now Derrick, that young lady is a friend of mine," he said pointing over toward Abby. "As I said, I'm not a cop. But I want you to know that I'm placing a restraining order on you all." He moved in close to Derrick, who was a few inches taller than Decker and was trying hard to save face in front of his friends and not give any ground. "If I hear that you've been anywhere near her again, I'll kill you." His look was cold, calm, and penetrating. "Got it?"

"Yeah," Derrick answered, then swallowed hard.

"Good," Josh said, then began turning to leave. But in a flash, he instead turned back toward Derrick and kicked him full force in the balls. Derrick went down to the ground instantly writhing in terrible pain.

"I mean what I say. Think about it," Josh said standing over him. It was a clear warning that he was to be taken seriously. He looked around at the other two and added, "All of you." Then he walked toward the back of the building where Charlie and Abby had been watching.

Charlie led Abby with his arm around her shoulder as the three of them walked around the back of the building toward the rear door of the bar. Josh paused a moment next to the three four wheelers, taking mental notes on the fresh mud found on the tires. There was nothing distinctive about them though and they themselves didn't prove anything. He had bluffed and it paid off. But now the coerced confession he obtained had lured him into the case. He now had something to occupy his mind besides a delightfully boring security report for an international transport company. The three entered the back door of The Chance.

"I need to use your phone," Josh said to Charlie as he dropped behind into the small office in the back of the bar. Charlie took Abby to the front and sat her down on a barstool. He then walked behind the bar and poured her a glass of water.

"Oh my God. He was..." Abby was still a bit stunned more by what she witnessed as opposed to what had happened to her. "He was amazing," she finished.

"He's someone you don't want to fu... fool around with!" Charlie said, catching himself realizing he was talking to a young lady.

"Where did he learn to do that?" she asked, her eyes wide with wonder.

"He was a cop for years," Charlie answered.

"Yeah, but that wasn't at all police like."

"You know Abby. You're nobody's fool that's for sure," he said. "I've known Josh a long time and he doesn't take a lot of shit from people. He's one tough son-of-a-bitch. But at the same time, and don't you tell him I said this, but he wears his heart on his sleeve."

Abby thought about it for a moment, then asked Charlie, "How did you guys meet?"

"I tended bar back in Chicago years ago. He was a customer from time to time. You know bartenders. We do a lot of listening."

"So does Josh. I end up doing almost all of the talking."

84

"I bet that's nice though." Charlie leaned onto his elbow, resting on the opposite side of the bar.

"Yeah." Abby looked down, shying away a bit. Then looked back up having made sure she was composed. "I haven't had anyone to talk to in so long that I suppose I've talked his ear off. Half the time he probably isn't listening anyway!" she laughed.

"Well, I know one thing for sure, kiddo. Josh likes you. He'd of thrown you out if he didn't. Trust me," he assured.

Josh came out from the back office and sat down on a stool next to Abby.

"Anything?" Charlie asked.

"We'll see. Called a friend. He'll be calling back soon. If you'll let me know when he does," Josh said.

"I'm not making that hike up there again just to let you know he called," Charlie said being intentionally difficult.

"I'll hang around town for a while, ok?" Josh retorted. Charlie nodded his head. But Josh also didn't want to leave Abby alone until Derrick and the others had gone.

"So, you're back into it," Charlie said to Josh.

"I don't do that anymore," Josh insisted.

"Do what?" Abby asked.

"He's a hell of a homicide detective," Charlie answered.

"Was," said Josh.

"Why 'was'?" Abby asked. She knew he had worked as a detective, but not homicide or why he had left.

"Are you hungry?" he asked her, changing the subject.

"Yeah. I didn't get a chance to eat."

"What do you say we go down to the diner and grab a bite?"

"Sure," Abby said, looking up into his face. Then she focused on his eyes.

"You ok?" Josh asked, thoughtfully.

"Thank you, Josh." Abby's eyes began to well up with tears. "I mean, not just about this, but about letting me stay and talk your ear off." Feeling vulnerable for the first time since running away, she suddenly leapt over into his arms, wrapping hers around his neck in a warm embrace.

It took him by complete surprise. Josh slowly returned the embrace, wrapping his seemingly large arms around her and holding her close. He looked over to Charlie, who was watching them from behind the bar. Charlie smiled and gave a nod of approval. Under his breath so that only Josh could hear Charlie said, "Well, look at you."

22 – London

As she approached the café Molly spotted Anne sitting inside along the far wall away from the entrance. She was wearing large thick sunglasses and seemed hunched over. Molly walked in and when she saw her up close she was horrified.

"What on earth happened?" Molly asked.

Anne hesitated then cautiously answered, "I took a tumble, that's all."

"A tumble?" Molly asked astonished.

Anne gave no reply, but she was visibly trembling, her hands struggling to maintain a grip on her cigarette.

"What happened Anne? Tell me." Molly persisted, fearing the worst.

"I told you." Anne murmured, but then in what was seemingly a small act of defiance she removed her sunglasses revealing a deeply purple and swollen right eye, and a laceration just under her left one. The bridge of her nose was also swollen and purple, and she seemed to be having a difficult time breathing. Molly also noticed a cane leaning against the empty chair next to her.

Molly covered her mouth as if to physically hold back her shock. "No! Tell me who did this to you." Molly insisted as she took Anne's hand in comfort. She could feel her hand continue to tremble, so she squeezed it tighter.

Finally, after some effort, Anne said, "You know, you really are a lucky girl Moll." She made a strenuous effort to sound sincere. "You have someone who will always take care of you, you know? He's nothing like I thought."

"You mean Gordie?" Molly asked in a hushed voice, matching hers.

Anne spoke very slow and deliberately. "He really does care. A kind hearted man." Then she looked up into Molly's eyes, tears welling up in her own. "He and his friends, stopped by and we had a nice chat." She continued slowly, carefully pronouncing each word as if she were reading from a script. "And I was told, I mean asked, to let you know that I think Gordie is a wonderful man." Then she squeezed Molly's hand with all her strength and said, "You can count on him, he's always watching – over you." She said ominously.

Molly nodded. She understood the message all too well and she understood that Anne was saying much more than what she was ordered to say. To keep her safe, Molly would also have to play along.

"I have to go now." Anne said. She let go of Molly's hand and with great effort and in great pain slowly took to her feet with the help of a cane. Molly also helped her up.

"Stay for a while, tell me..." Molly began.

"No!" Anne interrupted. "I really must go. Now." She insisted. "Don't worry. Don't call me Moll. I love you... so don't ever call me. Okay?"

"I love you too." Molly answered.

Anne slowly made her way out of the café with each step seemingly calculated in order to prevent herself from falling. Molly sat down, buried her head in her hands and began to cry. 'How could it have come to this?' she thought. 'It is all my fault... I should have been stronger...' More importantly she pondered, 'What am I going to do now?'

Somehow, over the next fifteen minutes she managed to finish a cup of tea and compose herself. She walked out and noticed two of Gordie's mates sitting outside at a pub across the street having a beer. They both gazed at her with menacing eyes that left no doubt that they meant business. Then one of them gave Molly a wink and a smile.

A chill ran through her. She turned and hastily made her way to the underground.

23 – Moscow

A pretty young girl stood at the gate of Domodedovo Moscow airport with Valery Zhukov. The older, heavyset Russian man was dressed in a dark business suit. It was busy, somewhat chaotic, with people crowded down the terminal passageways in their effort to get to and from their flights. They stood together awkwardly waiting. Finally, a tall, thin man emerged from the crowd of passengers having just arrived. He wore a stylish, plain white dress shirt, no tie, comfortable gray slacks and he was chewing gum.

"Mr. Chase," the Russian man began, "This is Nonna."

"Call me Gordie young lady." There was no reply. "Ty govorish' po-angliyski?"

"Net," she answered.

"Shit Zhuk, this is going to be a long flight," Gordie complained. Then he grabbed Nonna's chin and turned her head back and forth as if he was inspecting a slab of meat. "She's a young one now, ain't she?"

"She'll just sit quiet," Zhukov said in a thick, monotone Russian accent. He sounded cold and deliberate. "I've explained everything to her. She is happy to see America."

"Right. I'll bet she is, ain't cha little girl?" Gordie said condescendingly bending slightly down to her and exaggerating a smile. He finally let go of her chin.

"Here." Zhukov handed Gordie a brown envelope. He opened it and took out the girl's passport, visa, and wiring information for receiving payment.

"Nice," he said, repackaging the paperwork but holding onto the girl's passport. He opened it and looked at it.

"Damn Zhuk! Where'd you get her anyway? She's barely fifteen."

"She is shy and dumb," he answered. "She will do."

"Yeah, but I was hoping you'd bring me one of those beautiful Russian women you know? One of the big ones!" he gestured to his chest holding his hands out suggestively.

"Do as you please," Zhukov said coldly. "Just hold the papers."

"Right. Well, the Doctor wants you undamaged little girl, so I guess we'll have to behave ourselves. Eto normal'no dlya tebya?"

"da" Nonna answered, not knowing what she was agreeing to.

"And remind the doctor that *we* are running out of patience. This is the last one. If he does not produce the code with her, we're finished. As is our dealings with you." Zhukov warned.

"I'm just a messenger. I'm sure there are other jobs you got for a guy like me?" Gordie asked looking to be reassured.

"Perhaps you already know too much for your own good?" Gordie said nothing in reply, understanding the implied threat. "Two weeks. That's it. No more. Be sure the good doctor understands that... and you. If he is not here with the code, he is dead," his thick accent trailed off.

Gordie was less frightened than angered by the implication that he would also suffer the same fate if the doctor was not successful. He looked sternly into Zhukov's eyes and didn't blink. If he could have, he would have preferred to kill the Russian then and there. Zhukov handed Gordie two airline tickets, turned and began walking away.

Nonna watched as he left, then looked up at Gordie. He turned to her and, still agitated, he pinched the sides of her lips forcing her to pucker. He turned her head to the left, then to the right again with some force.

"You've got beautiful big eyes there," Gordie said. "Oh how I could make those big brown eyes cry." She just looked up at him, not understanding a word he said. He let go of her face and said, "Come on, we've got a fucking plane to catch."

The two walked off together and two hours later boarded a plane bound for Chicago.

24 – Highland

It was a bright and beautiful day. The autumn air was growing crisp and the sun illuminated the rich colors of the leaves still rustling on the trees. The trail around Josh's cottage was long and winding and there seemed no better way to spend the afternoon than to enjoy a long, peaceful walk.

"Who was she? Do you know?" Abby asked.

"Who?" Josh answered.

"The girl," she said. "Was she..." Abby paused trying to find the words.

"Dead?" Josh said.

"Well, yeah. I mean, who was she? What did she look like?"

"She looked dead," Josh said coldly.

"Well I figured that."

Josh stopped walking, turned to face her and said, "Some things you just don't need to know."

"I want to know."

"Why?" Josh asked.

"Because she was somebody. Someone somewhere is missing her. She was a little girl at one time and her father probably thought the world of her. His little princess! She felt happiness and joy. Sometimes cried herself to sleep, you know. Things we all do... I'm just curious."

"You're personalizing this."

"So? Is that bad?"

"You can't allow yourself to become attached like that. It'll eat you up trying to explain the unexplainable. 'Why bad things happen to good people' sort of thing. There's a real ugly truth about humanity Abby, and it's really horrible what some people are capable of doing to others. There is nothing to gain by hearing about it, or trying to figure it out because there is no answer. And you're better off just letting it go." Josh turned and resumed his walk, but Abby didn't follow. He stopped a short distance away. "Are you coming?" he asked without turning back around.

She was lost in thought, trying to soak in everything she just heard. His words hurt. In a single moment he was able to destroy a great deal of her optimism. For the first time since meeting Josh, she felt alone.

"Don't you think someone should give a damn? Shouldn't someone do something?" Abby asked scornfully.

Josh turned around, "You mean me?"

"Someone," she said. "I feel like if we don't care than no one will and then what? Nothing?"

"Why don't you go home?" Josh asked her.

Abby stood in silence for a long time, staring back at him.

"What the fuck is your problem?" she said to herself but so he could hear. Josh turned and began to walk away when she added, "Ripples never come back." He stopped and looked back at her. "Ever wonder if all the pain in the world began with one stone thrown. Then another, and another. It doesn't take much to get people going at each other. And you can't turn it back, it's too late to stop it. You just have to 'let it go' and life will be fine. Then one day I realized I could be a ripple myself and just go away. No one would care, or notice. And you know what I learned? I learned it's true! No one noticed! There're no posters of me anywhere. I'm not on the side of a fucking carton of milk! I've been gone for months now and no one has ever come looking."

Josh looked around knowing he had opened up something he hadn't intended. She continued in a non-emotional, factual and somewhat angry tone, "I'll go if you want me to, but I won't go back home. There is no *home* for me. My parents are both dead and no one gives a damn. I think I had a sister, or at least I remember someone older than me who was around a lot when I was very small but I don't know who she was, or is. My aunt and uncle are fucking drunks and drug addicts. And I have no fucking clue why I'm not more fucked up than I am. Why I'm not shooting up dope, dropping acid with a bunch of shithead friends and fucking every guy who wants a little action. But I'm not. But if I had stayed any longer I might just be doing all those things. I just figured, no one is ever going to hand me my happiness. I have to go find it for myself."

She took a few steps toward Josh whose back was still turned. He hadn't moved a muscle but had listened intently. She kicked some fallen leaves casually. "Actually, no. I'd be dead by now," she added. "No way I'd let some prick get the best of me. I'd be dead, just like that girl you found. And no one would care. 'Nothing to see here!' Just another stiff who ran up against fate. No big deal. No reason to give a shit." Abby strolled past Josh and resumed their walk. Josh followed.

"Everyone is forgotten eventually," Josh said, as if talking to no one. "Most people are forgotten within a generation. Many before they even die." Slowly he caught up to her pace and said, "We don't make the rules. It's a very cold-hearted world. Nature does its thing every moment. It creates and destroys in the same breath. And once you get burned by it you come to realize just how much nothing matters anymore. There are no heroes, Abby. We all just wait our turn."

"Wow, that's really cynical, Josh. You might be the next Tony Robbins!" Abby cracked sarcastically.

"No more cynical than your 'what if' story. You think I haven't heard it all before?" he asked, then he took her gently by the arm, stopping and turning her around to face him. "You don't need to know all about this. You don't know what you're getting into. Seeing a victim... Trying to understand why... Murder is something you just don't get over." They began walking again.

"All the more reason," Abby said.

"All the more reason for what?"

"To do something." Abby stepped in front of him and grabbed his arms, "Don't let her be forgotten Josh, please!" Josh just stood there looking down into Abby's deep brown eyes as they gazed up in desperate hope at him. "Did you ever believe that everything happens for a reason? I heard that one time at church. I thought, 'how ridiculous! What a way to cop out of all the shit happening in the world.' But now I'm not so sure. She's here, in Highland of all places. Why? Because I'm here? Or you?"

"Abby..." Josh started

"It could have been me, Josh. And I feel like I'm her only voice. I don't want to let it go. I don't know why, but she needs a voice." They stood there for a moment. Then Josh resumed walking away when Abby added, "Maybe that's why you isolate yourself in that cottage like you do. Or why you left the force maybe? You got too close? You personalized it?" Josh stopped. It seemed like minutes passed before he spoke.

"You know," Josh began as he turned around to face her, "You are an amazing young woman, beyond your years really. And I envy your idealism, but the fact is..." He caught sight of her eyes as they shifted to the ground in surrender. He didn't like the thought of bringing this beautiful, bright, wonderful young lady standing in front of him into what he considered the dark reality of the world. But he could see he was now directly causing her pain, and that felt even worse.

"Abby, don't ever let some old shit like me ruin your optimism. I just seem to be stuck in the darkness. I can't let it go." He shook his head, "You just... Well, I'm not worried about you."

"Why not?" she asked.

"Because, despite everything, you hold on to your humanity. And it's beautiful. Maybe I've forgotten how to do that. I sit on the porch and look out toward the lake, the sunset, the colors on the trees... but all I see is darkness. Pain. You can't just wish it away. It follows you wherever you go."

Abby smiled at him. "I know that feeling. I feel trapped," she confided. "Like a bird in a cage. I want to fly away but I'm tied down and I can't go anywhere. All I can do is imagine and sometimes that's just not enough anymore. I used to imagine being on my own, being free, away from everything." Tears began to drip from her moist eyes. "And... I'm really scared."

Josh put his arm around her and they resumed their walk. "You are something else," he said.

She quickly composed herself again and after walking a while in silence she said, "You know, I heard somewhere that there's beauty in dark places. Not sure I believe it." She wondered if he knew what she meant.

"I need a drink," Josh sighed.

"I know a place we can get a beer," Abby suggested.

Josh chuckled and squeezed her close for a second, like a proud parent. He stopped and turned her around to face him. She looked up at him again with her deep, curious eyes. He put his hands on her shoulders as if he was about to say something very serious. "How about some ice cream?"

She smiled and couldn't help but burst into laughter. Then, for some reason, her eyes welled with tears and the laughter turned into crying. It was long overdue. Josh pulled her into his arms and she wrapped hers around him tightly.

"It's not your fault Abby. That I can tell you."

In that moment she began to let go of a lifetime of pain and running away. She cried hard. He stroked her hair and kissed the top of her head. After a long while they continued their walk through the woods.

"I'll do what I can for her," he promised.

25 – London

It was a sickly sour – her stomach felt like it was twisting and turning slowly. She had just began to notice it distinctively, but when Molly thought about it she realized it had been slowly building in her for months. Her life was no longer normal. Her appetite had diminished, her nerves were on edge, and she was finding it difficult to concentrate and focus. Was it the Holy Trinity project? Her first real chance to work on an original piece for a church? Or was it the stress of her relationship with Gordie?

Had he changed? 'Not really,' she thought. He had always been domineering toward her, but only recently had he forced her to act on his behalf, like her visit to the bank. On several other similar missions as of late she delivered envelopes, wired funds, and made a couple of phone calls. She asked no questions. She feared to do so. She had even neglected the pictures she snapped on her phone of the documents at the bank. But now he had crossed the line. She couldn't stop imagining what Anne had gone through, or the sight of her limping away. She felt she had to learn more about what he was up to.

Molly took out her phone and opened the images she had snapped of the documents at the bank. She zoomed in on the first and reviewed the basic wire transfer instructions. Money was transferred from her account to a Swiss bank in Zurich. There was a name, Valery Zhukov. It sounded Russian, so the Russian documents now seemed to make sense. The second page looked like an itinerary with times, dates, and flight information. "Gordon Chase" arriving in Moscow. "Gordon Chase" and a list of names including, "Lucya Averin, Nonna Petrov." Lucya's name had been circled. Below Lucya's name it read, "Flight 067 to Chicago, USA." And she could barely make out a final flight for "Gordon Chase" to London. All were dated from a couple weeks ago. 'But hadn't he just returned to London yesterday?' she thought.

'Nonna?' Molly wondered. 'Who is this person?' Barely visible due to the image being blurred and cropped at the bottom was also a financial figure of "£50,000 upon delivery." Molly flipped to the third page. It was written in Russian and also had financial figures on it. It was short, and had a wild looking signature which she was unable to comprehend.

She wasn't sure what to make of any of it. The money and secretive nature of her instructions, Mr. Stephens at the bank, and now the apparent physical abuse of her friend Anne, all made her very uneasy. But she was still in the dark. For all she knew the documents were a normal part of his job.

Still, she was determined to find some answers. But she knew Gordie would not offer them. 'How dangerous was he?' she asked herself. Just the thought sent a literal shiver down her spine. 'No, it can't be. Can it?' she thought.

Gordie had always told her he was in the international logistics business. It involved a lot of travel and odd hours. She never thought much more about it until he began asking her to perform such tasks. She uploaded the images to the 'cloud' and erased them from her phone. She sighed and put on some music in her headphones. She sat down and began to reconstruct her personal project that Gordie had smashed earlier. She had been reluctant to pursue it again, but it had become instinctively important to her – an emotional outlet that connected her with a sense of hope. She placed a clean pane of slightly frosted glass onto her desktop and picked up a pencil.

Just as she was about to begin drawing onto the glass, she stopped. She had noticed the pencil was shaking. No, it was her hand. She watched intently as she tried to hold it still, but it would not stop. The tiny, rapid, impulsive movements back and forth hypnotized her. For a moment she felt her strength slipping away as if the pencil was trying to scribble out a warning to her. A tear began to swell in the corner of her eye, but she half blinked and opened them wider. Her brow curled, she closed her eyes, and took a long deep breath. Determined, when she opened her eyes and looked again the pencil was quite still, resting with ease in her hand.

26 – Chicago

"Who's there?" her soft voice attempted to shout but could only just manage a whisper. It was as if she was coming out of a very deep sleep.

"There, there now, just relax Nonna dear." She heard his voice clearly. He spoke passively and without emotion, even though she didn't understand much more than her own name. She took a deep breath, but with even the slightest move her head throbbed with excruciating pain.

"Who?" she said again, in Russian.

This time a Russian voice, a woman's, answered, "It's all right dear. Just try to relax, the pain will not last much longer."

She managed to open her eyes exposing an incredibly bright, foggy world around her. She was reclined. Her limbs felt lifeless and heavy. She was incredibly high on nitrous oxide, the dentist's 'laughing gas.' Even when she spoke she felt as if she hadn't said anything at all, that it was someone else actually talking.

"Where is the egg now?" Nonna asked, 'or was it someone else?' she thought.

"What egg is that Nonna?" the gentle Russian voice seemed to echo in her brain as if it was a giant hallowed out tin can. Every sound amplified like a tidal wave shuffling back and forth, side to side through her head. She took a deep breath, allowing more nitrous oxide to infiltrate. She suddenly relaxed.

"Nooooonnnnnnaaaaa…." The woman's voice called softly but it sounded as if she were screaming echoes into her ear at point blank range. "Are you there sweetie? Noooonnnnaaaaa…?"

"I can't, please!" she barely murmured. Her own voice being equally painful to hear.

"What egg darling? What egg?"

The Doctor turned off the light.

From Nonna's perspective the light emptied into darkness and she stopped squinting. It seemed as if instantly a weight had lifted from her head and although still in pain, it was much more bearable.

"There. She should be ready anytime now," Dr. Sullivan announced calmly. The sound of latex gloves being removed with a snap followed. "Don't remove the restraints. She mustn't move for a few hours."

"Nonna?" the woman continued to speak to the girl, their conversation continuing in Russian, trying to wake her from her groggy slumber again.

"Mother?" Nonna responded.

"Yes dear, tell me what you were holding?"

"My egg mama, where is my little egg?"

"I will help you find it Nonna, tell me what it looks like," she asked.

"Little, silver, sparkling…" she answered

"Like a Fabergé egg?"

"Yes! Do you have it? I lost it. Do you see it?" Nonna was almost panicking.

"I think I see it. How is it decorated Nonna? Tell me how it is decorated."

"Shiny and silver, and blue."

"Blue? What is the blue Nonna."

But Nonna seemed to drift back into sleep. Then she was startled by a firm hand on her shoulder, jerking her back and forth with force and a sharp male voice, in English, "Nonna! Come on now!"

She opened her eyes wide and looked into the dimly lit room, up at the woman who had been talking with her in Russian. Her hair was pulled back tightly and all she could make out was the oval of her face. She looked old to Nonna, somewhat frightening like some witch out of a fairy tale trying to pass herself off as caring and kind.

"Now dear, that's right. Tell me, how your little egg was decorated?" she asked.

"Serebryanyy (Silver). Blestyashchiy (Shiny). Sverkayushchiy (Sparkling,)" Nonna answered.

The woman bent down over her face and getting very close she said, "A takzhe? (And?)"

Nonna paused for a moment, then seemed to go into a small trance, again as if the nitrous oxide had taken control and she was speaking involuntarily, without hesitation and in English. "3729543...sully4.3.5395... mag86... 25... double... GX1=1... GX2=25..." she continued to speak, now beginning to articulate a specific fractal encryption code which sounded like gibberish to the woman. But not to the man sitting next to her.

His face lit up with excitement that he was barely able to contain. He pushed his thin wire rimmed glasses up onto his skinny, boney nose, and smiled from ear to ear. Within an instant he began to chuckle, then laugh out loud with considerable exuberance as Nonna continued to recite the code.

It was precise and as clear as if she was reading it off a piece of paper. She could tell it was her voice talking, but to her, still groggy from the gas, it seemed as though it was someone else speaking. She had no idea how, or what she was doing.

"Yaytso (the egg)?" the woman interrupted urgently. "Nonna! Yaytso!"

Nonna suddenly stopped reciting the code. She closed her eyes as if she was thinking hard about it. She then opened them again and looked straight into the woman's eyes.

"Sapphires," she said matter-of-factly and in English. "The egg is covered with bright blue Sapphires."

"AH!" came a sharp voice amid the shadows in the back of the room. Anita quickly caught herself placing her hand over her lips in a vain attempt to contain her enthusiasm.

"May I try?" she asked.

"Certainly," Dr. Sullivan answered.

Anita stood up and made her way over to Nonna who was illuminated with only a very soft golden light. "Nonna dear, tell me again about your egg?"

"Serebryanyy. Blestyashchiy. Yarko-goluboy... sapphires." Nonna smiled at the vision she now had of a beautiful Fabergé.

"Ah huh!" Anita again had to stifle her excitement. She turned to him saying, "Oh Sully! This is absolutely incredible!" Her eyes were wide and bright, sparkling with extreme lust at the very thought of what this experiment meant.

"Indeed, my dear," Dr. Sullivan answered. "But now comes the true test." He rose from his chair and walked back over toward Nonna and looked down over her as she had drifted back unconscious. "The implantation appears successful. We must now be able to extract the same."

"She can already! She just said it," Anita said.

"No, no, no," He corrected. "it would take her hours, if not days to repeat the entire code and program sequence. We don't have that kind of time. The code they provided is over 400 kilobytes of information. That's about two to three hundred pages," he said proudly with a smile. "She must rest tonight. Tomorrow, we will begin the extraction process."

He began to remove the eight electrodes from around her head. Then he gave Nonna a shot of medication through the I.V. that ran into her left arm. "This will help you sleep until then, my dear."

Anita walked over to her, gently stroked her forehead, saying adoringly, "Sweet dreams princess."

27 – Highland

Josh stood with his SCCY 9mm pistol aimed and ready to shoot. The morning air was crisp and he could see his breath misting around his face as he drew long, steady breaths of the cold air. The sky was glowing bright, but the look in his eyes was stone cold. The gun resting in his hands was perfectly still, his finger poised on the trigger. Slowly he squeezed the trigger until suddenly a shot smacked through the air and punctured a paper target, about 25 feet away, mounted in front of a sand pile behind the cottage.

Abby's heart was racing after being startled by the shot. She watched as Josh continued to unload the weapon into the target. Two, three, four, five, six, seven, eight, nine, ten, all rattled off as he moved slowly to his right. Every shot hit within a couple of inches of the target's center. Once stopped, he exhaled and released the clip. He walked over to a table he had set up outside his back door where Abby was standing.

"You don't pull the trigger. You squeeze it with the middle of your finger," he instructed. He handed her the empty magazine. "Here, try loading it."

Abby reached into a small brown paper bag full of ammunition and began placing the rounds into the magazine as he had shown her.

"You're a natural," Josh said, admiring her progress.

"I doubt that," she quipped as her hands were shaking. Within in a couple of minutes she had finished loading the magazine and placed it into the grip, pulled the slide back and released. The gun was ready to fire. She held it carefully and moved herself to the front of the table and in front of Josh who reached his arms around her to properly position her hands around the weapon.

"Just relax," he spoke loudly into her ear though it seemed more a whisper due to the ear plugs. "Remember what I've told you. Breathe slowly and grip it firmly but not too hard. Look at your target. Front site with your dominant eye. Take a nice deep breath... and squeeze."

Abby had never fired a gun before and she was shaking. Josh backed away leaving her to shoot on her own. After a few tense moments, Abby lowered the weapon without removing her hands from it. She looked down in front of her then closed her eyes. She took a deep breath. Then in a single motion she opened her eyes, raised the gun and squeezed the trigger. Her eyes blinked at the sudden crackle and kick back of the gun. But it was a great relief! She smiled and lowered the weapon again.

"Holy shit, Abby! Where'd you learn to shoot like that?" Josh shouted.

"Did I hit it?" she asked.

"Hit it? Hell yes you hit it! You hit the fucking bulls-eye!" Josh said proudly.

"I must've had a great teacher I guess."

"Try it again," Josh encouraged.

Abby slowly rattled off the rest of the rounds, most of them hitting the target but a few running astray. They removed their ear protection and Josh began to reload.

"Not bad. Not bad at all," Josh said.

"I don't know. I think it can be easy to get addicted to this!" Abby said excitedly.

"Well, targets are one thing. It's more important that you know your way around a gun just in case."

"I appreciate it, but I can run especially fast!" Abby quipped.

"Yeah, I noticed you packed your bag last night," he said.

Abby looked sullen and furrowed her lips. "I thought I might be going."

"It's getting cold these days. Ever think about hunkering down for the winter somewhere?" Josh asked. When Abby didn't answer Josh added, "You can't run away forever."

"I've learned it's better to be on the move." Abby felt compelled to rebuild her inner strength once again after feeling vulnerable the other day during their walk.

"Well, I think you should stay. And I may be gone for a while anyway, with this case now. And if you're going to be here I want you to be prepared." he said as he finished loading the magazine and handed it to Abby for another round of shooting practice.

"Prepared? Do you really think those guys will come after me?" Abby asked.

"No. I think Derrick and his friends won't want to have anything to do with you now. But consider it a life lesson. Better safe than sorry, right?" Josh asked.

"Right," Abby agreed with a smile. She took the loaded magazine and slide it into the grip with a much more confident force. She replaced her ear protection, turned toward the target, lowered the weapon again, and raised it in a single motion preparing to fire.

"Hold up!" a voice called out suddenly and loud. It was Charlie who had been making his way to the cottage but was nearly in the line of fire.

Startled, Abby jerked the gun slightly to her left and pulled the trigger. A shot tore off in the direction of the voice, nearly hitting him.

"Holy shit!" Charlie yelled. Josh quickly grabbed Abby's hands and lowered the gun as she continued to grip it.

"Charlie? Come on out!" Josh shouted.

"Damn you Josh! If you know it's me then why'd you shoot?" Charlie shouted as he emerged from the woods along the pathway that lead up the hill to his cottage and from there into town.

"It was me Mr. Webber. I'm so sorry!" Abby called out. "Josh was teaching me how to shoot and I guess I let one get away from me." Abby was quick to put the gun down onto the table.

"Oh, I see." Charlie said as he approached. He smiled and added, "Don't worry, I'm alright. Just giving this guy a hard time's all. It wasn't that close," Charlie said taking a deep breath as if he had just finished seeing his life pass before his eyes.

"You really shouldn't come up unannounced," Josh said poking fun at Charlie.

Charlie turned to Abby and said, "You really need to find a better teacher."

Abby chuckled, "He's a great teacher, I promise. It was my fault, I'm so sorry."

"No, no. It's fine," Charlie insisted. "Call came in from the M.E. and wanted to know why he should run more toxicology. What's he supposed to look for specifically?"

"Abby, Charlie looks like that hike has really worn him out," Josh said mockingly. "Can you go get him some water?"

"Really? Worn me out? I'll remember that," Charlie said in response to Josh's dry wit.

"I'll just go inside so you can talk, how's that?" Abby asked.

"Right," Josh said. Abby walked in the cottage and shut the door.

"I'm not sure. Why'd he ask?" Josh said.

"Said he checked for any drugs in her system but found nothing unusual. A little alcohol, some traces of amphetamines. Nothing 'too out of the ordinary'. Those were his words," Charlie said.

"Did he check on the blue mark behind her ear?"

"Yeah, said he didn't know what you wanted him to look for. Said the bruises were made just after she died, so it doesn't look like an accidental overdose."

"She was found in the woods and placed there by a group of thugs acting as stooges for someone getting rid of a body. I didn't think she just found herself naked and lost in the middle of the woods."

"Yeah, so now what?"

"No drugs. I didn't expect that," Josh said as he stood thinking for a moment. "Would you keep an eye on Abby for me?"

"Sure. Where you going?"

"Chicago. I'd like to borrow the old man's boat," Josh said referring to Chief Haig. "Is it still in the water?"

"Yeah, it's where it always is," Charlie answered. "Why are you taking the boat?"

"Because that's what I'm looking for. The 'Dream Catcher'."

28 – Chicago

"Now my dear, just hold still," Dr. Sullivan said rhetorically as he inserted the long thick needle into Nonna's neck, just behind her jaw and under her right ear. He squeezed the syringe gently, forcing the dark blue 'sapphire' liquid up into her cerebral cortex. The I.V. kept her safely unconscious and the Russian nurse who accompanied Nonna sat next to her monitoring her blood pressure and pulse.

The doctor removed the needle and turned to his left to face his laptop. He typed a command into the computer application and a tone signaled that it was ready to receive information.

He placed the electrodes onto Nonna's skin, all around her head. Once they were in place he pressed a function key on the computer. The screen changed and the program began functioning.

"And now the download begins," Dr. Sullivan said.

"Will it take long?" Anita asked. She was seated in the far corner of the room, observing the entire process from the shadows.

"It should be almost instantaneous once it finds the pathway containing the code," he said.

"This is so exciting!" Anita could barely contain herself.

"It is, indeed," Dr. Sullivan added, "the dawn of a new era right here in this little office." His face glowed as his beady eyes widened under his thin gold rim glasses.

"Right here in this little girl!" Anita almost squealed with delight.

A few minutes passed, yet the computer had not detected the neural pathway as expected.

"Humm... Perhaps a bit more of the sapphire derivative." Sullivan re-inserted the needle and injected more of the blue liquid.

"There! You're picking up something now," Anita said as she monitored the computer that was reading Nonna's brainwaves and translating them into discernable information. This was the essence of the 'Sapphire' technology which up to this point worked well enough to relay strong symbols or images, especially those attached to strong emotions. But could it find a massive amount of information not associated with emotion? The first round with Nonna proved successful. Now for the computer to capture and 'download' exactly what had been implanted prior.

"It's not enough. These items are images associated with her current condition," he responded. "That damn blue egg again. So close!"

"Her pulse is slowing a bit," the nurse advised.

"Blood pressure?"

"Looks good."

"A little more?" He squeezed another milligram of sapphire into her brain.

"Anything?" Anita asked.

He waited a moment, then becoming frustrated he said "No! Nothing! Stupid Russian bitch!"

"Be patient with her, she's only a child," the nurse retorted.

"A child?" he turned toward her and began rebuking. "The mind of a child is the perfect model. It is a clean slate upon which to write my code! Like a sculptor shapes the marble into beautiful works of art and interpretation, I too possess the power to shape the mind of a child! Unless she's already a mindless form of human debris! What has your government given me anyway?"

"They give what it is you ask for," She added with broken English and her strong Russian accent. "a young girl who is not to be missed. Who is little educated. Who is, as you say, clean slate! I am to keep her safe."

The computer sounded an alert, which broke up the argument. The doctor turned toward the screen and observed a portion of the coded information he was hoping to find.

"Yes! There it is! Finally."

"I knew it would work Sully, I just knew it!" Anita chimed in, bouncing a little in her chair as she placed her hands up to her mouth in excitement.

"Perhaps she's not as dumb witted as I suspected," Dr. Sullivan said in a soft but cautious tone.

"She's a good girl," the nurse replied defensively. She had clearly developed sympathy and attachment to the young girl.

A few minutes passed before the Doctor realized another problem. "This is some sort of redundancy," he said becoming frustrated once again.

"What do you mean?" Anita asked.

"It's not capturing anything more than this. And the conductivity is slowing."

"She should not stay under much longer," the nurse stated.

"I will try something different," said Dr. Sullivan.

He reached for the needle again, and inserted it as before.

"No more!" the nurse argued.

"Mind your business," he rebuked her sharply. "I need to decrease the interference. The brainwaves are being distorted."

He began to push the needle deeper up into her brain, slowly moving it back and forth as if adjusting the antenna on an antique television set. He knew that this would most likely cause permanent brain damage, but he didn't care. His goal was to retrieve the code. He'd work on a more refined process that would not cause significant injury, or death, later.

"What are you doing?" the nurse asked.

"Shhh!" he replied, keeping his eyes on the computer screen. Then he moved the needle even further. Nonna's entire body shivered. Her left hand suddenly grasped the nurse tightly.

'Everything's spinning!' Nonna shouted in her mind. 'Help me please! I am falling! Help, help! I can't stop! I'm going to fall... I'm going to...'

"There!" Dr. Sullivan announced. He had inserted the needle almost up to its limit and began injecting the 'sapphire' liberally in order to drown out the girl's conscious brain activity.

"Stop it! She's scared!" the nurse complained.

"Keep her under!" the doctor snarled.

"You're going to kill her!" the nurse warned.

"There it is! The code is downloading! It's working!" he was becoming very excited. Anita grinned in the background as the nurse was struck with panic and horror. The girl's eyes opened wide and began rolling uncontrollably around in her head, violently shifting from side to side, top to bottom, and around and around. Her muscles in her arms and legs were flinching, jerking this way and that, uncontrollably. Dr. Sullivan wrapped his right arm around her head in an effort to hold her head steady. But soon her entire body began flopping around in the reclined chair.

"Lay on her!" he ordered. "More Propofol!

"No! Stop it now! Stop it now!" the nurse insisted.

"Do it!" he shouted.

Anita leapt up from her chair and laid herself down over the girl, holding her securely in place.

"Do as he says!" she snapped at the nurse like a disobedient servant. But the nurse just slowly backed away from the entire scene in shock and horror.

Anita reached up with her right hand and squeezed the I.V. drip bag, forcing an indeterminable amount of propofol into the girl's system. Within seconds, Nonna had relaxed, but was now barely breathing.

"You're killing her!" the nurse warned.

"The code is coming!" the Dr. Sullivan confirmed. "It's almost finished! It's absolutely amazing!"

Anita smiled as she lifted herself off the girl's virtually lifeless body.

"You did it! You're a genius!" she said.

"I couldn't have done it without you my dearest," he replied.

An alert tone sounded. "It's done!" Dr. Sullivan exclaimed.

The nurse quickly rushed back over to Nonna and placed an oxygen mask onto her face. But there was no response. Her lips had turned blue and she had now stopped breathing.

Doctor Sullivan removed the interface connection between the electrodes and his computer. Then he carried the laptop to his desk with such care as might be given to a fragile new born baby. The nurse was left alone in fighting to revive little Nonna.

The glow of the computer screen seemed to hypnotize Anita and Dr. Sullivan, admiring the data it had retrieved. Their eyes were aglow with reverence as he showed her page after page of the code, giggling as if they were indeed excited new parents.

"We've just witnessed the dawn of a new era! A giant leap into the age of cybernetic life!"

"She's dead," said the nurse solemnly. She ended her attempt at revising the girl.

The Dr. turned around, only just becoming aware of the fact that his patient had passed.

"Damn!" he said loudly. "I would've preferred her alive. Your Russian friends want a real-time demonstration. Oh well, the experiment needed to work first and foremost!" he said intensely.

"I am to keep her safe!" The nurse broke down weeping in the corner of the room.

"I'm sure we can find another one," Anita tried to reassure. "You are so close now!"

"Close? No! I have it now! It would have worked for sure. Damn Russians! Sent me this garbage." The nurse looked appalled at him. "We must find someone quickly." He stared at the young girl, calmed down, and appeared to come to his senses.

He leaned over to her, stroked her forehead, and whispered as he gazed into her lifeless eyes, "In time, little one, your sacrifice will be remembered. When death is but a shadow and can no longer touch us."

29 - Chicago

It had been a fairly smooth crossing, making the voyage from Highland to Chicago in just under four hours. Josh spent the better part of the day cruising to and from the few Chicago marinas still open and mooring vessles. At Belmont Harbor he spoke to the owner of a small trawler who had fished out of the harbor for years, but never recalled seeing the 'Dream Catcher.' The fisherman directed him south to Burnham where he figured a lot of doctors and lawyers kept their boats so as to be near downtown. En route, Josh pulled in and scanned Diversity and DuSable harbors but they were mostly empty and there was no sign of the craft. Monroe harbor was near downtown but mainly moored sailboats. He passed it by. When he finally arrived at Belmont he needed fuel which provided a good opportunity to speak with the help who could tell him more about the vessels that frequented.

Josh scanned the harbor before pulling into a slip. Burnham Park Marina was near downtown Chicago and was still fairly active even this late in the season. The attendant knew the 'Dream Catcher' well but didn't know when she'd be back in port. But he had the right place and he decided to rent a slip for the night, planning to spend the evening lying in wait on the boat. He walked over to the store to pick up some basic supplies. On his way back to the boat, as luck would have it, he spotted her just entering the harbor. She moored a short distance from his slip, and two younger looking men, wearing thick sunglasses and grungy looking baseball caps and jackets, hopped off and proceeded to walk into town.

Josh dropped his supplies off to his boat then walked over to take a closer look. The 'Dream Catcher' was a 42 foot sport cruiser, sleek in design, and probably only a few years old. The 'Dream Catcher' was the only significant recreational vessel still in the water. She was handsome indeed, seating six or more in the cockpit and a nice sundeck stretching across to the bow.

"Hello!" Decker called onto the boat, but there was no answer. "Hello! Anyone here?" he called again, but no answer. He took out a stick of gum, put it in his mouth and began to chew. He placed the wrapper in his pocket and without hesitation proceeded to climb aboard with a calm confidence.

He knew what he was looking for – something out of the ordinary. But in this case, that meant almost everything. The boat showed signs of having been host to a party of sorts recently. Empty cups and beer cans were littered all around, a few in the cup holders still partially full. He made his way down into the cabin. Several articles of men's and women's clothing were strewn on the floor and the slight stench of marijuana smoke lingered in the air. A storage closet door was wide open with its contents spilling out: a few lines, a toolbox with the usual assortment of tools, and several large fishing knives.

'Must have been some party' he thought as he continued to chew his gum while opening several drawers and cabinets. He was looking more than searching, waiting until something relevant stood out. He was patient and methodical. As a detective, Josh learned to trust intuition first, then follow the evidence wherever it may lead. It had always served him well.

An askew cushion caught his eye. In the compartment below it he found a couple of life jackets and a clipped stack of yellow and pink papers – invoices. He flipped through the papers until he found a receipt for an engine repair. The owners of the boat were listed on the invoice. It belonged to three men: Kurt Flowers, John Reeves, and Dr. Eugene Sullivan. He folded the pink colored paper and placed it in his coat pocket.

The bedroom door was ajar, light shining from the porthole above made it easy to see in. The king size bed was not made and more clothing was scattered rather indiscriminately around the room. He checked the nightstands. On one stood an empty fifth of rum, in the drawer a half empty pint of vodka, an open pack of cigarettes, some condoms, and a remote control for the TV. On the opposite nightstand were the remains of a few joints in an ash tray. The impression left on Josh was that the boat was likely being used by one or more younger men. Certainly not the condition in which a mature man, a doctor, would typically leave his boat.

He made his way back up to the cockpit and searched around for more information that might be helpful. He located a set of keys to the boat and the GPS. He turned it on hoping to review the 'Recent Destinations' file, but they had been deleted. He looked under 'Memorized Destinations' and found, among others, several more remote locations in Michigan including Highland. He noticed another object tucked inside an open storage compartment to the left of the steering wheel. He was able to get a good look at it – a Glock 19 pistol.

Having found nothing else peculiar, Decker began to make his way down to disembark when one last thing caught his attention – a bag of fast-food trash tucked far under the table. He almost paid it no mind but despite the messy condition of the boat it bothered him. He turned back retrieved and opened it, tossed out the used hamburger and fry wrappers, and located the receipt in the bottom of the bag. It was dated eight days prior, from a fast-food restaurant in Highland.

30 - Chicago

Dr. Sullivan walked south onto the DuSable bridge spanning the Chicago River. It was a cold, blustery afternoon and raining lightly. He wore a dark fedora hat and a long tan trench coat. Mid way across he stopped next to a tall man dressed in a black leather jacket and a Chicago White Sox baseball cap who had his arms resting on the railing, looking over the river scene below.

"You're a Sox fan?" Dr. Sullivan inquired.

"I always pull for the home team," the man answered in his rough cockney accent.

"I need one more."

Gordie took a deep breath and puffed on his cigarette. "What the fuck happened this time?"

"That's none of your concern," Sullivan answered.

"The fuck it isn't!" Gordie said sharply and pointed his finger into Sullivan's face. "If you don't deliver in the next week we both go down, you ass!"

"She survived it, calm yourself," Sullivan said, taking control of the conversation. "She just didn't live long enough after. I've got the solution. It's like tuning a radio. I've passed over the right frequency twice, now I know it. I'm absolutely certain. Trust me."

"I don't trust you at all," Gordie replied. "They're not gonna give us another one. She was it." A moment passed before he added, "I ought to do the old Commie's a favor and dump your ass in this river straight away."

"With me goes the code, making the technology useless. They know it and you do too. So I suggest you help me find someone else. And fast. Do you have any ideas?"

The two stood in silence for a time before Sullivan added, "We can't just snatch someone off the street. It needs to be a girl, they are more emotional, more responsive to the procedure. Someone who won't be missed. Even after the delivery – the Russian's won't be letting her leave."

"What would happen to her afterward?" Gordie asked curiously.

"She'll undergo testing – further experimentation with the formula and technology. We'll push things to see just how much we can accomplish." Sullivan said, remaining purposely vague. "If that doesn't kill her, the Russians will finish the job to be sure. But in all likelihood she'd remain a vegetable the rest of her life, eating food from a tube."

"Humm." Gordie said as he puffed on his cigarette and exhaled into the rain. "Alright then. Yeah, I got an idea of someone. She's been looking for a change of scenery and I think it's time to give it to her."

"Who?" Sullivan asked.

"Girl I know back home. Just need the airfare and the usual accommodations."

"I don't pay that, they do."

"Not anymore. They find out you knocked off another one you'll be the one they experiment on next."

He didn't need to think about it long. He took his wallet out and handed Gordie several hundred dollars of cash.

"She needs to be unharmed and healthy. The more willing the better. The more naive the better," Sullivan explained his criteria.

"She's an artist, and she's available. That'll do."

"Right," Sullivan added, untrusting of Gordie's judgement.

"What's today?" Gordie asked.

"Tuesday."

"Right then! I'll have her here by the weekend."

He stuffed the cash into his jacket, flicked his cigarette into the river, and walked south to catch the train to the airport.

Dr. Sullivan stared down toward the water below and pondered. He'd have to deliver this time, or else.

31 – Chicago

A quick Google search of Dr. Eugene Sullivan provided Josh with some basic information. He was a certified sleep pathologist with over thirty years of experience; many positive comments made by patients, many long published reports on sleep research over the years, and more recently a study on the effects of a new chemical treatment for Alzheimer's. He had also served on a variety of boards and community service projects throughout his career, but nothing recently. He appeared to be a leader in his field but had apparently gone covert with his latest research, not wanting any publicity beyond the vagueness of a radical sounding memory restoration treatment.

Then he found a newly published YouTube video of Dr. Sullivan's convention speech. He noted the date and time of the convention – October 6. Eight days prior to when the girl's body was discovered and three days prior to the fast food receipt. The video was over two hours long with Dr. Sullivan's keynote speech near the end. 'An intriguing speech' Josh thought.

His detective senses tingling, Josh decided to pay the doctor a visit. Dr. Sullivan's listed office was a modest, small, and isolated unit on the 9th floor of a fairly obscure medical building. The receptionist worked for the entire floor and offered no additional information, or personality.

"Doctor Sullivan is out." She said prudishly.

"When is he expected back?" Josh asked.

"The doctor makes his own schedule."

"And he keeps it from you?" Josh asked quizzically. She found no humor in the comment, conveyed no emotion, and said nothing further. "Perhaps I'll just wait here for a while." He paused for a response, but there was none forthcoming. He took a seat near the elevator.

After a short wait and series of wary glances with the receptionist, Josh got up and began to explore the lobby. Her phone rang which occupied her long enough for him to wander off unnoticed. He walked down to the end of the narrow hallway, then turned right and walked down to the end of an even narrower hallway to a small corner office, very plainly marked with Dr. Sullivan's name. He knocked. There was no answer. He tried the knob. The door was locked. Josh removed a lock pick set from his pocket, selected the double round pick and proceeded to unlock the door with minimal effort. The room was dark; he went in shutting the door behind him.

The office consisted of a small, but unfurnished, waiting area and an examination room. It was very sparse. A few dark bottles were lined up on a shelf above a counter where a laptop computer was opened. The laptop was connected to a gray metal box from which protruded a series of wires connected to electrodes. It looked like what you might find with an EKG machine. Oddly, there was no desk, only a small table in the corner below the window opposite him. In the center of the room a large leather chair was partially reclined. Behind the chair, mounted on some sort of rack, were a series four lights. He imagined they'd be quite bright and hot when lit. It was clear they could be positioned above the chair if needed. The only other item of interest was an I.V. bag on a stand between the leather chair and the counter. A small tray was attached to the stand and held a long, fairly thick needle.

Suddenly, the sound of keys turning the tumblers of the door lock startled Josh. He quickly walked back into the waiting area, his right hand instinctively reaching around his back coming to rest on his pistol. The door opened slightly, then stopped. A moment later it continued to open, ever so slowly.

"Who's there?" the man's nasally voice demanded in a stern tone.

"Dr.. Sullivan is it?" Josh asked.

"I said, who's there?" the man repeated, even more sternly than before.

"Josh Decker. A friend of yours recommended me. Kurt Flowers." Recognizing the name, Sullivan cautiously entered.

"How did you get in here?"

"The door was unlocked."

"Mr. Decker, I am not accepting new patients at the present time." Dr. Sullivan stated and motioned Josh to leave.

"I apologize for showing up unannounced, but if I could just have a minute of your time." Josh gave no indication that he was about to leave. Curious, Dr. Sullivan showed him into the examination room and gestured to a chair opposite the reclined leather one.

"What do you want?" Dr. Sullivan asked tersely.

"I suffer from amnesia," Josh answered.

"Terribly sad."

"I was hoping you might be able to help me," Josh said. "Or I you."

Dr. Sullivan looked carefully into Josh's eyes, squinting slightly, trying to detect anything unusual. He offered no reply.

"Not much of a view," Josh remarked in order to break the silence by referencing the brick wall of the adjacent building outside the window.

"I prefer less stimulation when I'm with patients. Sleep, you know. That is the goal," He suddenly grinned exceedingly as if it was forced, his thin glasses repositioned themselves as a result.

"Your speech at the convention, amazing."

"Thank you. You were there?"

"No. A friend sent me a link to it on the internet."

"How nice."

Josh was watching the doctor carefully, trying to read his body language as well as to continue his look around the office.

"I'm curious about your research, Doctor. Who are your patients?" Josh asked.

"I treat extreme sleep disorders, usually those connected with some sort of trauma. One man had spent the better part of two years with no substantial sleep."

"Trauma?" Josh said, this time sincerely intrigued.

"Real or imagined," Dr. Sullivan responded. Josh raised an eyebrow. He didn't expect that kind of answer.

"Does it matter?"

"Of course it does. Real trauma is something tangible. Treatable." Dr. Sullivan explained. "Imagined? Well, one should never allow ones imagination to run wild for fear where it might lead," he smirked.

"I was referring to that needle. It looks terrifying," Josh said nodding to the needle on the tray.

"I would think amnesia is far more terrifying," Dr. Sullivan said.

"Well, it is painless at least," Josh said. "What do you use that for?"

"Therapy. And often medically induced sleep."

"And you can recover someone's memories?" Josh asked.

"Recover? Well, sometimes. It is a matter of relaxation and the proper stimuli." Dr. Sullivan answered.

"In your speech you mentioned treating Alzheimer's. How's that working out?" Josh asked.

"Progressing," Dr. Sullivan answered politely. "When did you first notice the symptoms?" Dr. Sullivan took up a small memo pad and a pen from his white coat pocket.

"Actually, it was only about eight days ago." Josh said.

"Eight days?" Dr. Sullivan looked back up at him.

"Yeah, about that. I think so anyway," Josh gave a slight chuckle and pointed to his head. "That's about as much as I remember."

"Ah-ha. I see."

"I was out on the boat, dropping a line, you know. I enjoy fishing. Do you have a boat?"

"Yes," he replied, his eyes squinted slightly as he adjusted his spectacles and looked up at Josh.

"You get out on the water often?" Josh asked.

"I'm quite busy," Dr. Sullivan said growing a bit impatient.

"I understand. In your speech you mentioned being able to store memories like you store computer files. Any success?"

"A few," Dr. Sullivan said.

"That's kind of like fishing, isn't it? I mean, you go out there, drop a line," Josh gestured to the I.V., "and see what bites. Hoping for that *dream catch*," Josh stared directly into Dr. Sullivan's eyes, which glared back into his. It was a contest of wits not unlike playing Poker. Neither man blinked. Josh continued, "But I guess every fisherman has a fish story. You know, a little embellishment here and there about the one that got away. His mad fantasy of finally landing that one dream catch!" He took a moment to read Dr. Sullivan's reaction. He didn't move a muscle.

Very slowly and deliberately Dr. Sullivan answered, "We all have our *dreams* now, don't we?" The reference was not lost on Josh as he was reminded of his own nightmares. He shifted his head slightly. After a long pause, the staring contest ended as Dr. Sullivan continued, "You don't have amnesia, do you Mr. Decker?"

"If you say so," Josh said coldly.

"I say, Mr. Decker, that..." Dr. Sullivan paused to replace his notebook and pen into his coat pocket, and placed his hands on his knees, "that will be all."

Josh slowly stood up and left the office. Upon his exit, Dr. Sullivan rolled his chair over to the table and picked up the phone. He dialed a number and it was answered quickly.

"Follow him," he ordered, then pressed the release button on the phone. He dialed a second number, which also answered immediately.

"Josh Decker. Find out who he is. Whatever it takes." he said, listened, then hung up the phone.

32 – London

It was evening when Molly reached The King's Head pub and sat down at the bar. She took out a white envelope and opened it. The letter was short and to the point. Her services would not be needed for the Holy Trinity restoration project. While it didn't surprise her, she still felt dejected.

"What'll you have Moll?" asked the bartender, Jake.

"Old fashioned," she answered.

"You okay?" he asked, noticing her expression. Molly just nodded her head. A moment later Jake returned with her drink and inquired, "You want to talk about it?"

"Do all bartenders have to pass an exam to act as psychologists as well?"

"Only the ones who can't make a bloody drink."

She tasted her drink, then replied, "Then you must be a fantastic shrink!"

"Come on love, what's up?"

"I didn't get the commission."

"Oh damn. I really thought it was in the bag, no?"

"So did I. Until my last meeting."

"What happened?"

"It's nothing. Just... just stupid, that's all."

"Well, you still have a commission here, as promised."

"Yeah, thank you," She said sarcastically and smiled.

"I know it's not the Sistine Chapel or anything, but I've saved that there window just for you," he said pointing to a large rectangular pane of glass in the dining area.

"I don't know," she paused to take a sip. "On second thought, a bar's as good as any place isn't it? Maybe just right for my work. You'd admire anything when you're pissed."

"Hey, I mean it you know. I think you're amazing. That Gordie's a lucky bloke to have you! How's he doing anyway?"

"I don't know. He's out of town again. Not sure when he'll be back."

"Well bring him in next time. And this one's on me."

"I will. Thank you."

She sat sipping on her drink, staring back and forth between her napkin and the mirror opposite the bar. In the reflection she could see the clear window pane where Jake wanted to place one of her works. Then she noticed herself sitting at the bar as if she was looking at a stranger and thought, 'What would I think of her? Her eyes look tired. She certainly isn't happy. I feel badly for her. Stuck there with no hope. But she keeps trying. Her eyes look tired, but they are not the eyes of someone who gives up.'

As she finished her thoughts she noticed a man sitting at a table behind her. He was well dressed in a gray suit sans the tie. He looked quite proper, handsome, and active. And she recognized him. It dawned on her that she had seen him before that very day. He was at the train station... and at the cafe when she stopped in for tea.

She felt a sudden chill thinking that he might be following her. She finished her drink, picked up her portfolio, and walked out the front door. She turned right, crossed the street, and proceeded down a row of many high end shops displaying Rolex watches, formal dresses, and jewelry stores with an array of diamonds, emeralds, and sapphires.

Walking briskly, she suddenly stopped at the front of a shoe store, turning to look at some shoes in the window. She carefully glanced back toward the bar. She saw the man exit. He began walking in her direction but stopped at the corner. He stood there as if he had no place else to go. After a moment he took out a cigarette and lit it. The street was bustling with window shoppers and tourists walking around in the area, and yet she thought he seemed out of place.

She turned and walked on, then took off to cross the street. Slipping her hand into her pocket she withdrew a Pound coin and dropped it. Then she stopped and turned to pick it up. As she did she glanced back. The man was gone from the corner. She stood up and walked on.

Upon reaching the Underground she stood on the platform which was crowded with people heading home from work or out for an evening's entertainment. She looked back toward the stairway just in time to see the man emerge. Her heart began to pound. He looked around, saw her, and began to walk in her direction.

Molly moved further away down the platform, at times pushing people aside in order to get farther away. Nearing the end she stopped and looked back for him. It was impossible to see through all the people on the crowded platform. She couldn't spot him. The train arrived and she proceeded to board.

"Mind the gap," the automated subway voice warned. The train was on its way.

"Next stop Victoria station," the conductor announced a while later. The majority of people exited the train, as did Molly. She looked carefully around the platform as she moved up the stairs on her way to transfer to another train. She saw nothing, but continued to be aware as she made her way through the station.

Fifteen minutes later she boarded the train for Croydon. It was far less busy than the main lines in the city centre, and there was no sign of the man. It was a thirty minute ride and she started to breathe a sigh of relief. Then the door of the car opened. There he was, the man in the gray suit, no tie. He quickly sat down at the far end. He made no eye contact.

Molly began to visibly shake. She noticed her hand pulsing on her knee as she sat watching him carefully. The ride seemed to last an eternity. Finally she stepped off and moved fast to get out of the station. It was another ten minute walk to her flat, but she didn't waste any time. Her walk quickly turned into a sprint. Then, as she turned the final corner before her building she ran right into another man, starling her.

"Hey there little girl! What's your name?" a jacked up young man bellowed as Molly bumped into him. "What's your hurry?" he said, grabbing onto her by the arms trying to hold her in place. His friend just stood by and began to laugh.

"I'm sorry," Molly answered, nearly out of breath. "I'm terribly sorry. Let go!" She pushed him away and continued her run home.

"No need to rush off now baby! Come on back here I've got what you want!" his voice followed her as she reached the door, his friends laughter echoing in the distance. She turned the key, got in and quickly shut the door behind her. She waited, looking out the window, but saw no one. After a few minutes she walked upstairs, entered her flat, and locked the door. Twice, just to be sure.

33 – Chicago

"Hello, my name's Anita" said a beautiful slim built blonde who only a couple of minutes prior had taken a stool around the corner of the bar to Josh's right. "You're from Chicago?"

"Originally. Not anymore."

"I don't think I'd ever get used to the cold!" she said as the bartender returned with a vodka tonic. She was beautifully made up in a skin tight, short, dark red dress with a black pattern that ran down her body like a supple silk web. It was low cut with straps and she wore a thin black scarf.

"You do look a little underdressed for this weather," Josh commented.

"I know! I wasn't really thinking. I live in L.A., you know, a place that is warm enough for humans!" she laughed.

"Here for business?" Josh asked.

"I'm a realtor. We're having a convention and since I was the top salesperson in my office this year, I got to come."

"Well, despite the cold I'm sure you'll have a nice time."

"I already have!" Anita said. She pulled out her phone and began to show Josh pictures of several places in the city including her standing in front of Buckingham Fountain, without any water flowing, and the city skyline in the background. A photo of her in front of Wrigley Field, the Picasso, the Calder, and the Cloud Gate in Millennium Park, which looked like it had been taken just before she arrived.

"You've gotten around today."

"Two days, so far."

"Not much time spent at the convention?"

"As little as I can! I have a friend who lives here and he's been taking me all around."

"He has, has he?" Josh asked with mild disappointment. She smiled and threw him a very obvious flirtatious look.

"He... and his wife. Yes."

"I see. Well, in that case I'm excited for you."

"Thank you. I think I'd like to come back in the summer though. Look, I got goosebumps! I'm still cold!" she laughed and held out her arm toward him. He placed his hand on her arm and indeed there were goosebumps. He gently stroked her in a vain attempt to provide some warmth.

"You have really incredible hands, ah, I didn't catch your name," She said.

"Josh," he answered.

"Josh?" she pressed for his full name.

"Decker," he said.

"Mr. Decker, it's nice to meet you," she smiled.

"Well, you look lovely. Are you going out tonight?" Josh asked.

"Thank you. Yes, well, maybe. I was supposed to meet another old friend of mine tonight. He was taking me out to see Rigoletto at the Chicago Theater. But I'm not really into opera and I'm not real crazy about this guy."

"So you're thinking about bailing on him?"

"I was thinking just that. If I had a good enough reason to anyway. Wanted to stop in for a drink to make up my mind."

It had been a long time since Josh enjoyed the company of such a stunning woman. Her perfume, long straight blonde hair, haunting eyes and smile had successfully worked their magic. He realized he was still holding her hand, what's more, she was still holding his.

"So, have you made up your mind?" he smiled.

"I think I have. Are you staying nearby?"

"Actually, no," Josh had planned to spend a cold night on the boat, but Anita's insinuation was obviously far more enticing.

"I have a room at the Hilton, just down the road. I was supposed to meet my friend here but if we leave now, I could avoid an unpleasant situation," Anita smiled, raised her eyebrow and tilted her head as if to make sure the hint was clear.

Josh left some cash on the bar and proceeded to walk her to the door.

"Oh, it's so cold!" Anita cried in a most appealing feminine fashion as the wind rushed through the doorway. Josh put his arm around her and she wrapped her right arm up and around his back, inside his jacket, and squeezed. She seemed delicate despite an air of confidence and intelligence.

"You said you were from Chicago originally. Where do you live now?" she asked.

"A little place on the lake," he answered.

"This lake?" she asked pointing out toward Lake Michigan. "Where?"

"Highland."

34 – Highland

"So why did he leave the force?" Abby asked as she sat in The Chance bar, drinking a soda and eating a hot dog.

"It's just not for everyone," Charlie answered.

"He told me he left for the money."

"Well, there you go."

"I don't believe him," she said. "You two are close friends?" Charlie nodded. "How did you meet?"

"After the war I started tending bar in Chicago and he just came in one day and I guess you could say we just hit it off," Charlie began.

"Vietnam?" Abby asked.

"Yeah. Another war to end all wars," Charlie smiled.

Abby quickly grew curious, but the look that flashed across Charlie's eyes at the thought of the war made her decide not to press it.

"So, Josh walks into a bar and sits down, that's it? Not very exciting," Abby probed.

"Honestly?" Charlie offered.

"Yeah. What was he like? He's really cynical about life. I worry about him, you know?" she said.

"You worry about *him*?" Charlie said admiringly. "Ain't that something. Young lady, I'm not into this whole idea of destiny, but I'm happy you're around him. He needs to know someone is worried about him, besides me."

"You worry about him?" she asked.

"I do," Charlie answered. "He's a good man, never doubt that. Loyal, honest, and he's nobody's fool, believe me. He has a sharp intuitive nature. And I've never seen him proven wrong."

Abby smiled. "So he wasn't always so cynical? What happened? It had something to do with his decision to leave the force, right?" She asked.

"That's not for me to say," Charlie answered. Abby looked disappointed. "The day we met was a day I'll never forget. It was the day Josh Decker saved my life," Charlie began.

"He saved your life?" Abby asked in amazement.

"He was off duty, end of a long day for him, and it was after midnight. I was tending bar, getting ready to close and in comes this guy. As soon as he walked in I knew it was trouble. Three others had been in the bar for a while. None of them made me feel too great. My help had just left and I had called for last round. So, as I said, the guy walks in and immediately the other three jump up and pull their guns. They were all working together, see, and there I was with my back to them and my hands on the register. I could see them in the mirror."

Abby had stopped eating and was listening intently. "My God," she uttered.

"They were serious too. They didn't want just the money. I was sure I was going down that night. Three years in Nam and I'm gonna go down like this? 'Hell no' I said. I was ready to pull the pistol I kept under the bar but it meant turning around to get it. I was very close, but if I moved I was dead. They demanded the money and as I opened the drawer I noticed him, out of the corner of my eye. It was like he just appeared in the doorway."

"Josh?" Abby asked. She could tell Charlie's story was really getting to him. He had slowed his speech, looked down to the bar, then up to the ceiling, all but avoiding contact with her young eyes.

"Josh Decker. I didn't know him. He wasn't in uniform, so I didn't even know he was a cop. Well, a detective really. But I saw he had a gun in his hands. The seconds felt like minutes. But it came and went so fast. I couldn't believe it.

"They hadn't been very loud, but that's what made them seem all the more deadly. Then Josh's voice broke over everyone. It was so quiet, yet deafening – because it was unexpected. He said, '*I wouldn't do that.*' Four deadly words.

"They all turned and started to take aim at him. Four to one, but it wasn't enough. Josh took them out one by one, systematically, as if he had all the time in the world to set up, aim, and shoot. The first guy was the one who had walked in. He seemed the most dangerous, maybe because he was sober. Hit him right between the eyes. The second was the guy closest to me, got him right in the chest. He went down before he knew what hit him. The third was actually the guy closest to Josh. He fired but was panicked and missed, just as Josh nailed him in the chest. The fourth guy was the lucky one. Josh was moving fast now and only hit him in the gut. They say he fired his gun as he was hit – his round landed in the ceiling. Now they weren't just standing around waiting to be shot, you know. They were moving targets looking for cover, preparing to shoot back. But it happened before you could catch your breath.

"By the time it was all over I had my gun drawn as well. But, of course, that didn't matter. No, in all my time in Vietnam, I never saw anyone handle a gun better then Josh Decker."

Abby was silent and trying to digest the story she just heard. Finally Charlie added, "I suppose he's a bit cynical at times. You might be too if you've seen what he's seen. Done what he's had to do. He has his fears like any of us. More human than most if you ask me. But in that moment, when he needs to be, he can be ruthless, cold, and precise."

It took her a moment before she could respond. "I thought those things only happened in movies," Abby commented. "It's amazing you weren't hurt."

"I admit I was scared. We both were. But I was never afraid to die. I've always been at peace with it," Charlie said.

"Is that why he left the force?" Abby asked.

"No. That was a few years prior," Charlie answered. He was now looking back at her. "Need a refill?"

"Please," she answered. "So why did he leave?" she asked again.

"That's something I'll let Josh share with you – if he wants. I wouldn't push it," he said as he filled her glass with soda.

"I won't. I think I bother him enough as it is," she said, taking her first bite of food since Charlie began his story.

"You're not a bother to him, believe me."

"Not sure I do," she said. "Do you think he's happy?" Abby asked with concern.

He thought about it for a moment, then answered, "Happier than before."

"Before what?" she asked.

Charlie smiled at her. It was the kind of smile a proud grandfather would give to his granddaughter. "Before he found *you*," he said.

35 – Chicago

Anita's spacious hotel room overlooked the dark great lake with thousands of twinkling lights stirring about along the shoreline. His arms were still wrapped around her slim waist, her arms securing his head against her breasts. They had just finished and she slowly lifted herself off of him and made herself comfortable, snug up into his side, now out of breath.

"That was... wonderful," she searched for an appropriate word, her eyes for once telling the truth.

"It was," he agreed.

"Oh! I never do this!" she giggled like a teenager.

"Really? You sure seemed to know what you were doing," Josh smirked.

"No, silly! I mean hook up with a handsome stranger while on a business trip. It's not like me."

"Well, for what it's worth, it's not like me either."

"What do you do, Josh?"

"Not much."

"Not much? Come on, I don't believe that."

"I'm a security guard."

"Security guard? Like a night watchman?" she asked.

"More or less," he answered, being cryptic.

"Well is it more, or less?" she insisted with a beautiful smile and silky smooth fingers that gently stroked his chest and chin.

"Mainly consulting. I offer advice to companies about security. Stupid stuff really." He turned to face her and began stroking her ass and thigh. "They pay me to tell them what they could get out of a decent video posted on the internet."

"Well, you must be worth it," she paused to kiss him. "You must have done something before to have made you such an expert."

"I was a cop," he admitted.

"A cop?" Anita said in a sexy tone. "I'm impressed," she said kissing him again. "So why did you stop being a cop?"

Josh couldn't seem to answer immediately, but after a moment's hesitation he said, "Money."

"Money is exactly why I got into real estate. There's kind of a rush when you close on a *big deal!*" she said intending a sexual innuendo. Then she kissed him and crossed her naked leg over his waist.

"A payoff?" he replied.

"Exactly!" she said and kissed his chest again. Then she rolled over and got out of bed, a solitary dim desk lamp back lit and accentuated her beautiful figure.

"Do you want some Champaign?" she asked.

"Sounds good," he answered. She poured a couple of glasses, replacing the bottle in the silver ice bucket. He sat up as she sashayed over and sat cross-legged next to him at a right angle so she was facing the open window high above the city – showing no inhibition whatsoever.

"Cheers," she said handing him a glass.

"Cheers."

"Ooh! This just sent a shiver through me!" Anita giggled. "It's going to make me cold again. You'll have to warm me back up," she smiled at Josh.

"I don't think that will be a problem," he smiled coolly.

She held up her glass taking note of the bubbles sparkling in the light.

"Oh, I love how the bubbles sparkle. There're like beautiful tiny gems, pulsing with energy. You know my favorite?" she asked rhetorically. "Sapphires." She smiled. "That's another way to warm me up. I adore how they feel against my skin, how they seem to penetrate so deep into your soul. Pulsing... full of energy and power."

"Oh?" Josh asked growing interested.

Anita looked over him and gazed wondrously out the window into the duality of the city lights and darkness, and her own reflection in the dark glass.

"Everybody goes for the diamond," she began. "Its clarity and sparkle are supposed to dazzle and impress. I always found them too cliché, too safe, too cold. I always needed to be different than others. I never had to work hard for attention, so I took it upon myself to work hard for the right kind of attention. The kind that would satisfy me." She took a sip of Champaign, never taking her eyes off the darkness outside. "The kind that demonstrated how they were kissing your ass!" she said with a cunning smirk. She licked her lips and smiled at herself in the glass.

The contemplation continued, "No, I never played it safe," she laughed. "Now, a sapphire can take you in, seduce you." She shifted into her best sexy voice and began slowly touching herself all over. Her body motioned slowly up and down from her somewhat crouched position, enjoying the moment, watching herself becoming sexually aroused in the window. "You can gaze deeply into a sapphire, and it's like an ocean. A world full of secrets, crystallized into a tiny blue ball."

Josh's intrigue suddenly changed as the image of a tiny blue ball spontaneously conjured up the thought of the strange bright blue mark left on the neck of the woman found in Highland. While he pondered, Anita continued without interruption, "It's like truth or dare. It's daring you to probe deeper and deeper, further and further than you ever thought you could or would go." She began touching herself sexually, her eyes never leaving the window. "They are the essence of passion, the fire of your soul." Her self-gratification grew slightly more intense. "Oh! Sapphires!" Anita said with pleasure and embraced herself tightly, her head tilted back, eyes closed. She took a long, deep breath, letting the air out slowly through her puckered lips.

"Do you know what I mean?" she asked having snapped out of her brief trance. But Josh was lost in thought. "Josh?" she inquired.

"Yeah. Well, I don't know really. I guess I always preferred rubies."

Anita finished her glass of Champaign and leaned over to Josh. "Oh no my dear. Always sapphires."

36 – London

"Where've yah been?" Gordie demanded as Molly entered her flat, her keys and a bag of groceries in hand.

"Oh! Gordie. You startled me." She said, looking worried. She shut the door. "You could've called me, no?"

"Sorry love" he said as he walked over and kissed her. "I said, where've yah been?"

"I paid a visit to my aunt." She continued to the kitchen, put down the bag and began to unpack.

"I see," Gordie said, sternly watching her every move. "Is that all you've been seeing?"

"What do you mean?"

"No one else coming knocking around on your door?"

"No. Why would you ask?"

"Jakey tells me you've been hanging around. Looking maybe?"

"I didn't get the commission. I went to have a drink."

"Ah, I see. I'll have to straighten Jakey out then won't I," he said as he walked back to the living area and sat down.

Molly thought for a long moment, then asked, "Did you have someone follow me?"

"What?" Gordie answered.

"Did you have a man follow me?"

"What are you talking about?"

"Last night a man followed me from the bar all the way ho... to Victoria station," stopping herself from saying 'home'.

"What'd he look like?"

"Not sure. Dark hair, grey suite. He didn't wear a tie."

He thought about it for a moment. "Just your fucked up imagination." He took a sip of a drink he had made.

"I don't need to be followed."

"Did you hear me? I said, it's your imagination. No one is following you. Ok?"

"Right," she said doubtingly.

"Listen, I'm off again tomorrow."

"Oh," Molly said returning to the kitchen.

"I think you ought to come with me, love."

"Come with you?" Molly asked, surprised at the suggestion.

"Yeah. Business there won't be long and we can have a good time, you know. And it'll get you away from this place for a while."

"You never ask me to go with you when you're working."

"Well, this time I made an exception. For you." He smiled at her. "Whaddaya say?"

It occurred to her that this may be an opportunity to find out more about his job. Maybe she'd find some answers to her suspicions or perhaps a reasonable explanation for the bank runs and his unorthodox schedule. She also considered that perhaps this was his way of turning a new leaf. But if nothing else a change in scenery would offer a chance to get away from her frustrations for a little while. He was capable of tremendous charm when he wanted. But she retained her doubts.

"You got nothing else going on now, with the commission gone and everything." He could tell she was hesitant. "Come on then. Whaddaya say?" he smiled innocently, with a hopeful expression.

"I don't know," she smiled. "I still have a lot to do..."

"Come here." He grinned and patted his lap. She walked over and sat down. "I've missed you," he said and kissed her. "And I'm really sorry about the commission. You deserved it. You'll get one soon." They embraced and he quickly moved on to her neck. When she was the object of his affection, it made her more a believer than a doubter.

"I've missed you too," she said, though as she said it she felt awkward and insincere. "Where are we going?"

He broke from licking her neck, "Chicago." Then he began to unbutton her blouse.

"Chicago? I was hoping for someplace a bit warmer."

"Maybe next time, love. But my business is with a specialist doctor in Chicago. Got some incredible things he's working on. I think you'd like him. He's like an artist really. Dreams, visions," he interrupted each descriptive with another kiss to her chest. "Psychological interpretations, boats, museums, and his lady friend is really into the art scene."

"Sounds interesting."

He resumed kissing her chest down to her bra. "I'll introduce you."

37 - Chicago

BANG! A deafening shot rang out!

Bang! The short echoes again, and again, and again, eventually trailing off.

He frantically looked around the room. 'Where's my gun?' he thought.

'I want answers!' the sharp shout was louder than ever before – the pain echoing in his brain.

'But I didn't know...'

'Answers!'

'That wasn't so bad...' said the soft voice

'What if I did it?' he thought. The dread plunged through his body like a surge of adrenalin.

'My gun... where's my...'

'Don't go! Don't go!' it was Abby's voice.

'What?'

'I want answers!' the man's fist pounded on the table and the room itself shook.

Josh sat up suddenly in bed, dripping in a thick sweat and breathing hard. The sun was rising over a silky smooth Lake Michigan. He squinted as the bright beams of light came streaming into the window. His head ached from the Champaign and the intensity of his dream. He looked around the hotel room. He was alone. Anita's purse and coat were gone, but the scent of her sweet perfume lingered.

He took a deep breath and calmed himself down. It had been a night to remember and he was disappointed that she had left so early. As he dressed he noticed the hotel key card lying on the desk. Growing curious, he placed it in his pocket and proceeded downstairs to the lobby.

"Room 1231," he said as he placed the card key on the front desk counter.

"Yes sir." The clerk typed in the room number on the computer. "You're all set. Hope you had a pleasant stay." He resumed his work sorting through a stack of papers.

"Could I get a copy of my bill please?" Josh asked.

"Sure thing... Mr. Zhukov?" The clerk asked.

"Yes," Josh answered, surprised to hear the name. He did not recognize it.

"Just a moment." He proceeded to print the bill and placed it on the counter. "Everything has been charged to your credit card. Is there anything else I can do for you?"

"No. Thank you." Josh picked up the paper and walked away. He looked at it carefully. The credit card number was truncated so it was no use trying to trace it. 'Valery Zhukov' was the name listed on the receipt and the address was sure to be a nearby commercial business by the look of it. It was clearly not Anita's who was supposedly from L.A. He pocketed the receipt, now more curious than before.

Josh spent the morning visiting his old stomping grounds at CPD. He had made a couple of calls after finding the body in Highland, one of which was to his friend and former colleague Marty Bowen. Marty was a CPD detective and had pulled recent records on missing persons and homicides. He also had the results of a background check on the owners of the boat including Dr. Eugene Sullivan, all per Josh's request.

"He's clean." Marty remarked regarding Dr. Sullivan. "And several homicides came up over the past couple weeks."

"Anything unusual?" Josh asked.

"This one struck me, but it's not my case. Paul Thomas. A young guy, late 20s, found behind a trash bin in an ally on the north end. He was shot at close range. It stood out since he's white collar, no record, and it was in a pretty decent area. No physical evidence, no motive. Seems random. Not much to go on."

"Except?" Josh baited his former colleague.

"You know, when you asked me to look for anyone the M.E. said had a bright blue mark on his neck, I thought you were high on something. What the hell gave you that idea?"

"It was there?" Josh asked, surprised at his hunch.

"Yeah, it was there. Take a look." Marty pulled up a

picture on the computer of the Medical Examiner's report. It showed a bright blue mark just behind and below Thomas' right ear.

"The victim we have in Highland had the same mark. The M.E. in Michigan didn't catch it and when I pointed it out to him he didn't think much of it." Josh said.

"Well, neither did Scotty." Marty replied, referring to the M.E. who worked the case. He had earned the nickname from the Star Trek character who worked engineering "miracles" helping the crew get out of trouble. This "Scotty" always seemed to find things others overlooked, thus performing his own "miracles." His findings had put many criminals behind bars that would have otherwise walked.

"Why not?" Josh asked.

"Said it was a bruise. Possibly he was hit by something to knock him out, then shot."

"No. He was shot first. It's too precise." Josh added.

"What are you, an expert now?" Marty teased. "Scotty says so, so it's so."

"Scotty's not aware of my victim. And this mark is more than just a bruise. There's a brighter blue color to it in the center, exactly like hers. How do you explain that?"

"I don't." Marty said. "But as I said, this isn't my case."

"What else do you know about Mr. Thomas?" Josh asked.

"He lived alone. Parents live in Kansas City which is apparently where he went to college. According to his social media he worked at Nexus Pharmaceuticals here in Chicago. He was a rising star based on the interviews. And all of this I'm not even saying to you." Marty added in order to cover his discretion.

"I'm sorry, I didn't catch any of what you just said." Josh replied.

"Bastard." Marty said under his breath and with a smirk. The two had a long history and trusted each other like brothers. It was mutually understood that since Josh was no longer a detective everything they were speaking of was off the record.

"Where was he found?" Josh asked.

"Outside the Essex Hotel. Down in the ally along the back

side, behind a trash bin." Marty said reviewing the notes.

"Do you have surveillance from the hotel?" Josh asked.

"Yeah. Shows him leaving just after one in the morning. He was staying there that night apparently." Marty said as he pulled up a series of short video clips and played them. The first showed Paul Thomas exiting the elevator and walking down a hallway toward the service exit. He was alone and holding a large manila envelope. The second showed Thomas exiting the building by a back door near the service elevator. Josh made out three laundry carts lined up near the doorway; apparently the back door was adjacent to the laundry facility. Then a final clip showed another man entering the hallway only a few minutes later.

"He's the first one to go through that door after our victim left." Marty explained. "He's wanted for questioning, but we have no idea who he is and no one's seen him." The man was tall, short hair, thin build, he wore sunglasses, a black suit with a white shirt, and no tie.

"I know I like to wear my sunglasses in the middle of the night." Josh observed sarcastically. Then he saw something peculiar and paused the video.

"A laundry cart is missing," Josh noted.

"So it is." Marty agreed.

"Do you have more of this video?"

"Yeah." Marty opened up the original video before it had been edited into clips. He scanned through until Josh stopped him.

"He's pushing a cart outside. Does he bring it back?"

They scanned the rest of the video.

"No. Not through this entrance anyway." Said Marty.

The video finished with the man walking in again and then under the camera filming the hallway from above. A second camera pointing in the opposite direction toward the hotel lobby picked up the man's walk toward the elevator. He pressed the call button and a moment later the door opened. A young woman stepped out and the two engaged in brief conversation before getting on the elevator together.

"That's her!" Josh said. "That's my Jane Doe in Highland."

38 – Chicago

"Joshua Decker!" Dr. Sullivan began as Anita sat down across the small table at The Walnut Room restaurant. He had already been served with a glass of wine.

"You have something?" she asked.

"Yes my dear, you managed to get more than enough for us to learn all about him."

"Well, who is he?"

"You must have spent quite a bit of time with him. Zhukov was impressed by the amount of detail you provided."

"We had a nice, long talk." Anita smiled and extended her hand to rest upon his. He held up a piece of paper and reviewed the notes.

"Yes, well... He was a detective with the Chicago Police Department until a couple years ago. He retired after a shooting incident, even though he was exonerated of any wrongdoing. He presently works for a small international security consulting firm. He is known to be intelligent..." he lowered the paper to the table and looked over into Anita's eyes, "and extremely dangerous."

"Impressive," Anita smiled seductively as she squeezed Sullivan's hand.

"Is he now?"

"I meant you!" Anita gently licked her lips. "How you are able to learn so much about someone so fast! How your mind works so diligently, brilliantly..." she leaned over and then whispered, "and yet you make it look so effortless."

"And a source informs me that he lives across the lake in Highland." The doctor finished and the couple ordered lunch before resuming their conversation.

"What are you going to do?" she asked.

"There is another opportunity that presents itself. I've learned that he has a young girl living with him. A runaway... that no one would miss."

"Ah, I see!" Anita smiled as she understood what this might mean.

"Young, female, gets mixed up with a former cop who is, perhaps, not entirely stable. Could be tragic if anything happened."

"Tragic indeed." She agreed.

"I feel compelled to take her safety into consideration. Arrangements are being made. An opportunity like this is too good to pass up. She's already so close." He took a sip of wine. "And I wouldn't have to rely on the Russians, or whether or not this English girl will be suitable."

"Is she already on her way here?" Anita asked.

"Gordie has left to retrieve her, they should be here tomorrow evening. She'll serve as a back-up. There isn't much time," he added.

"How can I help?" Anita asked.

"You can entertain her until I have rescued the runaway."

"Entertain her?" Anita said obviously disappointed.

"Yes, she needs to be occupied while Mr. Chase picks up the girl. It'll only be a couple days. Take her to a museum or something. Just keep her occupied and out of the way."

"Oh Sully. If she were a handsome man I'd be fine with it. But another woman... from England?" she began to pout.

"It's important. Do it for me, my dear. Do it for us."

"Fine." she pouted.

"If all goes well, and I think it will, we'll be in Moscow within a few days. And then... my work toward immortality can begin in earnest," he said smiling like a kid in a candy store at the thought of his dream coming to fruition. He took another sip of wine. "Now, tell me more about him."

"He's handsome, and quiet. I had to do a lot of talking. But if he were a physician he'd of bought anything I wanted to sell him."

"Is that so?" Sullivan feigned surprise.

"Like most men he had only one thing on his mind." Anita smiled, pleased with herself.

"Like all men around you," Sullivan complimented, then shook his head, "I sometimes wonder if the 'Sapphire' would be nothing more than an endless pornographic fantasy machine if I used it only with adult males."

"Oh, most definitely." Anita agreed.

"So, what did you *sell* him in order to obtain his information?"

"Come on Sully, it wasn't like that," she tried to reassure.

"Don't take me for a fool. I know exactly what happened. I just want to know. I want to hear you describe it."

"We went from the bar to my room. I poured some Champaign, and then I let him explore…"

"I see," Sullivan said, seemingly becoming aroused.

"I watched his face the entire time. He seemed very lonely. It was so easy."

The waiter interrupted with their salads and two glasses of Pinot noir.

"Even the slightest glance from you can bring a man to his knees. But to allow him to experience your full beauty – my God, that is enough to overwhelm him completely. So much so that I do wonder sometimes about you, my dear," he smirked.

"I may have sold him my flesh, but I sold my soul to you long ago," she licked her lips before resuming her meal.

39 – London

The Victoria Apollo Theatre in London's West End was not sold out, but was bustling with activity as the final guests were being seated for the evening's performance. Peter Hawks sat alone, high in the top balcony wearing a long dark coat, over a gray suit, white shirt, no tie. He was carrying an umbrella, not uncommon in London, as it had been raining occasionally throughout the day. He stood about six feet tall, slender with a strikingly handsome face, a chiseled jawline and defined cheek bones. He was middle-aged, charming, and spoke with a sophisticated English accent. The dark red colour of the seats faded to black as the house lights dimmed. Several of the back rows were empty, a handful of patrons were scattered here and there, but no one too close.

Once the show began, a second man emerged from the aisle and walked into the row, sitting down next to Hawks despite plenty of other empty seats. He was older, early sixty's, and a little out of breath.

"Not a sell out?" he whispered, tongue in cheek.

"A patron of the arts," Hawks answered. "It's been a while Syd. I'm glad you're still a fan."

"I wouldn't miss this performance for anything," he said. "In fact, I was willing to pay quite a bit for these seats."

"Can't see much from here, I'm afraid." Hawks said.

"Far away. Good thing you have eyes like a Hawk," he said.

"I hear things. I hear things more than I see them. You know?" said Hawks.

"You shouldn't believe everything you hear," Syd said.

"Oh I shouldn't, eh?" The two men were talking in slow whispers, looking mainly toward the stage as the musical's overture began to crescendo throughout the theatre. Hawks leaned over and continued, "I don't care for what I've heard Syd. It's quite disturbing to hear you have been screwing the wrong sort of women. The kind to whom you should never tell a secret, or pay for what you could get for free down at the pub." The lecture continued, "It makes me look bad. And now it looks as though it has cost me one of my young men. Perhaps you should think about retirement."

"Who?" Syd asked, sincerely surprised at the news. But he was also trying to gage Hawks' reaction to see if the news was even true.

Hawks looked directly at him for the first time and said, "Chicago. Paul Thomas. I think you know about it by now. He was set to deliver some vital information."

"Peter," Syd spoke in an exaggerated, reassuring tone. "Here. This will make things right." He reached into his coat pocket and pulled out a ticket stub. "Best seat in the house."

Hawks took the ticket, looked at it, and placed it in his shirt pocket. "I don't care for this show." he said.

"These things are not an exact science!" Syd insisted. "But I've always been a man of my word and I promise you'll enjoy the view from that seat. I have more where that came from I assure you," he said confidently. "You take care of me and I'll take care of you my friend."

"I've never known anyone more loyal Syd. You've never let me down," Hawks said and extended his hand which Syd shook.

As Hawks then began to stand, his umbrella jabbed Syd in the lower thigh. "Oh pardon me," Hawks quickly added. He stood up preparing to go when he turned back around to face the old man. He bent down, placed his hand on his shoulder and squeezed a bit saying ominously, "I do hope you enjoy the rest of the show. They say it's over before you know it." Then he walked down to the end of the row and turned toward the front of the balcony to exit. Syd remained behind, now rather nervous.

If he had done it just right, the old man would be dead in a few days. Loaded into the metal tip of his umbrella was a tiny cylinder from which he had fired an incredibly small projectile as he jabbed him in the leg. A tiny round pellet the size of a pin head, was shot into Syd's thigh. The tiny pellet contained ricin, a powerful enough poison that even a dose the size of a couple grains of salt would be sure to kill him within a few days. Shot at a high velocity, it would feel like a tiny rubber band snap on the skin. The jabbing of the umbrella tip was more than enough to disguise that minor pain and it would also serve to deliver the pellet securely through his slacks and into his skin, practically unnoticeable. It was also virtually untraceable. But in their line of work, there would be no mechanism for him to seek help in any event, even if there was an antidote.

As he left the theatre Hawks handed the ticket Syd had given him to one of the ushers. He then continued downstairs and out to the street for a smoke.

The usher quietly proceeded to the seat which was printed on the ticket, a lower level seat along the far right back side of the house. He felt around the bottom and toward the back until his hand came across an envelope. He quickly placed it in his pocket, proceeded out of the theatre and dropped it off to a beautiful young woman working the coat-check counter named Tina.

Tina was a petite Irish girl a little over five feet tall with short red hair, a lovely young smile, smooth pale skin, and a cute little figure. She proceeded to place the envelope into the coat of Mr. Peter Hawks. A few minutes later, Hawks crushed out his cigarette and walked back in to retrieve his coat. He handed Tina his claim check. She promptly retrieved his coat and he gave her a fiver.

"What are you doing after the show?" Hawks asked her.

"Planning to meet my man for a drink with his mates," she answered with a pretty smile and her delicately mild Irish accent.

"That sounds lovely," Hawks said as he reached over and took her hand, drawing her toward him. He kissed her cheek and moved his lips closely toward her ear. Her perfume smelled incredibly light and sweet, matching her soft skin and personality. She found herself compelled to take a deep breath and closed her eyes. "St. Ermins, 304," he said.

As he pulled away, she gave him a sweet, seductive smile which answered him in the affirmative. Hawks walked out, hailed a cab and was off. In his coat pocket, as expected, he found an envelope with a series of documents. He began to scan the names, dates, figures, and places. He recognized most of them as players in the organization he had been infiltrating and observing for quite some time. It was good information, exactly what he had expected out of the old man. But he had grown uncomfortable with Syd's reliability in recent months. He had learned that Syd was no longer credible with the Russian contacts with whom he had fostered a relationship over the years. Hawks now feared he might try to bolster his standing with them by offering some information on his current assignment. That was too much of a risk. It was time to pull the plug on old Syd. But he did regret that it had to be like this.

He scanned the papers which included the usual suspects and contacts he had been keeping tabs on. There was some new information on money wires and drug shipments. Both Lucya Averin and Nonna Petrov were listed, each with a red checkmark next to their name. Molly Wheeler was also listed, but he expected that. Though it was good information nothing seemed out of the ordinary until he scanned the final page and noticed a new name. It caught his attention instantly, recognized from years ago: Josh Decker, Chicago. "How interesting," he thought out loud.

Late that evening, Tina knocked on room 304. Hawks answered and she entered. He shut the door and then swiftly picked her up into the air, swung her around and landed her flat onto the bed. They embraced and kissed passionately as he quickly and easily slid her out of her dress. She was one of his favorites, for many reasons. She was someone who kept an eye on others, ran special errands, never asked questions, and always delivered reliably and splendidly. She was totally compliant both on the job and in the bedroom, desirous to be positioned however he wanted. The love making went on for some time until finally both were exhausted and fell out of breath onto the pillows.

"Oh!" she moaned. "That was so incredible Pete," she said as she tried to catch her breath.

"You're ravishing as always my dear," Hawks complemented. After a few moments, he pulled her near to him, spooning her small body easily up into his and asked, "Did you follow the old man?"

"Yes. He went to the pub, then walked to a flat. I have the address."

"Keep it. Pay him a visit in a day or two and let me know how he's doing," Hawks instructed.

"A visit? What kind of visit?" she said seductively.

"Not that kind. Be creative. I just want to make sure his health is up," he said.

"Is he sick?"

"I believe so," Hawks added. "Sad really, but I don't think he has long to live."

"Oh, that's sad." she said, reveling in his strong embrace. "What's the matter with him?" she asked.

"I don't know. Probably just something that didn't agree with him," he said sarcastically.

"Will I meet you back here in a couple days then?" she asked hopefully.

"I'll find you," he said. "Like I always do."

"I can't always break my plans at the last minute you know. Richard might get suspicious," she said.

Hawks tickled her and said, "He should be. With a sexy girl like you." He kissed her ear and began to work his way down her neck. Soon things began all over again.

40 – Chicago

"Do you recognize this woman?" Josh asked the receptionist as he showed her a picture of his Jane Doe that was printed from the surveillance video.

The lobby of the Nexus Pharmaceutical's suite was impressive. Smooth dark slate floors, polished to a bright shine, reflected the bright white LED lighting above. Large white leather couches and a tinkling fountain in the center of the lobby set the mood of wealthy serenity. The receptionist counter was only a few feet tall but topped with a thick slab of black marble with tiny flakes of gold dust sprinkled below the polished surface. It was Paul Thomas' employer, and seemed a logical place to start investigating his connection to the Jane Doe in Highland.

The receptionist was barely twenty, a gorgeous dark haired girl with bright indigo colored eyes. It was clear that she was comfortable being the company's luscious eye candy. Josh's blunt approach, along with the photo, left her momentarily speechless.

"I... I think so... Wait. Is that Kristina?" she said as her jaw dropped. The photograph clearly disturbed her.

"Kristina who?" Josh asked impatiently. When there wasn't an immediate answer he gently reached over the counter and placed the photograph in her hand.

She looked up at him with her beautiful large round eyes, blinked her elegant lashes, and looked back at the picture. Her face turned serious and concerned. "Yes. Kristina Hanson." She handed the photograph back to Josh.

"Tell me about her," he said.

"She... used to... I mean, works here. She is very nice and kind. Would do anything to help you. It's like, you know how some people will offer you help, or say this or that in order to be nice? Well Kristy's someone who would actually do all those things. She's not just talk, she has a heart of gold." Keeping her emotions in check she added, "She would make good on the promises of others. She was... a beautiful person."

"Do you know what happened to her?" Josh asked.

"No. The police won't even say she's missing. I'm sorry, I shouldn't talk about her like she's... dead or something."

"You were friends with her outside of work then?" he asked.

"Yes, we went to school together. She got me this job too. She was so excited about her future, her new boyfriend." At this thought she teared up and quickly grabbed a tissue to prevent her mascara from running.

"Paul Thomas?" Josh asked after she recovered.

She looked up at him thoughtfully and asked, "How did you know?"

"Yes, how did you know?" a man walked in from the left corridor. An older, heavy set, gray haired man, he appeared to be an executive, dressed in a full three-piece suit.

"I'm following up on an order I placed with him," Josh answered readily.

"An order? For who?" he asked.

"Doctor Eugene Sullivan," Josh offered. The old man's face never flinched, but he clearly thought about his response before making it.

"Well I don't think it is appropriate for you to be upsetting my employees, Mr..."

"Decker. Josh Decker."

"I see Mr. Decker. Well, I suggest that if you have any inquires here you make them with me."

"And you are?"

"Busy," the old man said briskly.

"Perhaps then I'll make an appointment with your receptionist," Josh said. The man stood for a moment to contemplate the situation, then placed a file on the receptionist's desk. He looked at Josh and said, "You do that." And walked back down the corridor.

"How about lunch?" Josh asked.

"Mr. Jackson's assistant makes his appointments, but I can arrange for you to meet one of our sales representatives."

"What I meant was, where will you be going for lunch today?" he asked.

"I shouldn't."

"Shouldn't what?"

"I don't know." She was clearly uncomfortable talking with him.

Josh began to speak a bit louder, "Fine then, I'll be back next week to meet with your sales representative." Then in quieter tones he asked, "And your name is?"

"Cindy."

"Thank you, Cindy."

A couple hours later Josh spotted Cindy exiting the building to go to lunch. She was alone and he slowly made his way along side of her until she noticed his presence.

"I'm sorry about barging in on you at work like that. I didn't mean to get you into any trouble."

"You didn't. Mr. Jackson is just very... protective. Especially after what happened to Paul."

"You knew him?"

"Yes, he was one of our best sales reps. He was dating Kristy. She was madly in love with him."

"What was your impression of him?"

"He was nice. I mean, he was a slick salesman, you know. But you have to be in this business. It's pretty intense. A lot of wining and dining. He was good at it. I just hoped he'd be good to Kristy too. But..." She began to sob.

"He didn't hurt her," Josh said confidently. Cindy stopped walking and turned to him.

"How do you know? How do you know all this? Who are you?" she asked.

"I'm working with CPD, following up on some new evidence." They resumed walking toward a restaurant down the road. It was chilly out and both kept their hands inside their jackets as they walked.

"Was Paul working on anything peculiar? Anything out of the ordinary?" he asked.

"I don't think so." She paused to wipe her eyes. Josh feared a dead end and wondered if questioning Cindy was such a good idea. Then she added, "But Kristy mentioned he had found something suspicious going on at one of our competitors."

"Did she say what it was about?"

"Not really. I don't think she knew. Something about illegal drugs, like unapproved chemicals that were being shipped to one of their clients."

"What competitor?" Josh asked.

"Trans-Pharmaceutical. They were his big competitor. They're everyone's big competitor."

"Do you know anyone there?"

"No. I haven't been here too long. I just know she said that Paul had some big deal going on and she thought it was going to get him a huge reward, or promotion, something like that. She was hoping that would mean a ring on her finger, you know? I think she was dreaming, I mean, they had only just started going out. But she was so happy, and so sure. But then he was robbed and killed in cold blood. And Kristy... I'm still hoping she's okay."

"I'm sorry," he paused before continuing, "Kristina's body was found a little over a week ago." They stopped and Cindy turned to him again. This time she wasn't crying. She just stood motionless, in shock. "I don't know if it helps, but Paul had nothing to do with it."

"So that's it. Nothing more," she said. Josh looked at her in silence as she gazed off into the distance as if there was another world she could see across the busy, bustling street. "She was a really good person."

"Thank you Cindy. For what it's worth, this helps." Josh said.

Cindy just turned and walked off toward the restaurant. Josh watched her until she entered and then walked back down the road toward the lakefront.

41 – London

Molly had just left an interview, this time for a much smaller artistic commission at a hotel. As she walked down the street a beautiful red headed woman approached her.

"Molly?" she said excitedly.

Molly looked confused and tried to recognize the woman but couldn't place her.

"Molly! Seriously? It's me Tina!"

"I'm sorry, I don't think I..."

"Oh my God! Come along we need to catch up!" Tina said enthusiastically in her Irish accent and took Molly by her left arm and proceeded to walk down the road.

"Tina is it?" she asked.

"Don't you remember our days at Wellington?"

Molly was surprised at how much she knew and began to believe she really had forgotten Tina. After all, it had been almost ten years since her last day of high school. Molly stopped walking. "No, actually. I'm terribly sorry but I don't really..."

"Of course you do!" Tina interrupted loudly, then suddenly spoke quietly to her through a large smile, "We are old school friends and I know you're in trouble. I can help."

"What?" Molly's face grew concerned.

"Smile!" Tina whispered, then resumed, "Let's have some tea!" and she quickly whisked Molly down the road to a tea shop where they sat down.

"I'm sorry Molly, but you are being followed and if we don't become long lost friends very soon, I feel you may be in a bit of danger. So smile and order some tea so we can talk," she said in a happy manner but under her breath.

Molly turned as white as a sheet. A sobering feeling of dread sank into her. They ordered some tea and Tina prompted Molly. "Tell me a story about Wellington. A fun story."

"I ah..." Molly hesitated then thought of a story to tell. "The time... we... both performed the scene from Romeo and Juliet in the courtyard, on a dare. We were studying for literature and the boys teased us into it... um..."

"Oh yes! Of course! That was so embarrassing! Do you still remember the scene?"

"I think so," she answered.

"What was it?"

Molly rolled her eyes, becoming truly a little embarrassed. "The balcony scene, of course." She smiled.

"That's it!" she said excitedly then added under her breath, "Keep smiling and tell me the story."

"I was Romeo because I have the deeper voice. You were Juliet. And the boys just wanted to see us kiss." She grinned remembering the silly scene from her school days.

"Beautiful! We were terrible at our lines, I think we ended up just making them up."

"Trying to avoid the kissing!" Molly laughed, forgetting for a moment that Tina was never actually there.

"Oh Romeo! But we couldn't hold back forever. They wouldn't let us, would they?" Tina continued.

"No. They wouldn't until we…" Molly shook her head, "kissed."

"Ha, ha, ha!" Tina laughed. "Tell me, how was I?" she arched her eyebrow.

Molly grinned, "Not bad," and chuckled.

"I'm so happy to have run into you like this, Moll." Tina took her hand in friendship and slipped a small note in it. "Tell me what you do now, show me your portfolio," she prompted.

"Yes, okay," Molly said taking her portfolio and unzipping it. She had several large photographs of her work and some stained glass samples. Molly took this opportunity to read the note. It had a phone number written on it. As they were looking, Tina spied around the area and began to speak softly but seriously.

"Molly, I have a friend who works for the government. He will be here in a moment and I will introduce him as my husband. Listen to him and know that we can help you with your situation."

"What situation is that?"

"It's okay," she said. "Play along. You can use this real encounter to explain anything you might need to explain about what happened today. You can even bring it up to him if you wish."

"Him?" Molly said. Tina looked at her with an expression that conveyed the idea Molly knew exactly what she had meant. "I don't want to do that." Molly answered.

"Fine. Oh, here he is now." Tina sat up straight, smiled enthusiastically as if trying to get someone's attention, and waved. The man came into the café and proceeded to give Tina a hug and kiss.

"Oh Molly, I'd like you to meet my husband Peter!"

"Nice to meet you, Molly," he said as he extended his hand.

Molly gasped openly. "You!"

"My wife has told me much about you," said Peter, "Have a seat Ms. Wheeler."

"You're the man who was following me," Molly said almost gasping for air.

"Relax now. Everything is alright. Sit down."

Molly cautiously took her seat.

"You're right, I had the chance to follow you. To make sure you were safe."

"Hardly a way to make a girl feel safe, Mr...."

"Hawks. Peter Hawks."

"I don't appreciate you following me Mr. Hawks," she said with a touch of anger, "and I'll mind you to not let it happen again."

He took a moment before nodding in agreement. "Please listen to me first. I have a proposition for you, Molly," he said.

"I'm not interested. I haven't been..."

"You need to be interested my dear. Your life is in danger. But I can help – if you let me."

Molly's eyes shifted from side to side nervously.

"I'm with the government looking into a suspicious trail of money," he continued. "We have followed some transactions flowing from Russia to London, to China, back to Russia, the United States, etc. And they all have one thing in common. Your boyfriend."

"Well, I wouldn't know anything about that really," Molly said.

"No, I suspect you wouldn't. But you could learn about them a bit, no?"

"What do you mean?"

"We are interested in learning exactly where the money is going and what it is being used for. We know there is a contact in Chicago. An energy corporation in Russia, probably a front organization, but we'd like to learn more about Gordon Chase. He's new to this 'business' and I'm offering you the chance to help us, help you."

"What business?"

"He may be caught up in some illegal foreign activity. We're not quite sure yet."

Molly thought about this for a moment. It was making too much sense for her comfort. She was quickly coming out of denial.

"I don't see how I can help. He doesn't even come home all that often anymore."

"Your help would be to let us know when he leaves, where's he's going, who are his friends, that sort of thing. Keeping tabs on him and anything he asks you to do for him. If you begin to show such an interest he may just begin to involve you in whatever he is doing."

"And how does this spying on my boyfriend help me?" Molly asked indignantly.

Hawks paused a moment then said, "You're afraid of him, aren't you?" Molly just looked straight at him. Hawks nodded his head. "We've tracked more than just money. Your boyfriend is growing more and more dangerous, Molly. He is using you and may end up really hurting you if you allow him to continue."

Molly chuckled and smiled shyly. Then she shook her head slowly and looked down. She paused and thought about it. "I can't..." she couldn't finish the sentence.

Tina placed her hand onto Molly's and said, "This isn't just about you. He has hurt others as well."

"I'm leaving London, so I can't."

"Leaving?" Hawks asked. "With Gordie?"

"Yes."

"Where?"

Molly refused to answer.

"Chicago?" Hawks asked. Molly looked up, stunned that he knew. Hawks and Tina exchanged urgent glances. "When do you leave?"

Again, Molly was silent. She was trying to process everything she had heard and it all made sense. She realized that she had worked hard to deny her intuition and better judgement. Making excuses to herself about Gordie now felt like a terrible and intimate betrayal of herself. Her emotional connection with him had degenerated from admiration and affection to abject fear. But it had to stop now. She was determined, but how? She couldn't think. It was all too much too fast. As strong as she was, the fear he imposed on her over the last couple of years had done its job. But she would not continue to be a victim.

"Has he said anything about Chicago? What you'll be doing?" he asked.

"Only that his business was with a doctor who works on interpreting dreams or something. And that a friend would show us around the city, and to museums – art. Things like that." She spoke softly in a monotone voice.

"A doctor?"

"Yes."

"Molly, this is very important," he and Tina again glanced at each other. "This doctor is someone whom we are very interested in. He has a new technology that, if it works, would allow people to read the thoughts of others. He has been experimenting and he might ask you to participate."

"Me? To read my mind? Sounds like a bit of fantasy."

"It's very real, Molly. And if it falls into the wrong hands, it could be extremely dangerous. But that's the answer. That is what you can do to stop all of this. Help us find the doctor and this machine or whatever it is, and I promise you will be free of him.

Molly slowly shook her head. "He knows things. He checks on me. If he finds out, I'll…"

"The number on this paper, Molly, is Tina's number. Your old friend from your school days at Wellington. Contact her with your flight information and where you're staying in Chicago. We'll be nearby."

"Being one of my friends is dangerous as of late." Molly warned.

"I can take care of myself." Tina added. "Let's do lunch when you get back!" she brought back her enthusiastic demeanor.

"What do you say Molly? Does 'lunch' work for you?" Hawks said, implying an agreement to helping them.

Molly thought about it.

"It's the hardest thing to do, standing up to your fears. Standing up to a bully. Even when you know it's the right thing to do. It takes a very brave young lady," he said looking at her admirably.

"Lunch sounds nice," Molly agreed.

"Good! Keep us informed," Hawks said.

The two stood up, paid the check, and left the café arm in arm. Molly took her portfolio and proceeded to the Underground, making her way back to Croydon.

42 – Highland

"Josh is in the house everyone!" Charlie announced loudly as Josh entered The Chance bar.

Josh looked around, "There's no one here, moron," he said. Charlie chuckled.

"Need a drink?"

"What incredible intuition it must take to be a bartender," Josh said sarcastically.

"It is a skill acquired and enjoyed by only a select few," Charlie replied with a smile as he poured Josh a glass of whiskey. "How was Chicago?"

"Kristina Hanson. Twenty-three. That's our Jane Doe," Josh said producing the photo of her taken from the surveillance video.

"Oh yeah, that's her alright. What'd they make of the blue spot?"

"Nothing. Except they found the same thing on her boyfriend after he was shot in the chest a week or so ago."

"No shit! Wonder what it is," Charlie asked rhetorically.

"Also, we have an unknown man who entered in after her boyfriend disappeared out the back. And a name. Some Russian guy who paid for my hotel room. Probably unrelated."

"A Russian guy paid for your hotel?" asked Charlie.

"Yes. Actually, he paid for someone else's room," Josh said cryptically. "Anyway, they're running additional toxicology to see if anything turns up."

"And the boat?" Charlie asked.

"Belongs to a sleep doctor. A strange guy who just doesn't seem right. I saw his speech online. Guy thinks he can back up his brain like a hard drive and implant it into a new body. Living forever kind of craziness."

"And you thought Ted Williams was crazy for freezing his head!" Charlie laughed.

"I never said he was crazy. It's the fans who think that someday he'll be back playing ball again!" Josh said and took another sip. "Anyway, Marty's looking into it now. Should hear something in a few days or so."

"How is Marty?" Charlie asked.

"He's the same. Sitting behind a desk too much, but he's good."

"Yeah, sitting around for too long isn't good for you. Did he ask you back?"

Josh hesitated then answered, "Yeah."

"But you're back here now?" Charlie asked.

"I am," Josh said.

"So, what do you do now?"

He took a sip. "How's Abby?" Josh asked, changing the subject.

"She's good. Got to spend some time with her. Helped her practice some shooting."

"That's good."

"She's a good shot. A natural."

"Well, she'll be ready for prom night," Josh smiled.

"Oh yeah," Charlie agreed. "She's quite a young lady."

"I know."

"You know, she needs to finish school," Charlie began in more of a parental mode.

"I know that. Once she's eighteen she'll no longer be a runaway..."

"I mean you'll have to let her go soon," he interrupted.

Josh paused at this comment then said, "Yeah, so? She can leave now if she wants. I don't care."

"The hell you don't."

"What are you getting at Charles?" Josh asked pointedly.

"Nothing," he smirked as Josh took another sip. "I think she's good for you to be around. Kinda gives you a chance to... deal with things."

"No, that's just..." Josh took a long sip instead of finishing his thought.

"Hey, did you hear? The old man may not be coming back," Charlie announced encouragingly.

"So I heard."

"You know, I think it'd be a good thing for you."

"I have a job," said Josh.

"I know, I know. But hell, you don't have to give it up. Kel isn't here half the year as it is! And wearing a badge again would be good for you. Exactly what you need. Plus you'd be legitimate again!

"That's all behind me," Josh insisted.

"Bullshit. You're investigating right now. Except without a badge."

"Nothing happens here! What good is it?" Josh asked.

"It's not about the town, it's about you! I think it's time to move on Josh." Charlie suddenly got very serious. Josh didn't respond, just lost himself in thought. "You know, this whole case hasn't just fallen in your lap for no reason. And Abby? Yeah, her too. How'd she end up in your living room out of the blue?"

"Don't tell me you put her there," Josh said sarcastically.

"Come on! Of course not. It's fate telling you to get on with your life," Charlie said, but Josh seemed unphased and annoyed. "She worries about you. Having her around can help you deal with this, find some closure."

Josh just sat there, staring into his glass, thinking.

"You know what I feel like saying to you?" Josh asked.

"Yup. You want to tell me, 'What the fuck do you know about what I'm going through?'" Josh only nodded. "Except you can't," Charlie finished.

"Cause you know exactly what I'm going through," Josh finished the thought.

"Yeah, I do," he said, slowly.

"How old was he, do you think?"

Charlie's lips quivered, "Oh, 'bout eight I suppose. I can still see him. Half naked, running straight at us. And I..." he couldn't finish.

"Hell of a thing," Josh said.

"Hell of a thing," Charlie echoed.

"And you're over it?" Josh asked with a hint of sarcasm.

"No. You never get over it. You get used to it. I suppose if you ever really got over something like that, you'd have nothing left in you. No humanity. Nothing."

"I know the feeling," said Josh.

"I know you do. But Josh, your life ain't over. Not by a long shot. You have so much more to give. You can't run away forever." They were silent for a long time.

"Kristina Hanson," Josh said. "Abby asked me to help her. That she deserved answers."

"I told you, that girl's good for you," Charlie said.

"I know he killed her," Josh blurted out.

"Who?" Charlie asked.

"The 'Dream Catcher' himself. Dr. Eugene Sullivan."

"How do you know?"

"I just do. I saw it in his eyes. You can recognize the eyes of a killer. They're cold and lifeless. Like a shark."

"Yeah," said Charlie. "Unlike yours."

43 – Highland

Their voices all came echoing at once.

'Someone should've been there...' said the steady man's voice.

'I didn't know...' was it his voice, or someone else's?

BANG! A blast followed by fading echoes of a gunshot.

'I want answers!' shouted the angry man.

'That wasn't so bad... was it?' said the woman's soft voice.

Over and over again, turning frantic. They wouldn't end!

'I didn't know!'

'You should have!'

'Answers!'

'BANG!'

'You made me a promise...'

'Like a little butterfly, tied to a string...'

'Hope Josh... there is always hope...'

'Hopeless! I can't fly!'

'Where is it? Where are you?'

The room was empty now, only the sloshing of water could be heard as he threw himself down onto his hands and knees, searching. It was futile! The water was incessant! As soon as it moved it was replaced and he was growing more and more frantic.

Footsteps could be heard approaching, like in a television Western, slowly pounding on the boardwalk.

'Let it go... Joshua... the harder you pull the tighter the string... let it go...' Charlie's voice calmed him. He held his breath, his hands resting on the floor under six inches of rich, thick, red blood.

The footsteps approached and then stopped. He waited. His heart beat loudly in his chest, so hard he felt it may burst!

Then silence – the only sound, a fluttering of the most delicate wings rippling through the air. Its tiny motion eventually effecting drastic change around the world. Or so the theory goes. But would hope die with it?

Suddenly the door burst open! At the same instant he found his gun! He turned and aimed it into the doorway and... he pulled the trigger. But nothing happened. He held no gun. It had vanished.

He looked ahead to where he was pointing. It was Abby, standing there with a string around her and bright butterfly wings around her back.

"NO!" Josh shouted and sat up in his bed, again soaked with sweat and gasping for breath. He heard someone coming and reached across to the nightstand for his gun. As he whipped it around and aimed at the doorway, the curtain parted and Abby stumbled in. She had come running to check on him after he screamed.

"Huh!" she stopped fast. It was still dark out, but the light from her room blead through enough to clearly make out the gun.

"Josh?" She could see him breathing heavy, almost gasping for breath. "Are you ok?"

Realizing what he was doing, he quickly put the gun down on the bed and let it go. He placed his head in his hands and wanted to scream, but held back. Abby was visibly concerned and frightened. Josh stood up and walked to the far end of the room. On top of the dresser was an antique mantle clock. Out of no-where, with his right hand, he whipped it off the dresser and across the room, smashing it to pieces against the wall.

After a long moment Abby spoke, "Josh? What happened?"

He didn't answer. He put on a pair of jeans and his coat and slowly walked past her out to the front deck.

Dawn was about to break and the trees swayed gently in the wind which was growing restless with a brewing autumn storm, playing the trees like a musical instrument. A symphony of hallowed tones gently roared above their heads as if the gods themselves were waking, scheming, preparing to make their power known to mere mortals.

Abby approached slowly. She walked out, keeping her distance, saying nothing.

165

"Like in the movies, for every happy ending there's someone who lost. The loser isn't always an asshole. It's just a fact. You see someone win the girl's heart, you don't always see the other guy who lost it. No consolation prize. Just go home and deal with it. To be a winner you need a loser. I've known the loser. But I don't go there anymore." He turned around to face her and said, "Why did you barge in like that? I might have shot you?"

"You called for me."

"I what?" he asked surprised.

"You called, 'Abby!'

"I called for you," he repeated as if he needed to confirm it to himself. "I think you need to leave."

"If that's what you really want. But why?" she asked. It was starting to get light now, and he turned back and faced away, toward the lake beyond the thick woods.

"Without the leaves on the trees you can see the lake from here. They fall down like… like a fluttering butterfly." Abby was confused but appreciated the image. Josh continued, "I loved someone once. More than anything in the world. It was as if life brought us together. We didn't even have to try, it just clicked from the very beginning. Then one night, just like that, she was gone. Freak accident." Josh took a long pause and Abby sat down on the chair to listen.

"'Let her go' they said. You have to move on. 'I know' I said. And that's what I did. Went through the motions for over a year. Things were never right after that, but they seemed to get a little better. Just as I stopped remembering her for a moment, I would dream of her, only to wake up and start missing her all over again."

He looked up and could see the dark clouds moving rapidly through the sky above. He could smell the moisture that was soon to blow in. "The world never slows down and could care less," he continued, "It just does what it does. So that's what I did. One day I joined a squad to take out a thug on the south side. We went in, two went to the right, two to the left, and I went upstairs. As I climbed the steps I could hear the footsteps fumbling around. I reached the top… turned the corner… and there were three doors. The one straight ahead was the one. The door was open and I saw a shadow move. My gun was aimed and ready. Breathing, calm, steady as I ever was." Abby's eyes grew wide, her face pained with concern.

"I moved closer. Then he came around from the right side of the room into the doorway. He had a gun. I swore it was a gun." Josh paused and looked down. He placed his hands down on the railing at the edge of the deck. "I fired. I can still see him in my site. It was a perfect shot. But at that very instant... he moved. And I hit the girl he was holding hostage. I killed her." The sound of the wind kicked up blowing a cold chill around them with the sound of dried up leaves scattering about. "She was seventeen."

"You couldn't have known," Abby said as she wiped a tear from her cheek. She hated to see him in such pain.

"I did know. I saw her. He had a knife. She'd of lived if I had just... not rushed it." He paused then resumed as if only talking to himself. "I often wonder... if I had it to do again, would I have taken the shot? You always ask yourself, you know... try to prepare for that moment. But nothing prepares you. No training, no book. The decision is first instinct, then skill. You pull the trigger and it's over. And I play it over and over again. Slow motion, frame by frame. You know, I can still see her. She was terrified. And yet for an instant when she saw me I know she felt that I'd save her. Instead, I killed her."

After Josh turned around and faced Abby once again, "That was my last day as a cop. I lost the woman and the job I loved. I have dreams. And in those dreams I still see that helpless girl. Clear as the moment it happened. But not this time. This time... I saw you." He paused again and looked deeply into her eyes. "And that's why you need to go."

Abby looked away from him, trying to hold back her emotions, but she felt both sad and an incredible sense of responsibility. She wasn't prepared to just leave him behind. She stood up and walked into the cottage. A moment later she returned with a piece of paper that had been neatly folded, obviously a keepsake read many times before.

"My English teacher shared this with us. May I?" she asked. Josh nodded and turned back toward the lake. Abby read,

'tis a fearful thing
to love what death can touch
a fearful thing
to love, to hope, to dream, to be –

to be,
and oh, to lose.
A thing for fools, this,
and a holy thing,
a holy thing
to love.

For your life has lived in me,
your laugh once lifted me,
your word was gift to me.
To remember this brings painful joy.

'Tis a human thing, love,
a holy thing, to love
what death has touched.

(Yehuda HaLevi)

"I thought it was so perfectly beautiful. Especially when... my teacher, he died unexpectedly the following year. But I will always be grateful and happy to feel that kind of pain." Abby finished and folded the paper.

"Oh Abby," Josh shook his head. "Why you?"

"I don't know. Your cottage was empty!" she said, breaking the tension.

Josh smiled and turned toward her. She smiled back and gave him a little smirk. "Thank you. You know," he continued, "Charlie saved my life. I drank myself nearly to death in the days, or weeks after, I don't remember. He let me his place here. He stayed in his other one so it wasn't a big deal. I'd have blown off anyone else, I think. But he knew somehow. He knew.

After a while I pretended to pull myself together. A retired cop, friend of mine, owned a security consulting company, working for high-end companies all around the world. He gave me a chance to go anywhere. And I wanted to be as far from my life as I could be."

"Sounds nice. Get to see the world," Abby added.

"I hate it," he chuckled and shook his head. "It's not *me*. All these huge companies with more money than they know what to do with. Transportation companies, tech companies, drug companies..." he stopped mid-sentence. "Drug companies," he repeated.

"What is it?" Abby asked.

"Nothing. Well, something I hope. I need to get to town and use the phone."

"May I come with you?" Abby asked.

"I'd like that," Josh smirked and placed his hand on her shoulder. She returned by giving him a tremendous hug.

"I love you," she said. "Just wanted to say that to you at least once. You don't have to say anything." She let him go and ran into the cottage to grab her coat before he could. Josh wished he could have managed to get the same words past his lips.

44 – Chicago

The daylight filtered in through the curtains waking Molly early in the morning. She was feeling the jet lag now as she stretched her way outside of the bed sheets wearing only a spaghetti strapped top and bikini underwear. She expected to find Gordie with her but he had left shortly after they arrived and apparently never returned.

She yawned several times before finally standing up and pulling back the curtains, getting her first look at the city in daylight. Although her room was toasty warm, the view was of a cold, gray day. Up only a few stories, the buildings nearby were mainly made of old, dirty brick with languishing old fire escapes clinging to their sides.

She walked over to the desk and picked up the hotel directory. A post card fell out onto the desk. The picture was of the beautiful shoreline, with a bright, deep blue Lake Michigan caressing the sandy shore, and the Chicago skyline bathed in bright beautiful sunshine. "Chicago" was boldly written in the upper left hand corner. The image contrasted with the cold reality outside her room. In that moment of introspection, Molly took up a pencil and scratched out a haiku.

Eternity's touch
Ripples on a frozen lake
Yearn for spring to free

Her creative bent rarely ventured into verse, but her loneliness, now amplified by her strange surroundings, had found a momentary voice. She tucked the card back into the directory, planning to retrieve it later. Then she heard a knock at the door. She walked over.

"Who is it?" Molly's English accent was clearly evident.

"Anita Reynolds. Dr. Sullivan sent me," a voice calmly spoke, barely audible through the door.

"Ah, just a moment." Molly answered. She looked into the closet, saw a white robe provided by the hotel, and hastily put it on. Then she opened the door revealing an elegant woman, dressed in sharp black pin striped business suite with a dark red blouse – the top two buttons left undone. Anita strutted right in without so much as an acknowledgment.

"Oh, I thought you would be ready to go," Anita said smugly.

"Ready to go? Um, to go where?" Molly asked.

"I was asked to show you around the city. What is it you would like to see?"

"Oh! How nice," Molly said, but Anita gave a stone faced expression that left Molly feeling uneasy, as if she was a grave inconvenience.

"Well, I thought my boyfriend was going to show me around actually..." Molly began before being cut off.

"Well, it's up to you but I have already taken the day off from work for you, so I'd appreciate it if you would make up your mind."

"Of course. I mean, if you'll give me a moment I'll change and get ready." Molly took some clothes from her bag and quickly entered the bathroom to prepare and get dressed.

Anita walked around the room, snooping into Molly's bag, then her purse. She opened her wallet which contained British currency and a credit card. She then opened Molly's passport and looked at her picture and privately scoffed at what she thought of as Molly's 'precious smile.' She read her date of birth quickly revealing her age, 28. 'Perky young thing' she thought.

"What kind of things would you like to see?" Anita asked in a raised voice so as to be heard in the bathroom.

"I understand there are many museums in Chicago. I'm a bit of an artist," Molly answered.

Anita continued her stroll around the room, finally sitting on the bed and curiously placing her hand inside the sheets and blankets, feeling the entire center of the bed. It felt warm on one side, cool on the other. "Hmpf" vocalizing her contempt. "They have jewelry at the Art Institute. Among other... art," she said unenthusiastically.

"That would be wonderful," Molly answered from the bathroom.

Anita stood up and looked out the window. "It's cold today. I hope you brought a jacket."

Molly opened the bathroom door and walked out, dressed in blue jeans and a gray sweatshirt. "I did. Ready to go?" she tried smiling, hoping to break the icy chill her escort had thus far provided.

"Dressed like that?"

Surprised, Molly paused and quickly looked herself over saying, "How should I dress?"

Anita sighed, "It's no wonder," she spoke out loud but to herself. "That'll do. My car is parked out front."

Molly grabbed her purse, a light black jacket, and followed Anita out the door. Before the door closed, Molly remembered, "I forgot the room key!" and she went back in to retrieve it from the desk. Once the door closed behind her she sarcastically mumbled, "This is going to be fun."

45 – Highland

The wind had subsided by evening after a dark gray day. Abby lay on her bed reading *1984* by George Orwell. With the isolation of the cottage she had quickly become an avid reader of the classics and although initially she had no idea what it was about, it didn't take her long to become intrigued. The idea that 'Big Brother' was always watching and the way the Ministry of Truth delivered its propaganda all seemed to resonate with her views of the modern world. 'To think this was written so long ago and yet so much of it seems to be coming true!' she thought.

Winston, the main character, intrigued her the most. He was lost, void of feeling for so long, and all he wanted was to love and to be loved. She thought of how beautiful and elemental this desire was and how it could drive us to push both societies and self-imposed boundaries. She was fascinated and from time to time would stop reading, close the book, roll over onto her back holding it to her chest, and gaze up toward the ceiling in contemplation. She had a lot of questions, and enjoyed simply asking them in her mind over and over. 'Was love the definition of God, or a path that blinds us to doom?' 'Is there anyone that we can really trust?' 'Are you alive without love?' 'Are we nothing more than what we are nurtured to be?' 'Can a human be programmed and controlled into conformity, a soulless creature like a worker bee?'

The book invited her to question her world and examine what she thought was true about it, particularly her own humanity. She also thought about Josh. The more she thought she should leave the more the felt she should stay. She wasn't unlike him. She too had run away from a painful past, felt unloved and, more significantly, felt unable to take the risk of loving someone else. She was glad she had told him she loved him. It was the truth and nothing else needed to be said or done. But now what? In any event, she was looking forward to discussing the book with him when he returned. She admired how he was able to find a different perspective of things, even if it was cynical.

It was during one of these contemplative moments that she thought she heard something just outside her window. It was dark, the far side of dusk, and her lamp was the only light on in the cottage. She was comfortable, in sweatpants and a t-shirt – it was expected to be cold overnight. She stood up, moved to the window and held open the curtain. All she saw was darkness.

Then another rustling sound came from outside to her left. She moved back and turned off the lamp in order to see outside with more clarity. She returned to the window and looked toward the back deck and doorway that entered into the kitchen. She couldn't make much out, the woods shadowing what little light was left. 'Was it an animal?' she thought. 'Probably. What else could it be?'

A distinct thud was heard from living room area, but it still seemed that it was outside. She turned the light back on and moved toward the curtain which hung in the doorway, the rest of the cottage was dark. The isolation and quiet atmosphere made any disturbance unique but this was the first time she had ever heard something so distinctive.

"Josh?" she called quietly. There was no phone, few lights, and no internet, but there was the pistol Josh had left for her on the hutch in the living room. Just then a light flashed outside near the front deck and simultaneously a loud bang accompanied by the sound of shattering glass blew in from the kitchen as the back door was kicked in with extreme force.

Abby shrieked and quickly made for the hutch and the gun. Her hands were shaking violently but she managed to reach the hutch, spilling several papers and trinkets onto the floor as she slide her hands across the top shelf where the gun was kept. Just as her hand reached it, she was suddenly jarred away violently and pushed down from her left. The gun fell, she could see it a few feet in front of her.

"I found her!" one man announced. The sound of heavy boots pounding on the old wooden floorboards now began to fill the room around her, but she was still free to move and quickly slide herself toward the gun.

A flashlight now flickered and then focused on her face from in front of her. It was bright and blinding, but she touched the butt of the gun and continued to frantically reach for it. Everything seemed to happen in slow-motion.

"Well now…" a second man's voice spoke from behind the bright flashlight. Abby continued to cry out when a man fell onto her back and grabbed her right arm, just as she had reached the gun. He lifted her arm and slammed it to the floor, forcing her to drop the weapon. He pulled her back by her hair and t-shirt and lifted her up to her knees. It all took only seconds.

She screamed, but her mouth was quickly covered with a cloth and her arms arrested behind her back by the assailant.

"Bring her in here." The man with the flashlight spoke and walked over toward her room, the light still on.

She was lifted to her feet and pushed in the direction of her room, her bare foot kicking the gun aside as she struggled and resisted. The man holding her was joined by a second in order to keep her under control. Together they managed to bring her into her bedroom and stood her in front of their leader. She recognized him instantly.

"What do we do now, Derrick?" one asked.

Abby continued to struggle until Derrick grabbed her by the throat with his left hand and began to squeeze.

"Let her go," Derrick ordered. The two others complied. She grabbed his arm and tried to remove it from her throat, but using his right hand he grabbed her hair and pulled it back hard. She squealed in pain. "Stop!" he demanded. "Stop and I'll let go." Slowly Abby stopped resisting, and he eased his grip. He moved his right hand to the back of her neck and pulled her close to his face. "There, there now, just relax little girl. This won't be so bad." He noticed her eyes were welling with tears as her face was overcome with fear. "You're trembling. Well it's okay to be a little nervous your first time," Derrick smiled as his two stooges chuckled.

Without warning and in full strength, Derrick squeezed her throat and threw her violently onto the bed with one motion. Abby gasped for air as she lay on her stomach.

"Now you little bitch, I'm gonna give you what I promised you before! But now I'm not gonna be so nice about it." He reached down and forcefully ripped off her sweatpants and underwear down to her ankles. The others chuckled more as he began to unzip his pants.

"Hey leave some for me!" the older one said.

"Yeah, me too," the smaller one, Johnny, added although he was visibly shaking and nervous.

"You'll all get your chance! When I'm done."

With his pants down he moved on top of her just when another voice entered the room.

"Stop it!" he said.

Derrick and the others froze and were silent. The footsteps slowly walked into the room and stopped.

"Get the fuck off her," he said in a distinctively cockney accent.

Derrick lifted himself up off the bed. "You said I'd be able to mess with her how I wanted."

"Not now. I need her unharmed," he added.

"Then when?"

"When I'm done with her, I'll give her to you. You can do whatever you like with her then, as long as it ends with her… disposed of."

He took out a small white cloth and a little brown bottle from his coat pocket. He dampened the cloth with the contents of the bottle and reached over to cover Abby's nose with it. In a moment, she was knocked out completely.

"Get her dressed and be gentle with her."

"Derrick began to zip up his pants when he kicked the end of the bed. "Yeah, fuck that," he said under his breath.

The man turned to Derrick and grabbed him by the shirt collar violently. He was wearing black leather gloves and dressed entirely in black clothes. The move stunned Derrick who was still holding his zipper.

"If she so much as suffers a broken fingernail I'll gouge your eyes out and piss in your eye sockets," he said coldly as if not a threat but a certainty.

"Yes sir, Mr. Gordie," Derrick answered.

"The boy's not here. I'll leave him up to you."

"Me?" Derrick questioned, clearly a bit frightened by the prospect.

"Yeah. Get rid of him, you know," Gordie lectured condescendingly. "Or else."

Gordie quickly looked around the room. He picked up her cloth bag and the book from the bed. "Bring her out to the car. Carefully," he instructed. Then he walked out of the bedroom, sat down at Josh's desk, took out a piece of paper and scribbled something onto it. He folded it, placed it inside the old book, and the book into Abby's bag. Then he picked up the Glock from the floor. He aimed it at an old picture of a married couple that was hanging on the wall. The frame was thick wood, an antique. The faces of the subjects were noticeably sullen for a newly wedded couple. Just as Derrick and the others emerged from the bedroom, Derrick carrying Abby over his shoulder, he fired the gun across their path in front of them, shattering the glass and ripping a hole into the picture.

"What the fuck?" Derrick shouted, stunned.

"Get her down to the car. Then finish the job. You screw up and I'll put a bullet through your fucking heads. All' ya!" He placed the gun in his jacket and walked out.

Derrick quickly followed, carrying Abby down to the car as instructed. The other two retrieved a few gallons of gasoline from behind the cottage that they had brought via their four wheelers and began pouring it out on Abby's bed and into the living room. They poured it over the antique furniture, Josh's desk and typewriter, the record player and records. They splashed it onto the books, the walls and pictures, the hutch and throughout the kitchen.

Once the cans were emptied, they walked out the back door and over toward Abby's window. The larger one threw a rock, shattering the glass. Then he struck a match and tossed it into her room. Instantly, flames erupted and quickly spread. Within seconds the entire cottage was ablaze.

46 – Highland

"A young girl, maybe fifteen. She was found in a trash bin on the south side, heavy drug area. Made to look random," Marty said.

"Not unusual in that part of town these days," Josh said as Charlie listened to his side of the phone conversation.

"Well, it might have worked except for finding that blue mark behind her right ear."

"Has toxicology come back on either of the others?" Josh asked.

"Yes. They found an unusually high concentration of some sort of aluminum oxide. It wasn't noticed before because it wasn't anything you'd expect to test for, and the body would have flushed it out eventually."

"What the hell is aluminum oxide doing in each of these victims?" Josh asked.

"Hell if I know. Scotty's looking into all that. He called it a neurotoxin. Said he'd call you as soon as he has something."

"Did the girl have any identification?"

"No. She was found nude in a trash bag. We don't know exactly where she was dumped because they only discovered her once she was at the incinerator," Marty finished.

"When did she die?"

"Within the last seventy-two hours. You want to come have a look at her?" Marty asked.

"Yeah. I'll head out in the morning. Have Scotty call me here tonight, okay?"

"Will do. He's working overtime on this one so he'll be here late. I'll have him call Charlie."

"Thanks Marty. Damn! It's almost ten o'clock and you're still working?"

"All thanks to you! It was your lead."

"I owe you one."

Josh hung up the phone and finished scribbling a few notes on a piece of paper. Charlie had left the office in the back to tend to a few customers in the bar. Alone with his thoughts, Josh starred at the paper intensely. He lightly circled the names of the victims over and over again with his pencil, never lifting it from the page and thus connecting each of them with wide loops. 'The man was shot. The women were poisoned somehow, but why?'

"Anything?" Charles returned and broke his concentration.

"I can't shake this feeling."

"What feeling?"

"This doctor in Chicago. Dr. Sullivan. He's got something to do with this," Josh circled the name "Dr. Sullivan" which he had written in the center of the paper. "My boss tells me there are some big time players in the pharmaceutical industry in Chicago. Now there's a chemical found in these victims... It almost sounds like some science fiction experiment." His tracing grew more intense as he spoke until the pencil lead snapped. He looked up at Charlie. "It's crazy."

"What is exactly?"

"Could this doctor be some kind of psychotic nut case experimenting on these people for some perverted scientific reason? Doesn't that seem just a bit ridiculous?"

"Once you've eliminated the impossible..." Charlie began.

"I know. Whatever remains, however crazy, must be the truth," Josh finished.

"Something like that," Charlie smiled.

"But to what end? I didn't think anyone took his speech seriously except him." They sat for a moment in silence before Josh continued, "And you're standing there quoting fucking Sherlock Holmes to me?" he teased.

"Why not. Combine his logic and your intuition and the criminals don't have a chance."

"Well, I'm not a detective."

"Hell yes you are," Charlie insisted. Josh just continued to look at the paper and slowly shook his head. "Why don't you just let it go then? Let Marty and CPD handle everything? Why not?"

"I can't," Josh answered.

"Exactly. It's in you Josh. It's who you are. And you need to let Josh Decker back out to do his job."

"It's not my job damn it!" Josh said, clearly irritated by Charlie's provocation. "What am I doing anyway, huh? This has nothing to do with me!" He crumpled up the paper and threw it across the office. "I don't need to be doing any of this. In fact, I shouldn't be doing any of this. You think this is healthy for me? You think getting back into the shithole of humanity is going to somehow make me feel good again? I was a part of that horrible world!"

"For God sakes Josh, get the hell off your high horse and realize that your place in this world is to help people! To protect them! And you can't do that by hiding in the woods the rest of your life!"

"I'm not hiding."

"Of course you are. And it's fine – for a while. But this is something very strange. Unusual, and so far you've been the only one who's caught on to it. Do you think that's all some sort of divine accident?"

The phone rang interrupting their heated discussion.

"Hello?" Josh quickly answered, still in a heated tone.

"That's my phone," Charlie said under his breath.

"Scotty, what have you got?" Josh said.

"Not much," said Scotty, "But it is strange."

While his nickname came from the 'Star Trek' character he couldn't have been more unlike him in terms of his physical characteristics. Scotty was a tall, black man in his late sixties and spoke with a calm, measured, tone.

He continued, "The blue mark is a bruise, but it is enhanced by a chemical reaction with the skin. The chemical is a liquid sapphire derivative."

Josh instantly perked up as he heard the word 'Sapphire.' "What's that?" he asked.

"Liquid sapphire. It is used as a protective coating on electronics to prevent scratches or moisture from damaging components."

"But it's not pure, it's a derivative?" Josh asked.

"Right. I don't know the breakdown. Probably mixed with a normal saline solution and a combination of some other chemicals, but there's not enough of them to identify."

"With that entry point behind the jaw, where do you think it would it be going?"

"My guess is the brain," said Scotty. "It was a large needle but I can't imagine what for. I don't think it's something you'd want injected into your system."

"Why kill someone like that? It has to have some purpose," Josh speculated.

"It is unique for sure. Someone put a lot of care into this chemical," Scotty said.

"Scotty, if you injected someone with this chemical, what would it do to their brain?" Josh asked.

"I have no idea. But it can't be good," Scotty said.

"If you had to speculate... Say I wanted to extract information from the brain. Would this chemical help in some way?" Josh asked.

"I don't think so. That's above my pay grade. I just identified the chemical. It's a poison, that's for sure," Scotty answered.

"Thank you Scotty. I'll be in touch."

He hung up the phone.

"Sounded interesting," Charlie said.

"The good Doctor gave a speech in Chicago about recording brain activity. Said he was going to preserve humanity. Gain immortality. It's all too crazy. Isn't it?"

"If you had told me about the internet thirty years ago, I'd have thought you were crazy," Charlie noted.

"Charlie!" a voice shouted from the bar. "Charlie!"

Both Charlie and Josh rushed out to the bar to see Dino, in uniform, and out of breath.

"What the hell is it?" Charlie asked.

"Oh Josh! You're here! Quick... Your cottage!"

47 – Highland

Although it was a long way around, due to the urgency of the situation the three men jumped into Dino's police cruiser and headed down and around the dunes, then back up toward the men's cottages. They could see the flickering light of the flames in the distance almost the entire way. Once they arrived, the worst of the fire was over. It was a total loss.

"Holy shit!" Dino said as the three exited the car and slowly walked down the path around the ravine toward the front of where the cottage once stood. They stopped short of the cottage as flames continued to lick what was left of the roof which had collapsed, and the branches of some surrounding trees. Charlie looked Josh over carefully and noticed that he had that same cold, icy look in his eyes, just as he had seen the moment they first met in his bar.

"Where is she?" Josh said stoically.

"Who?" Dino asked. There was no answer.

"Dino, why don't you go around back and look for the girl, Abby. She was supposed to be here, but maybe she had gone into town or something," Charlie said, the last part for Josh's benefit.

"Ok," Dino said and slowly made his way around the cottage to the back, using his flashlight and calling out Abby's name.

Josh moved in closer to the front of the cottage and noticed Abby's bag. It looked as if it had been tossed onto a shrub as if it was meant to be found. He opened the bag and found a couple of her shirts and the book she had been reading, 1984. Inside the book was a folded piece of paper. He opened and read it.

"They took her," Josh said as he held her bag.

"We don't know that," Charles said. "We'll look for her, she might have just run."

Josh had felt anger before and one of his gifts was his ability to manage and temper it into a productive course of action. But this cut him deep. As he and Charlie stood in silence, starring at the flames, it was as if the fire was no longer destroying and consuming but rather fueling an intense anger and rage in Josh like he had never felt before. But he had to control it.

"No," he said, breathing hard and deeply. "They have her." He handed the paper to Charles.

It read: "Josh Decker killed me"

"What the hell?" Charles said.

"It's not her handwriting. It's a man's. And it's meant to keep me tied up here with the police."

"Then at least we know she's not inside," Charlie said, trying to be positive.

Josh turned and looked at Charlie for the first time since their arrival.

"They took her, but they wanted to get to me."

"Now Josh..." Charlie began, trying to assuage him of feeling responsible.

"Hold on to that bag," he said as began walking briskly back down to his car. Charlie followed close, the smell of smoke trailing behind them.

"Josh..." Charlie said as they walked. "Josh, this is not your fault, you couldn't have known." But he simply ignored him and continued his determined march. "Don't do something you might regret! You don't even know who did this!"

"Those 4-wheeler tracks tell me where to start," Josh said, pointing to some fresh tracks that Charlie hadn't noticed. The tracks led part way up the path around the ravine. They were not prominent, but Josh had spotted them on the way up, even in the dark.

"Josh! Damn it, listen. What are you going to do?" Again there was no answer. They reached his car and he pulled open the front door, reached into the pocket on the driver's door and pulled out his SCCY pistol. He pulled the slide back and released it launching a bullet into the chamber.

"They came for me? Now I'm coming for them," Josh said as he got into his car.

"Josh, they couldn't have gotten too far, we need to call the State police and get their help," Charlie said in a vain attempt to keep him from acting recklessly out of anger. It was no use.

Josh backed up the car and tore down the hillside leaving a trail of dust and sand behind him.

48 – Chicago

"What's that? No, no..." she wanted to scream it, but her voice could only manage a soft whisper as if she was struggling to break free from the bonds of a very deep sleep.

"There, there, now, just relax my dear," she heard his voice clearly. He spoke passively and without emotion. "Do you remember your name?"

"Abby," she answered, her eyes felt as if they had weights on them as she struggled to look at the man speaking to her.

"Abby. What a pleasure to meet you. I'm sure you will be excited to go on a wonderful trip before you are brought back home again," he seemed to be speaking to her but she wasn't really sure. It was as if the world around her was a shadow of her awareness and she wasn't even certain that she had said anything either.

"Tell me about your friend, Josh," he asked.

"Josh!" she shouted, which only amounted to another desperate whisper. She took a deep breath, but even that slight movement caused her head to throb with pain.

"Yes, Josh. You remember him. Who is he? What is he like?" he asked.

She managed to open her eyes exposing an incredibly bright, foggy world around her. She was reclined. Her limbs felt lifeless and heavy. She was high on nitrous oxide and the light pierced directly into her eyes blinding her from making anything, or anyone, out.

"Where is he? Josh!" she cried.

"He's nearby and waiting for you Abby, relax. He knows all about this. He saved you and now we're going to help you," he said as if he was reading a script, barely able to feign sincerity.

"He's here?" she asked gasping for breath, trying to fight off the effects of the gas.

"Near, yes. He is. Now tell me about him? Is he dangerous?" he asked.

"No. He's nice. He made coffee," she answered.

"Coffee," he repeated. "Well, that's certainly helpful information Abby," he sounded agitated.

"The little bitch is a dud. Just get on with it," Abby heard a woman's voice say as if very distant, barely audible.

"I need her lucid to make sure she's unharmed," the man said.

"Unharmed," Abby repeated.

"Yes my dear. You are unharmed. Everyone is fine and waiting for you. Who do you want to see first?"

She tried again to open her eyes but the blinding light elicited tremendous pain from the back of her head and squinting was not effective.

"The light... turn off the light," she said, struggling to articulate even those simple words.

"In a moment my dear. First, answer my question. Who would you like to see first?"

"Josh. Where is he?"

"He is near. Very close now. Tell me about him."

"He is..."

"Yes?" he said growing impatient.

"So alone."

"Go on Abby. Why is he alone?" he prompted.

"He is... I think he's scared. He's by himself and – I wanted to run! I wanted to get the hell away!" she began crying.

"You're safe now, my dear. He cannot harm you anymore," he said.

"No! He wanted to be... I mean... I wanted to go away. I hate him!" she began crying openly.

"You hate Josh?" he asked.

But something strange began to happen as she grew confused. She was responding to various thoughts that seemed to float rapidly into and out of her mind. She wanted to say she hated Derrick, she hated her aunt and uncle, she longed to be free like that bird trapped in a cage. She was trying to explain all of it, but she knew what it sounded like. It wasn't coming out right at all. She wanted to explain that Josh felt the same way, trapped and alone. She wanted to explain how wonderful he was, and how much she cared for and even loved him. But none of it would come out right. This made her all the more frustrated which further jumbled her thoughts and speech.

"Yes," she answered. "I hate him. No... It was just that he is alone! No... stop it! It's not right."

"Abby dear! Relax. You are safe," he said, raising his voice.

"I know!" she began to cry. The crying seemed to help her focus. She was still squinting her eyes shut, but the effects of the gas were less. Her emotional outburst was allowing her to compose her thoughts. Somehow she made sense of the correlation and so she didn't allow herself to stop crying. She thought about the pain, and about how afraid she was. She thought about the murder, about death and how she no longer feared it.

'*'tis a fearful thing to love what death can touch...*' echoed through her mind as she spoke.

"He is..." she spoke deliberately and slowly through her tears and gasps for air. "He – will – find – me."

'*a fearful thing to love, to hope, to dream, to be and oh, to lose.*'

"No! I – won't – go! I won't..." she blurted out using what seemed like all her strength.

"Abby, my dear. Who is Josh Decker?" the man's voice asked, it sounded almost like background noise.

"No. I – don't – know- him," she kept crying to retain the slightest of clarity.

"Abby! Tell me now, who is Josh Decker!" he raised his voice and forcefully asked the question again.

"I am.... No! I..." she sat in the chair trying to rise up, but the restraints around her waist and her arms prevented her from much movement. She continued to search for the pain in order to maintain her tears which seemed to provide her lucidness.

"ABBY! Tell me now! Who is this Josh Decker!" the man shouted at the top of his voice.

'*Your life... your laugh... your word... this brings painful joy...*' echoed in her mind.

"NO! I – WILL – NOT!" she managed to scream, finally finding her voice through the foggy haze that seemed so overwhelming.

Suddenly she felt a strong hand push her down deeper into the chair and a mask placed over her nose and mouth.

"Turn it up," he ordered.

She could hear the gentle sound of gas flowing before she was quickly back asleep.

"Oh well," Dr. Sullivan said. "Since they didn't kill him I had to try. But this one's not so dumb witted after all. She's a fighter."

"You don't want to get information from her using the Sapphire?" Anita asked, having walked out from the shadows up next to the chair.

"No. I can't risk it until after the extraction in Moscow. Then we can play around with her until we uncover everything we want."

"She will be fun to experiment with. She seems to be quite attached. It would be fascinating to discover what leaders could do to induce such loyalty. Think of the possibilities in that! Being able to produce armies of loyal... well, for lack of a better word, servants." Anita smiled as she spoke.

"Indeed. Haven't I told you that great minds think alike?" Dr. Sullivan said sinisterly as he looked up at Anita upon finishing an adjustment to Abby's I.V.

He then moved over to his laptop and brought up the Sapphire program. He removed a small, blue colored flash drive from his pocket and inserted it into the computer. The flash drive contained an encryption code and acted as a key to unlock what he now called the Sapphire Application. Without the code the mind-reading and recording software he had developed was useless. He had written the program with numerous self-destruct mechanisms should anyone try to tamper with or hack the program's secrets. An abundance of caution until his security and funding were guaranteed. Between this software and his chemical compound, his entire life's ambition and potential fortune rested.

He placed a series of sensors onto Abby's head, just as he had done with the others. But instead of beginning the injection process, he filled a syringe with a similar blue chemical and prepared to administer it to Abby.

"I have fine-tuned the formula now to a precision that should prove to be perfect. Like bringing a projector into focus. A little more, then a little less. Now it's just right." He said.

"We can't afford it to be otherwise, can we?" Anita reiterated, acknowledging that time was critical if Dr. Sullivan's deal with the Russians was to go through.

"I couldn't have done it without you, my dear," he said. "Without you and your networking skills, I'd never be able to acquire the drugs and compounds necessary to have made everything possible."

She relished the compliment and placed her hand on his shoulder as he began to insert a needle into the I.V. and inject the formula into Abby.

"This will be the critical test. If she survives this tonight, she will quite easily survive the implantation and extraction process, while remaining fairly lucid. This should condition her body to the Sapphire similar to an inoculation, allowing her to build up a tolerance that is far in excess of what is necessary," he explained.

"Lucid enough to make it to Russia and through all the security?" Anita asked to clarify the importance of Abby being able to manage herself for the trip.

"Exactly. Turn off the gas, she won't be needing it to stay asleep. She is resting easy now." He looked at his watch. "I have an evening engagement in a few hours. Will you be able to check on her tonight?"

"Yes. I'll swing by after I have dinner with the English girl." Anita replied.

"Good. With any luck she will be ready in the morning – and fully subordinate for the trip."

"Well, why shouldn't she behave herself?" Anita added with a horribly fake smile. "After all, she should be damn grateful for the gift you're giving to her."

"Yes, I have big plans for you little one." Dr. Sullivan continued, now talking to Abby. "First, you will transfer some vital information to demonstrate the functionality and power of my little Sapphire, then you will serve as my first follower." He leaned over to her, talking directly into her ear saying, "I will preserve your mind and your soul, forever! I will give you something death can never touch. Immortality."

49 – Highland

He was proud of himself. He had stopped shaking. The entire incident had come and gone and Johnny knew he was in the clear. He walked through the living room as his mother lay passed out in front of the glow of the television next to a half consumed fifth of vodka. Typical.

Johnny opened his bedroom door and closed it behind him. He turned on the light and walked over to his desk. He removed a six inch blade from his belt and a set of brass knuckles. While he was not a large fifteen year old, he had been in several altercations since hanging out with Derrick. He was still learning, having lost several such bouts with Derrick and others.

He continued to undress, removing decorative chains that dangled from his belt and an earring. He walked over and looked into the small mirror he kept on his dresser. Ran his fingers through his hair a few times, puckered to himself, then looked down at his hands. They were steady. It had been a new experience for him and he was proud to have steadied up without a shot of booze or some weed. He smiled. Then he lifted his head and looked into the mirror again. From out of no-where he saw Josh standing sternly outside his bedroom window.

A shock of cold fear raced through him along with a shot of adrenalin. He felt it in his fingertips and his toes. His knees visibly buckled and he almost fell down as he instinctively began his flight from the room. He fumbled with the doorknob, pulling without turning it. He banged on the door and was finally able to whip it open. He raced through the living room, his mother remaining oblivious to everything. He made his way through the kitchen with the goal of making it to the garage and onto his four wheeler. He burst into the garage, slammed the door behind him and turned on the light. Josh stood next to the vehicle, his gun drawn and aimed right at Johnny. He froze, still catching his breath and visibly shaking.

"Don't move," Josh commanded. "What's your name, Johnny was it?" His voice was low, eerily calm, but patient.

"Yeah," he answered.

"You remember me?"

"Yeah."

Piss began running down his leg, unable to control himself. He squinted at the warm liquid running down his leg, wondering just how obvious it would look.

"I remember you too," Josh said after the piss began puddling on the garage floor. "There was a fire," he continued. Johnny didn't answer. Josh began to move to Johnny's left. "There was a girl there."

"She's safe. I promise. We didn't hurt her," Johnny blurted out as if his mouth was outrunning his mind which regretted saying anything as soon as he said it.

"Now Johnny, I have a problem," Josh continued in his muted but stern tone as he moved slightly closer to the kid, slowly around his left side. "You have a score to settle with me that's fine, you come after me. But I warned you all about anything happening to that girl, that there'd be hell to pay. Do you remember that Johnny?"

"Yes."

"So, I'm willing to believe this wasn't your idea. But to set it right and avoid the worst of what I'm going to do here, you need to tell me where she is, and who took her. Now." Josh stopped moving, his gun now pointed within a foot or two of the side of the kid's head.

"I don't know where she is, I didn't take her. Derrick took her down to the car, I just helped with the fire."

"So you all came for me and when I wasn't there..."

"No, no, not for you. He wanted the girl."

"Who? Who wanted the girl?" Josh asked.

"I don't know. Derrick said we were to get the girl. He said we'd take her and then torch the place. No one would ever miss a run-away. That's what he said."

"He say anything about where he was going, what he was going to do with her?"

"Derrick? No, man, he didn't take her. This Gordie guy did. He came from out of town for her. Gave the orders, you know."

"You know him?"

"No, this was the first time any of us seen him."

Josh grew more concerned as he thought through the prospect that it wasn't the local boys behind the abduction and that finding her might be far more difficult than he thought.

"Describe him," Josh demanded

"He's tall, thin, really short hair, like a buzz cut. Um, he had on a black leather coat or something. And he's from Australia or something."

"Australia?" Josh repeated.

"Yeah, he had an accent. Australia, or England, something like that."

"Where was he going?" Josh asked.

"I really don't know."

"Think!" Josh's voice heightened showing impatience. "How did he leave?"

"His car was parked down by the ravine. I didn't see it. We rode up part way from the back and walked the rest to be quiet."

There was a silence as Josh thought through what he had heard. Johnny continued to shake and began to weep.

"You said she wasn't hurt?" Josh asked.

"No, she wasn't hurt, I swear. He said he needed her unharmed. He put a cloth over her face and she was knocked out. Then Derrick carried her down to his car. That's all I know," he was practically weeping.

"Did Derrick say anything about this, Gordie person?"

"Just that he was some kind of big shot killer. That this was a huge deal for us. We'd move out to Chicago or something."

"Chicago? Why Chicago?" Josh asked.

"That's where he said all his connections were. We'd get paid and work there, you know."

"You really want to be a lackey who takes the fall for the 'big shot' criminal, Johnny?" Josh asked as walked behind him, lowered his gun and placed it back into his belt behind his back.

"No, I guess not," Johnny thought for a moment then added, "I'm sorry."

It became clear to Josh that this was more than a warning to him. The fact that they wanted Abby unharmed made two things very clear. One, since the professional had seen to the job personally, it was very serious. And second, that Abby was probably in Chicago by now and that further local investigating would be a waste of time. If he was going to be able to get to her before they had a chance to hurt her, time was critical. His blood was up but his thoughts were clear, sharp, and far from reckless.

"Johnny, I need you to lay low for a while. Don't talk to anyone for a few days. No one. You understand?"

"Yes sir," he answered.

"I mean it Johnny. If I hear you spoke to Derrick, or anyone else – anyone, I'm going to come back here and really hurt you." Josh placed his hands on his shoulders and squeezed firmly to drive home his point. "I might even kill you," he whispered.

Josh spun Johnny around and grabbed his shirt collar, pulling him close, looking him sternly in the eye and said with slow determination, "Don't doubt me."

"Okay, okay... I promise," Johnny said cringing with fear and anticipating the pain he was about to receive.

Josh looked deeply into his eyes for a moment, then let go of him. He turned and walked out the side door of the garage the same way he entered. Johnny fell to his knees, unable to believe he was okay. He truly was sorry. He began to cry hysterically as the gravity of the night's events finally began to settle in.

50 – Chicago

A streak of bright orange ripped through the high clouds over the city, touching down in a shining glimmer onto the lake. The view was amazing as Molly sat with Anita over dinner at the Signature Room atop the Hancock Tower. Modest as she was, Molly rarely found occasion to dress up. But when she did she was simply radiant. She hadn't packed for such a fancy dinner so Anita had taken Molly shopping earlier to buy something more, 'suitable.'

"It's so beautiful from here," said Molly admiring the view. Anita sipped a white wine and glanced quickly.

"Yes," she said. "It figures that the only sunlight of the day would come as it is setting."

"It's usually cloudy in London as well," Molly said. "Have you lived here long?"

"Five years now. Building up a client base. Making a name for myself."

"What line of work are you in?" Molly thought it strange that after spending the majority of the day together she still knew very little about Anita.

"I work with Doctors. Specialists really," Anita answered. Then her phone suddenly chimed. "Excuse me." She finished her glass of wine and began texting a response.

Molly continued to watch the sunset. She thought about how far from home she was and how isolated. Who around her could she trust? Gordie was missing, Anita was clearly not happy with showing her around, and this mysterious Doctor with whom she was supposed to meet had suddenly postponed their appointment. Was he wise to the plan to lead Mr. Hawks to him? It was all very unsettling. For the first time she felt truly frightened that there may be no way out.

"Excuse me," Molly said as she stood up to leave. Anita barely acknowledged. Molly approached the Maitre d' and asked, "Where will I find the loo?"

"Down this hall and to the left," he answered.

Molly entered the ladies room as two very chatty women were preparing to leave. Feeling a bit nauseous, she moved swiftly into a stall and shut the door. She just stood there, trying to hold back her anxieties.

"So William is planning to host the Simmons out at the lake front, you and Daniel really should come!" she overheard one woman saying to the other.

"Oh splendid! We'd love to! What day?"

"The weekend prior to Thanksgiving. It's always beautiful up there."

"I can't wait..." the voices trailed off as they left the restroom.

Molly spent a few quiet moments alone. She gathered her strength, emerged from the stall and approached the sinks. She ran some cold water over her hands and then her face. The towels were nice and soft, and she blotted herself dry and looked up into the mirror. What little make-up she had on had run a bit. 'How fitting,' she thought. She was feeling worthless thanks to Anita's aloofness toward her, the loss of the commission, and Gordie's ongoing contempt. 'Why?' she thought.

"What have I done that could be so wrong?" she said softly aloud. Feeling the tears coming on again, she stood herself up straight and took a deep breath. She looked at herself carefully and squinted her eyes in a determined fashion.

"No," she said. "I've done nothing wrong." She opened her purse, briskly applied some make-up and closed her bag once again. She forced a fleeting half smile of confidence at herself in the mirror before turning away toward the door.

As she returned to the dining room a man approached her.

"Good evening Miss," he said.

"Good evening," Molly replied with a smile.

"I ah, couldn't help but notice you as you left just a moment before and I... well I just wanted to ask if ah, if you might be interested in a drink."

Molly was surprised and flattered. He was very handsome and his unexpected attention was a bright spot in an otherwise gloomy day.

"I..." she thought about it for a moment. He seemed so sincere, unlike most, and Anita surely wouldn't be missing her. 'Why the Hell not?' she thought. "That's very kind. I would love to," she smiled.

"Great!" He gestured toward the bar, opposite the direction of her table, and she walked ahead of him and took a seat.

"What'll you have?" he asked.

"Gin and tonic."

"Gin and tonic for the lady and I'll have a Manhattan," he ordered. "My name's Brett," he extended his hand, palm side up.

Molly placed hers in his. "I'm Molly."

"Nice to meet you, Molly. You're from England?"

"Yes. I suppose it's easy to tell."

"Well, I can never quite hear the difference between English and Australian accents, so a lucky guess," he quipped.

She smiled and answered, "Well, I suppose we sound similar. But to us it's very distinctive."

"I see. Do you live here now or are you just visiting?"

"Visiting actually." The drinks arrived and they took a sip. "I'm sorry, I really didn't mean to mislead you. I've had a... well, a long day and a little pleasant conversation sounded very nice," she smiled.

"But you're with someone?" he completed her thought.

"Um..." she hemmed and hawed a bit before answering, "Something like that." As she said it she wished she was free. By her initial impression he was someone she wanted to get to know. It was sad, she thought, to have to cut it off before anything even had a chance to begin. But it wouldn't be right to do otherwise.

"Well, in that case let me offer you my undivided attention for as long as you wish it tonight," he smiled.

Molly couldn't help but beam at the thought. They clinked glasses and sipped on their drinks. It was then that Molly gazed over Brett's shoulder and noticed Anita sitting at their table with a man. She could only see the back of his head, but there was something familiar about him. Anita was sitting at a right angle to him and was smiling shrewdly over their conversation. She showed a level of emotion that had been lost to her all day. As her own small talk with Brett continued, she kept noticing Anita first leaning closer to the man, then sitting back with an eyebrow raised. A look of concern, followed by licking of her lips, a pouty face, then a cunning glare. It was strange, but their conversation didn't last more than five or ten minutes. The man wrote something down and handed her the paper. Anita took it, read it, then folded it up tightly and placed it down inside her blouse.

"I've always wanted to go to London," Brett continued. "I guess I just never had a reason." He was clearly on the verge of continuing when Molly saw the man sitting with Anita stand up, and turn around to leave. She recognized him immediately: Peter Hawks.

Startled at seeing him, she spilled a bit of her drink on herself.

"Oh I'm so sorry..." she began.

"No worries," he answered. "It's nothing," he reassured as he helped her retrieve a napkin and handed it to her. She looked up again toward the exit, just in time to see him leave the restaurant. 'What could it mean? Was she in danger?' For a moment she was completely distracted by such thoughts.

"Hello? Molly..." Brett spoke kindly trying to regain her attention.

"Yes. Oh, I'm sorry... Forgive me."

"It's alright," he smiled and chuckled. "Where'd you go there?"

She paused, then simply said, "I have to get back to my dinner. It's been very nice meeting you, Brett. I'm sorry."

"Not at all Ms..."

"Wheeler," she added.

"Ms. Wheeler." He took her hand and kissed it. Molly smiled, then returned to the table with Anita who now seemed lost in thought.

Finally, Anita turned to Molly and smiled slyly.

"My dear, you won't mind taking a cab back to your hotel, will you?" she said as she handed Molly several twenty dollar bills. She stood up and prepared to leave.

"What about dinner? Aren't you going to eat?" she asked.

"Enjoy dinner. Perhaps that young man you were talking to will give you a ride…" she cleared her throat, "uh-ha – a ride back to your hotel that is." She then walked over to the Maitre d' to retrieve her jacket and was gone.

In a moment of hope Molly looked back over toward the bar, but Brett was no-where to be seen. It wasn't every day a handsome man took notice of her. She was left to wonder if he might have been able to take her away from it all. Had she missed her chance to escape?

She turned back to the window hoping the sunset would divert her attention. But it too had diminished into a cold looking blanket of clouds and darkness.

51 – Chicago

After driving through the night Josh arrived in Chicago before dawn. It was calm and clear, a bit warmer but still a rather chilly autumn day. He had contacted Marty to keep an eye on the various marinas and to watch for the 'Dream Catcher' specifically, but he had heard nothing. He picked up some breakfast and began to stake out Dr. Sullivan's office building, sitting in his car across the street. By mid-morning he was growing impatient. Just as he was about to go into the building to see what the receptionist might know about Dr. Sullivan's schedule, he spotted the Doctor exit his car in the covered parking garage adjacent to the building and walk inside.

Josh got out and walked over to Dr. Sullivan's luxurious BMW and looked inside. It was empty with no signs of anything being out of place. He tapped on the trunk, hoping he'd hear Abby's voice, hoping he wasn't too late. But again, there was nothing. He walked into the building, took the elevator up to the 9th floor and stopped at the receptionist's desk.

"Dr. Sullivan please," he said to the stern, middle-aged receptionist. She was physically attractive, being tall and slender, but stone cold when it came to personality.

"Do you have an appointment?" she asked.

"No," Josh answered.

"I'm sorry, you will need to make one if you wish to see the Doctor."

"Is 'the Doctor' in at the moment?" he asked.

"I can put you in touch with his assistant and she can make the appointment for you."

"I'm afraid it's rather urgent. Is he in now?" Josh asked.

"He is not available."

"Call him."

"I will not. Here is his card, you may call for an appointment." She slide a business card across the countertop and proceeded to answer a phone call.

"Restroom?" Josh asked in a polite tone.

"To your right, then the first left." She pointed down the hallway opposite the one that led to Dr. Sullivan's office.

Not wanting to waste any time, Josh walked toward the restroom. He stepped in the nook which led to the two restrooms, just out of sight of the receptionist and turned around. She had watched him, but was now busily tapping away on her computer keyboard while on the phone. He stealthily walked out and down the hallway until he came to the stairwell. He walked up one floor, then walked across the building to the opposite stairway where he descended, successfully bypassing the receptionist desk on the 9th floor and entered the hallway just outside Dr. Sullivan's office.

Upon opening the door into the hallway he recognized the distinctive voice of Dr. Sullivan echoing from the main lobby.

"...out this afternoon. I will be back around six to pick up the supplies. Leave them in my office."

"Yes Doctor," the receptionist replied.

"Also, I'm going to be at the Rimpau Medical conference all afternoon so forward any calls from this list only," he ordered.

"Yes doctor."

"Forward them, do not have them call me directly, understood?"

"Yes Doctor," she answered obediently. "By the way, you had a walk-in this morning. He seemed very tired and agitated."

"New patient?"

"I think so, I saw him once before but he left before making an appointment.."

"Did you get his name?" Dr. Sullivan asked.

"No. I did give him your card," she said matter-of-factly.

"Next time get a name damn it. Always get a name, then send them to my assistant."

"Yes Doctor."

Knowing where the Doctor would be all afternoon, Josh could either follow him, or search his office. He quickly decided that he'd take the opportunity of searching the office now and catch up with the Doctor later. If there was a chance Abby was there he couldn't pass it up.

Once Sullivan left, Josh pressed his ear up to his office door. He heard nothing. He gently knocked on the door. There was no response. He removed a lock pick tool from his pocket and proceeded to work the locked door. It soon opened and he slowly turned the handle and moved inside retrieving his pistol from his belt in the process.

The room was dark with only a small amount of light filtering in from the window along the back ally. The office was as sparse as the last time he had seen it and he moved toward the back room carefully. The door to the inner office was slightly ajar – suddenly he thought he saw movement, a shadow on the floor inside the room. The leather recliner was just to the right of the doorway, the window would not have cast a shadow if someone were sitting in it. He drew up his weapon and moved stealthily toward the door.

Part of him hoped Abby was there and it was not too late. Part of him hoped she was not there, perhaps she got away or they hadn't started anything with her yet. He looked through the opening and could see the foot of the chair. It was dark, and a blanket was draped over it. He took a deep breath. Slowly he opened the door. He walked inside the room, aimed the gun toward the back, then around toward the opposite side wall. He exhaled and turned on the light. The room and the chair were empty.

Josh placed his gun back into his belt behind his back and proceeded to have a look around. He examined the few items that were in the room including the bottles of various drugs sitting on the counter and inside a cabinet. One was intriguing, consisting of a bluish hue. He opened it and smelled the contents. It had no odor. He placed it back carefully. He felt the chair – it was cold. He concluded that the doctor had not been using the office for much more than receiving mail and deliveries. He left carefully, so as not to be noticed, and headed back out to his car, planning to pursue Dr. Sullivan to the conference.

As Josh headed back across the street toward his car, a young black male approached him. He was oddly dressed in a uniform vest worn over his more grimy clothes apparently in order to legitimize his selling of theater tickets to locals and tourists.

"Tickets! Ticket Star! Best seats tonight," he said in a loud voice, greeting passersby along the busy street. To Josh it seemed he was a little off the tourist path, but not too unusual and paid him no mind – until he bent down to his passenger side window and tapped on the glass.

"Tickets sir? I have the very best seats in the house."

"No thanks," Josh answered, but took a second glance at the man. He looked familiar to him.

"Ah, but sir, this is a special, reserved seat for a fine performance this very afternoon! I know you will really enjoy this show," he said holding up a ticket to the glass. Affixed to it was a yellow post-it note which read, 'Decker.' "I hear it is a must see program," he finished his pitch and smiled, a gold tooth catching a glimpse of sunshine.

Josh rolled down the passenger side window and took the ticket.

"How much do I owe you?" he asked.

"No charge, it's on me my man! Now that's a matinee performance lover, enjoy." And he walked back toward the miracle mile.

Josh looked carefully at the ticket. It was for 3pm, at the Chicago Theater.

Josh arrived at the Chicago Theater just prior to the start of the performance. He was led up to his seat near the back of the balcony by a cute, petite red headed young woman. The balcony was virtually empty. The lights dimmed, and the show began – an acoustic folk band. Within fifteen minutes, he noticed the silhouette of a man walking down the left side of the theater. The man turned into his row and proceeded to walk slowly toward him. Josh carefully placed his hand on the butt of his pistol which was inside his coat pocket. He kept careful peripheral watch as the man approached while keeping his eyes on the performance below.

"Long time Josh," the man said in muted tones. He then proceeded to sit down next to him. He wore a sharp tan jacket and carried a small briefcase and umbrella.

"Hawks," Josh answered soberly. "I might have known."

"Is that any way to say hello to an old friend?" Hawks offered cheerfully in his fine English accent.

"You called me, so to speak," Josh answered.

"Indeed. I was surprised when your name came up the other day. Very surprised. I thought you had retired."

"Well, you know what they say."

"No, I don't. What do they say, Josh?" he asked.

Josh turned and looked Hawks straight in the eye. It was a look that Hawks interpreted correctly as one that was through with the pleasantries and meant business. As for Josh, Hawk's presence could only mean that the situation he had fallen into was much larger and far more dangerous than he had imagined.

It was Hawks who spoke next. "I needed to pull you off the street my friend. You were being watched."

"By you?"

"By those working for a mutual acquaintance. Dr. Eugene Sullivan. How well do you know him?"

"I couldn't sleep a while back. He gave me a pill," Josh said slyly.

"This is very serious Josh," Hawks warned.

"Okay, first you tell me. What about the good Doctor has caught the interest of MI6?" Josh asked.

"I consider you a friend, Josh," Hawks paused waiting for his agreement. It was not forthcoming. "My contact here in Chicago had obtained some sensitive information about a particular project the doctor had been working on when we lost contact with him. I'm here to retrieve the information."

"Paul Thomas?" Josh asked.

"You knew him?" Hawks replied.

"No. I came across his girlfriend."

"How so?"

"She was found dead near my home," Josh said.

"I see. I didn't know she was involved," Hawks remarked.

"Involved in what, exactly?" Josh asked.

"Listen, I just wanted you to know that I'm on the case and that you can stand down now."

"I don't think so," Josh answered.

"Josh, I'd really hate to see something happen to you."

"Would you now?"

"Yes," Hawks answered slowly.

"I know he's doing something that has to do with the brain. I'm guessing he's developed a way to read brain activity, maybe use it as a vessel of some sort where he could pass along information undetected. How am I doing?" he asked.

"You're damn good Josh. We're thinking the same, but we don't know if it's a fools errand or a serious bit of science."

"And you're here to find out." Hawks gave no answer. "He's praying on young girls mainly, and..." Josh paused not wanting to reveal too much. But then he thought he'd have to risk it in order to help Abby. He looked down toward his feet and in a hushed, vulnerable tone said, "Hawks, he has my friend."

"A girl?"

"Yes. She's a runaway, completely innocent. She knows nothing about any of this."

"That would make her more appealing to him. And complicate things."

"Do you know where she might be?" he asked.

Hawks sighed. "I'm not sure. I have a contact working this, but nothing has happened so far. Your girl being involved might explain why. But he's moving around a lot now, covering his tracks. He knows he's being watched."

"Why?" Josh asked.

"You're guess is correct. We believe he has developed a method of extracting sensitive information from the human brain. Advanced interrogation, if you will. Something our government would like to use on terrorists perhaps. But we don't have all the details."

"How has Abby interfered with your contact?" he asked.

"That's... all I can tell you," said Hawks.

"The killing has to stop," Josh said firmly.

"Well, perhaps it will. We need to know who he's working for, who is funding it. We suspect a Russian connection, but there are others trying to obtain his work before he ever delivers it."

Josh thought for a moment. "You're protecting him," he stated.

"I wouldn't say that."

"You son of a bitch. You want the technology! And you're willing to let innocent people die in order to get it."

"Don't get ahead of yourself old boy. We're both on the same side."

"The hell we are."

"Now listen. I called you here because I don't want anything to happen to you," Hawks began, but Josh interrupted.

"No, you called me here to find out what I know and to keep me from fucking up your mission." The two stared hard at each other for a long moment, the lights from the stage flickering onto their determined faces.

"He doesn't want her dead," Hawks began. "This may work out best for both of us. He needs her alive to prove his 'system' works. Once he has done that, we will move in and grab him. I will see to it personally that the girl is not harmed."

Josh took a moment to look him in the eye. Finally he said, "What a crock of shit."

"I have a much better chance at finding her than you, Josh. But I will tell you this. The man who took her is Gordon Chase. He's a pro, out of London. He's new to the game, but has proven to be extremely dangerous and he has your number." Hawks added.

"Well then why don't you try recruiting him?" Josh said sarcastically.

"I shouldn't be telling you this but I want you to believe me," Hawks said.

"Oh I believe you." Josh said in a menacing tone. A moment later he added, "You know Hawks, it's not supposed to rain today. You can put the umbrella away."

Josh stood up and slowly made his way out of the theater. And while he was more determined than ever to find Abby fast, he was aware that now he was also a target.

52 - Chicago

'So Paul Thomas was a MI6 contact...' Josh thought about the information he had just learned from Hawks as he emerged from the Chicago Theater. Cindy had mentioned he was involved with something related to Trans-Pharmaceutical – that and the strange reaction of Mr. Jackson, the owner of Nexus Pharma, at the mention of Dr. Sullivan's name made him believe that would be a good place to start. He debated it though. He was there to find Abby, not solve an international drug or espionage case. Still, he was most comfortable following his gut.

Dr. Sullivan was at a conference all afternoon, so he seemed harmless enough for now. He couldn't perform any procedures on Abby while he was there. He would ask Marty to have someone keep tabs on him. Josh began walking north back to where he left his car but then decided a cab would not only be faster, but safer. This was a tangled web more complicated than he had realized, and Hawks had resources – he was likely being followed by more than one individual. He hailed a cab, got in, and proceeded north along Michigan Avenue for a few miles.

Once inside the cab, he used his phone to look up the web-site for Trans-Pharmaceutical. The company was a monster. Billions of dollars in research and development, high-end cancer fighting drugs, and an entire experimental division. Offices were world-wide from London, New York, Mexico City, Tokyo, Shanghai, New Delhi, Greece, Rome, everywhere. Most were sub-divisions, but the parent company practiced mainly in the US. He looked up the Chicago office. He tapped on their directory of sales representatives. A list of names and contact information popped up, along with a photo of each.

Josh's eyes widened. He recognized her immediately. A stunningly beautiful blond, rich soft pink lips, and a smile that would make you agree to almost anything. Her picture was radiant.

"I'll be damned," he said softly, then loudly to the cab driver, "Do you know where the Trans-Pharmaceutical building is?"

"Sure, north Lakeshore."

"Can you get me there fast?" Josh asked holding out an additional twenty dollars.

"Oh I think so!" he said as he made a quick lane change in front of another car who laid on his horn in disgust. Then a sharp right turn down a narrow side street. The car noticeably moving at a faster, more erratic pace.

Now it all made sense. His encounter with Anita was no accidental meeting after all. She had found him at the bar… her hotel room… no, it was not her room, he remembered. It was paid for by a Russian. Valery Zhukov. She was the only one who could have tracked him back to Highland. From there the boys would've known about Abby. He had told her too much as they laid in bed together. He felt totally responsible.

With Hawk's arrival everything clicked. Now he could begin to move onto the offensive. But time was short. Abby was somewhere out there and if they hadn't already begun experimenting on her they soon would. And yet he cautioned himself. This will need to be done carefully. They could be using Abby to lure him, or even Hawks, into a trap.

"Trans-Pharmaceutical," the Cabbie announced as he slowed near the front entrance.

"Take me to the corner by the park," Josh ordered.

The cab rolled to a stop several hundred feet past the building on the lake side. The sun was out and the lake looked beautiful massaging the Chicago coast. Josh looked around carefully in every direction. He didn't see anything that looked suspicious. There was no sign the cab had been followed. He paid the cabbie and exited.

He stared over at the tall building that housed Trans-Pharmaceutical. He picked up a newspaper that someone had left in the trash and walked across the street toward the building. He sat down on a nearby bench and called the Trans-Pharmaceutical office.

"Sales please," he said into his phone.

"Anyone in particular?" the tiny female voice on the other end asked.

"Anita Reynolds," he said.

"She's not in at the moment but is expected back yet today. Could I have her call you?"

Josh looked at his watch. It was nearly 4pm. "She's been out all day?" he asked.

"She had appointments this morning and is supposed to be back to the office this afternoon. Any time now, actually. Can I have her give you a call?"

"Definitely," Josh said, and hung up the phone. He didn't have to wait for a call back. He had spotted her walking toward the building with another woman, a bit shorter, long brown hair, and plainly dressed by comparison to Anita's flare and provocative style.

He was only a hundred feet away as he watched them stop short of walking into building. Anita pointed to something behind the other woman, who turned and followed her direction with her eyes. The two seemed to exchange a nod but he was too far to hear what was being said. The other woman looked uncomfortable as she half extended her hand to shake Anita's, but pulled it down quickly after it was clear she would not be reciprocating. Anita just stepped backward, smiled, turned and walked into the building.

The other woman turned around and began to walk in the direction that Anita had pointed. Josh got his first good look at her as she walked past him – she was certainly beautiful, but there was something different about her. Her walk seemed slow and paced as if she was counting. Her eyes mainly gazed downward and looked tired. Then, suddenly the young woman looked up from her trance-like motion and locked on to his eyes, as if she sensed he was watching her. She didn't attempt to look anywhere else. It was only a tiny moment, but to Josh it spoke volumes. This woman was afraid. Just as quickly as she looked up, she looked back downward and never stopped walking. She turned toward a café outside the building next door and sat down beneath a table with an umbrella, a few trees providing additional shading. He continued to watch her but she made no motion, no attempt to look back at him, or around at anything.

A waiter from the café approached and took her order. Josh waited few minutes until she had been served, then decided to approach her. He walked over stopping just short of her table. She had an attractive profile with the wind gently blowing her hair behind her as she sipped a cup of coffee.

"May I?" Josh asked, motioning to the chair opposite her.

"Um, I suppose so. But I'm really not..."

"Are you alright?" Josh interrupted with a noticeably lowered voice that expressed both concern and urgency. Her accent made an immediate impression, connecting her potentially to Hawks. But she spoke beautifully, a subtle guttural tone which he found very appealing. But it was the look in her eyes, an expression that conveyed nervousness that he focused on immediately. She also quickly read the look in his eyes, sensing an underlying kindness subject to determination and purpose. In other circumstances a conversation would have been more welcomed, but he was a stranger among already confusing circumstances so she remained skeptical, not knowing who to trust.

"Why do you ask?" she feigned surprise, but her eyes looked up hopefully.

"The woman you were with – do you know her well?" he asked.

"No. She's been showing me around. I'm waiting for my boyfriend now."

"You're here visiting then?"

"Yes."

"I'm sure she makes quite the tour guide," Josh said sarcastically.

She cracked a smile. He conveyed a calming presence to her.

"Well, I have not really seen what I've wanted to see. Are you from Chicago?"

Josh ignored her question, he didn't have time for small talk. "How long are you staying in town?"

"Probably around a week? That's how long my boyfriend should need. He is here on business and I'm just... here I guess," she sighed.

"Really... are you okay?" he asked. She paused and looked at him carefully, trying to read his eyes, his intentions.

"Who are you?" she asked suspiciously.

"My name is Josh. Josh Decker." They sat silently for a moment before Josh continued, "Here is my card." He handed a plain white card with his hand written phone number on it. He looked at her in a soft reassuring manner and while he noticed tremendous strength in her features and her eyes, there was something more. He didn't want to push her. But his gut was telling him that she was somehow involved. "If you feel like you need anything. Call me." Josh stood up to leave, then stopped and asked, "What is your name?"

She placed the card in her small purse, looked up at him and answered, "Molly."

53 – Chicago

A tall man with short hair and a slender build approached Molly as she sat at the café waiting. He wore a black leather jacket, a white shirt, and dark sunglasses. As he approached he called out to her.

"Moll, let's go. Now," he demanded, loud enough to be heard by anyone nearby. His accent was English. Her reply was inaudible but she wasted no time and stood up to go. As she did, her purse caught on the arm of her chair and the contents spilled open.

"Jesus Christ you're a clot!" the man said, thoroughly annoyed as Molly quickly began to pick up the few items and quickly shove them back into her purse. "I've business, let's go," he said as he grabbed her arm and began walking her down the road, disappearing around the corner.

'That's him', Josh thought as he watched the scene unfold. 'The man in the video.' He made this conclusion despite being pretty far away. He was watching both the front of the building as well as the parking garage. He hoped Molly would be ok but he couldn't leave to follow them. He was waiting for Anita to emerge.

As the minutes passed he grew more and more anxious. What if he was wrong? What if he was not in time? The Doctor had a dinner appointment, but it was now getting late.

'I can't just sit here. I need to do something!' he thought. Frustration was beginning to get the better of him when finally, around six thirty, he spotted Anita as she drove out of the building's parking garage. He hailed a cab and followed her. She parked at an eight story brick building on the north side, only a half dozen blocks from Dr. Sullivan's office. He ordered the cab to pass by the building and stop at the next corner. He paid him and exited. He crossed the street and watched from a distance as Anita opened the trunk of her car. Then, she closed it having retrieved a woman's black leather briefcase. She entered the building through a side door.

Josh followed her in. By the time he entered, the elevator doors had just shut. He watched and waited to see it stop on the 5th floor. He walked to the end of the hallway to the stairs and climbed them quickly.

He carefully opened the door to the 5th floor foyer. It was nearly seven, after business hours, and there was no one in sight. The floor consisted of a carpeted hallway, an empty receptionist desk with a sign-in sheet, and at least a dozen doors lining both sides of the hall. The hall was clear so he moved toward the reception desk. In addition to the sign-in sheet, there was a small rack of business cards. The cards varied, but most were psychologists who practiced in the floor's small individual offices. He noticed a few kept night office hours. 'Could she be coming to see her shrink?' he thought.

A door opened and Josh moved quickly into the waiting area which was out of sight from the hallway. He peeked around the corner to see who it was. Five doors down on the right emerged Anita. She turned, locked the door, and removed her phone. She began texting someone. As soon as she was finished she began walking toward the reception area, still looking down at her phone. It gave Josh just enough time to pull his head back and find a position between the far wall and a vending machine. He was not well concealed. One glance over in the general direction and she'd see him. But there was no-where else to go.

As Anita walked into the reception area her phone chimed. She stopped, in plain sight of Josh. She looked at her phone and read the incoming text message. Then she slowly lifted her eyes and slightly opened her mouth. It was as if she knew she was being watched. Without moving her head, she tried to look around the waiting area. She was sure someone was there. Afraid to turn around, she slowly began walking toward the end of the hall. Her pace soon turned into a run as the adrenalin flowed through her. Josh moved out into the foyer to see where she was going when he heard the stairway door being thrust open and only caught a glimpse of her blonde hair as she quickly made her way down the stairs.

He began down the hallway to follow her when something stopped him. It was more of a feeling than a thought. He turned around and walked slowly toward the office from where Anita had come. He pulled out his pistol.

'She may try to call to warn anyone who's in there,' he thought. He twisted the doorknob slowly and carefully, it was locked. It was a simple lock, wooden door frame, and time was critical. He'd have to move fast to catch up to Anita if he were to confront or follow her further. So he decided to kick the door in.

With his gun by his shoulder, Josh took a deep breath and kicked the door with his right foot, just to the left of the latch. The door flung open instantly. The room was dark, the light from the hallway filtered in. There was a red glow coming from some equipment on a table. The room itself was not large, with the window being opposite the doorway the first thing Josh saw was his own silhouette in the window. Just below, facing away from him, was the back of a large reclined chair.

He moved in cautiously, but swiftly, saying nothing. He found the light switch on the wall and turned it on. He lowered his weapon, "Oh my God."

He rushed to the chair.

"Abby! Oh my God, Abby..." he said as he removed the gas mask and began to tap her cheek in an effort to wake her. He shook her gently and stroked her hair as he continued to call her name.

"Come on Abby, I know you're there. Come on!"

Then he thought to check her neck, behind her ear. He moved her hair back and inspected both sides of her neck. There was nothing.

"Oh thank God!" he said. "Come one Abby, wake up now!"

He noticed she was connected to an I.V. but was not sure what disconnecting it would do to her. He checked her vitals. She was breathing slowly, had a slow but strong pulse, and she was starting to become responsive. Josh pulled out his phone and called 911.

"I have an unconscious female, possible drug overdose. I need an ambulance right away!" He proceeded to give the operator the building information, but then hung up.

"Abby! It's Josh. Talk to me now, come on... you're okay, you're okay..." he repeated as he dialed another number.

"Marty! I need you here right away..." he proceeded to tell him where he was. "I've got her Marty. I found Abby. But I need your help."

He put the phone down as Abby gave a slight moan and moved her head toward him. Now on his knees next to the chair, he put his face next to hers, one hand on her cheek, the other behind her head, rubbing the back of her neck.

"Abby? Abby, can you hear me sweetheart?" he said.

She moaned a little louder, then in a faint whisper answered, "Josh?"

Tears welled up in his eyes. He hated being emotional, but he couldn't hold it back. He had not slept in over thirty six hours and it was as if the weight of the world had suddenly lifted from his shoulders.

"Abby," he said. "You're okay. Oh thank God... I got you."

"Josh," she answered, barely managing to open her eyes. "I'm sorry."

"No, no, don't be sorry," he said quickly wiping a tear from his eye. "I found you... I found you."

She managed to open her eyes wider and focusing on his. "You're the only one who's ever cared enough to... to look for me." she ran out of energy as she finished.

Still kneeling, he lifted her up to him and hugged her. He could hear sirens approaching from the streets below.

"I'm here Abby. You're safe. It's going to be alright. I promise."

54 – Chicago

"How is she?" Marty asked as he walked briskly toward Josh who was in the hospital waiting room.

"I don't know. They haven't said anything."

"I'll see what I can find out."

"That Lieutenant has been asking me a lot of questions," Josh said as the lieutenant approached, this time accompanied by a young female uniformed officer.

"Detective, do you know this man?" he asked.

"Yes Lieutenant, he's working in a consultative capacity with me on this. There are some corporate security issues that he's following up on."

"Well that may be but it doesn't preclude him answering any questions about..."

Marty interrupted, "He's also former CPD. I know him, it's fine."

The lieutenant was not happy with the answer. "I'll have to raise this with my captain."

"Good. I know your captain. Have him call me directly," Marty said and gave him his card. The lieutenant walked away. "Stay here." Marty told Josh, then began to walk toward the nurses station, the uniformed officer trailing right beside him.

"Is that Detective Decker?" she asked anxiously.

"Yes, it is." Marty answered a bit reluctantly. "I don't know you..."

"Officer Heather Balogh, sir."

"Nice to meet you." Marty said as they shook hands. Her hands were softer than he expected. "You must be fairly new to the force, I know most of the officers in this precinct."

"Yes sir, been on the job three months now." She was very pretty, young, and seemed anxious to get involved. He couldn't help but shake his head a little, wishing for a moment he wasn't already married. She was next to him as they arrived to the nurses station. "Any information on the girl, Abby Lowell?" he asked as he showed the head nurse his badge. She picked up an iPad and tapped on a few prompts and read Abby's chart.

"She's stable. The doctor is running some additional tests on her, but she should be fine. She's still in treatment." She answered.

"Ok. Let me know as soon as I can see her. She's a witness and I need to talk with her."

"I will." The nurse promised.

"Good. Thanks." Marty turned and headed back toward Josh in the waiting area.

"I've only been hearing sketchy details about this girl, what happened?" Officer Balogh asked.

"Did you respond to the call?" Marty asked.

"No, I'm pulling a late shift here at the hospital all night where nothing happens." She answered. By now they had reached Josh.

"She's still in treatment, but she's gonna be ok, Josh" he said.

"Thank you, Marty" Josh said.

"Anytime. And thank you for getting me out of bed! I didn't need any sleep tonight." They stood quietly for a moment. "Would you excuse us?" he asked Officer Balogh.

"Of course." She said, but couldn't help but smile at Josh saying, "It's very nice to meet you Detective. I've heard so much about you." She said smiling at him. Josh nodded, quickly dismissing her. "Well, I'll let you know if there's any update." She walked back toward the nurses station.

"I'm not gonna ask what's going on with all this, but how exactly do you need me to help?" Marty asked in order to gage the situation, knowing that if he got involved it would become more official and Josh's hands would be a bit more tied.

"I need you to guard Abby. She's still in danger."

"I can't stay here."

"Marty please. She's... it's just very important to me," Josh said in a heartfelt manner. Marty knew Josh well and the look on his face spoke volumes.

"I'll put a couple of uniforms on it. But I got to give them a reason."

"She was almost murdered, isn't that a good enough reason?" Josh said growing impatient.

"Yeah, well... you would think." Josh stared at him. "Don't worry, I'll think of something."

After another moment of silence Josh began again, "Also, Hawks is in town."

"No shit. Then I don't wanna know about it. Do you know how much paperwork that guy has generated for me?"

"I know. But if he's here then you can bet the CIA, FBI, or whoever is nearby as well. They want the technology."

"If they are near that'll limit what I can do for you, you know."

"I know. All I need is a name and some background before they decide to move in and shut you all out."

"What kind of information?"

"The man from the hotel video. Slender, tall, shades," Josh described.

"Yeah, I remember."

"I saw him just a few hours ago."

"Where?"

"Outside the café next to the Trans-Pharmaceutical offices off Lakeshore. He picked up his girlfriend and I think she's in danger.

"Jesus Josh, you got to give me something more than what I already know if you want my help with this," Marty complained.

"I have a name, Gordon Chase. He's some new muscle out of London. He would've been making trips in and out of the US probably. I think that's the guy in the video. Can you see if you can dig up some more details on him?"

"Yeah. I'll get on it right away. What are you going to do?"

"I'm going to find him. And put a stop to all of this."

55 – Chicago

'All is well. Meet you at 9.' Dr. Sullivan read the text as he was getting up from the table following dinner with two colleagues. He was looking forward to spending the night with Anita, something he would much rather do than spend the night with his wife.

The three doctors had made their way out of the restaurant and into the hotel lobby when the second text came in. 'Someone is following me! What do I do?'

"Gentlemen, would you excuse me," Dr. Sullivan motioned to his phone and walked over to a more secluded corner.

He texted back, 'Check on her again. I'm on my way there.' He made his way toward the valet and presented his parking stub. After a few minutes his car pulled up and he got in. This time the phone rang.

"How is she?" he answered, convinced that she was nervous and not really being followed.

"She's gone! We've lost her," Anita said in a panic.

"What? What happened?" Dr. Sullivan growled.

"I told you, I saw someone! Just out of the corner of my eye. Someone hiding and spying on me."

"Who? Did you see him?"

"No. I pretended I didn't see anything, and walked out. Then I texted you. Now there's police cars and an ambulance..."

"Get out of there. Meet me at the Essex. Go there now," he ordered.

"Okay," she answered. Then she added, "Sully dear, we can still use the other one."

"Yes, I know... Look, it's getting late. I'll call and have her ready. You swing by and pick her up. I'll set up the equipment in my room at the Essex. Take her there and wait for me. I'll meet you at 11, in the lounge.

"I will," Anita answered.

He ended the call, and dialed another number. A man answered and Dr. Sullivan began, "The girl's gone. We'll need yours after all. Get her ready. Anita will be picking her up shortly."

"Yeah? That's all fine but what 'em I supposed to tell her, eh?"

"Oh for Christ sakes, just tell her you're going to a party. Anita will pick her up shortly and take her to the Essex. But I need you to get rid of Josh Decker."

"Why, where is he?" Gordie asked.

"Why? Why do you think? He found the girl and took her which wouldn't have happened if you had done your job in the first place!" Sullivan said with great agitation.

"Hey, you can't blame me that he wasn't there now can ya? I got the girl, just how you wanted. The local kid was to finish him."

"Listen! Decker cannot be allowed to interfere again. This is our last chance and we leave tomorrow, got it? Or do I need to explain it in more primitive terms for you?"

"So you don't know where he is then?" Gordie asked with condescension. "How am I to get rid of him if I don't know where the hell he is?"

"I will find him." Dr. Sullivan thought for a second and added, "I will arrange for you two to meet, at 11 o'clock. I'll let you know where. Get the girl ready and meet me at the Essex in an hour."

"That's clear on the other side of town," he complained.

"Just be there! I'll explain it then." He ended the call as he drove off.

56 – Chicago

"Get dressed!" the bedroom door burst open instantly stunning Molly as she was just falling asleep. She hadn't been able to sleep much since arriving in the United States, anticipating the call to meet with the doctor or from Mr. Hawks to update her. The shock would assure that she'd not get any rest tonight.

"What is it?" she asked, agitated.

Gordie turned on the light. "I said get dressed."

"Why?"

"Why?" he repeated, not used to such defiance. They stared at each other momentarily, Molly with an unusual curl in her brow that expressed determination. "Because I'm leaving and you're going to a party." Gordie went into the closet, put his gun down on the dresser, and began changing his clothes to go out. For a moment Molly wondered if she could get to the gun quick enough. But it would be suicide.

"I don't want to go to a party, Gordie. I want to sleep," Molly grumbled.

"You're going! They'll be here in a few minutes to pick you up." He finished changing and turned around to face the bed again. Molly was still sitting up in bed, dressed in a plain white cotton nightgown. "Well?" he taunted. She looked away, refusing his request to get up and get ready. He picked up his gun, walked over, and sat down next to her on the bed.

He placed the weapon up against her stomach and slowly used the muzzle to pull the sheet down revealing her soft bare thighs. She was sitting so her knees were bent with her legs curled up slightly below her. She breathed slowly, controlling her fear quite well. He began to move the muzzle of the gun up her leg, beginning with her ankle, over her calf and thigh, and then straight back into her stomach.

"Look at me," he said softly. Molly looked up. "You know I can take what I want." He placed the muzzle of the gun upon her upper chest, pushing her enough to force her into a slightly reclined position. She propped herself up with her arms refusing to lay down.

"Yes," she said obediently, hoping to disarm him by offering no overt resistance.

"Good," he answered and returned the gun to her stomach, pushing it into her with some mild force. Molly held her breath, but kept very still, refusing to be shaken. From there he used the gun to trace the side of her body up and over her left breast. Positioning the muzzle around the strap of her nightgown, he eased it off her shoulder. Molly took a noticeably deep breath, but never stopped looking at him. Then he slowly moved the gun across her chest.

"A tiny twitch in my finger. Less than a second..." he said with his face very close to hers. Then he whispered, "I could end you any time I want."

"Yes," she said again.

He then moved the gun to her right shoulder and again used it to slowly pull the strap off. From there he slid the gun back over her chest and pulled the dangling garment down until it fell resting at her waist. "Good girl," he said.

There seemed to be a long moment of wondering and anticipation, as he looked coldly at her. It was then, at what should have been a profound moment of terror that Molly was able to reach past her fear and look upon him differently. She wondered where *HE* had gone wrong. His cold, almost lifeless eyes seemed vacant of humanity. But how? At what point did his life turn to violence, anger, and even fear? At what point does a person go from hope to hopelessness? The short train of thought confirmed in her mind that she was right. It was nothing she had done. He had been like this long before they ever met. And while she was tempted to feel sorry for him, she dismissed the emotion before it could begin. She'd have no pity for someone who inflicted such pain and suffering onto others. She had been living under this cloak of fear and misery for far too long. Her anxiety almost seemed to vanish. If he pulled the trigger it wouldn't matter to her, she would be free in death. If not, she would find her own way to freedom in life. It was the predominance of this thought which kept her calm and somehow confident. She simply believed.

Gordie leaned closer to her, placing the gun down to the bed just to her left by her waist. As he moved closer, she leaned back in order to deny him for as long as possible, until she was flat on the bed. He took in a deep breath as he moved his face from her neck, down to her chest, and back again. He was less than an inch from her skin, but never touched her. It was as if he was soaking in her scent. She could feel his breath cascading over her body as he exhaled. Then when he put his face directly over hers she could feel the butt of the gun pushing onto the side of her right wrist. He looked her in the eyes. Then suddenly his brow curled and he sat up.

"So get dressed," he ordered.

He stood up and walked out of the bedroom. A moment later the door shut and he was gone.

Molly quickly got up, put the nightgown back on, and ran to her purse. Despite her demeanor she knew she was in danger and needed help. She looked for and retrieved a small piece of paper. Knowing Gordie would check her phone, she quickly used the hotel phone to call the number on the paper. A voice answered.

"Hello, Mr. Hawks?" Molly asked.

"Yes?"

"I'm leaving soon."

"Where?"

"I don't know. All he said was that I have to go to a party."

"Is he there now?" Hawks asked.

"No."

"Okay, I'll send someone over right away to pick you up and take you to a safe place."

"Okay, what should I bring? What about this doctor?"

"Don't pack anything, I'll have everything you need. Dress for a party. We don't want him to think you're doing anything wrong."

"And the Doctor?" she asked.

"I'm trying to locate him now. We'll set up your meeting with him as soon as possible. I'll let you know. And Molly..."

"Yes?"

"When you meet with the doctor keep your eyes open for flash drive that looks like a large, blue, oval sapphire. There is a code on it. That's what we're looking for. When you see it, text me and we'll move right in for you."

"Okay," she acknowledged.

"Good girl." Hawks finished and ended the call.

Molly put down the phone and began to feel very uneasy about the haphazard arrangement. She walked to the closet and put on a simple yet sleek v neck black dress with spaghetti straps, the length stopping at mid-thigh. It was the second dress Anita had purchased for her during their shopping spree. As she went to the bathroom to apply make-up there was a knock at the door.

Molly walked over and asked, "Who is it?"

"It's me Molly." She recognized the voice.

She opened the door and saw Anita.

"Are you ready to go?" she said with a smile.

57 – Chicago

"She's going to be fine," said the Doctor.

Josh looked down, his body language expressing a tremendous sense of relief. "What eh, what was it she, I mean, what did they do to her?"

"They had her sedated, but it was dangerous for her not to be monitored carefully. She's shown some confusion and amnesia as a result, but that's normal and she should be fine in a few hours. We'll keep her here overnight for observation. She can go home tomorrow."

"Thank you Doctor," Josh said.

"Do you want to see her real quick?" he asked.

"No... No, I need to get going. I'll make sure someone's here for her tomorrow," Josh said.

"That's fine." The doctor walked off.

Two uniform police officers had arrived just as the doctor came out to speak with him. Josh walked over to them and handed one his card.

"If anyone comes asking about her, call me," he said.

"Will do, Mr. Decker," he replied.

Josh walked down the corridor to the stairway and made his way down and out to the parking lot. He got into his car which Marty had arranged to be delivered as he was waiting for news about Abby. Before he could start the engine, his phone rang.

"Already?" he said out loud. He answered the phone, "Hello?"

"Good evening Mr. Decker."

Josh paused, the voice was unmistakable. "Dr. Sullivan."

"I wondered if you would answer your phone this late in the evening. Apparently you've been busy."

"Well, Doctor, I guess I just couldn't... sleep," Josh retorted.

"Ah, 'To sleep per chance to dream.' You know, I actually thought about putting that quote on my business cards when I was young. How puerile. Isn't it funny how the mind works Mr. Decker? How it grows and takes in new information, knowledge.

It begins as infants. Raw data of colors, shapes, and sounds from its surroundings. Then, over time, as the neuropathways are developed the brain begins to sort and organize everything based on experience. The child begins to recognize and react. Like grooves in a vinyl record those paths are assimilated over and over again into something new and exciting."

"It must thrill you to be able to play such a 'record.' Is that what you're all about; reading the thoughts of others before you murder them?" Josh said in an attempt to rile the Doctor.

"No, Mr. Decker. What thrills me is what my work will mean in terms of progress! Humanity is just like that infant. Ever evolving and learning. From hunting and gathering to settling down into civilizations. Law codes, punishments, causes and consequences, we are continually learning to do things better and more efficiently. It has been the trend of humanity and I am about to play a significant part in that progression.

"By taking away people's lives?" Josh asked.

"No, by preserving them! Death is all around us and yet it seems so primitive. We've evolved, created artificial intelligence and become the creators of new life! We can build our own lifeboat to immortality! I have developed a method where I can implant and extract immensely complicated data strings to and from the human brain. And thus, I will soon be able to preserve the data of an entire mind! And someday soon I will implant that data into another human brain, thus creating an everlasting existence!"

"Sounds like the delusions of a mad man," Josh answered.

"The mind *can* be mapped, I've done it! The data can be retrieved and new data implanted. *I have done it!* Can you imagine reducing the learning curve of an individual by simply implanting academia directly into their minds with complete accuracy? No, my work, Mr. Decker, will *save* lives! By imposing morality into the brains of humans, making savagery a thing of the past!"

"Whose morality?"

"The morality of consensus. I believe it was Rousseau who said that 'whoever refuses to obey the General Will is then compelled to do so by the whole body. He will be forced to be free.'"

"So in the name of liberty, you propose to end suffering and immorality?" Josh asked.

"Exactly. Only the brave push the boundaries of the frontier, the great unknown. But that is progress. And death along the way has always been part of that progress. I am merely a pioneer."

"So murdering someone for your own glory is now justified?"

"That's a relatively shallow summation, but it is essentially correct," Sullivan answered.

"Well then, perhaps I should kill you for the glory of having prevented the imprisoning of humanity according to your 'general will'?"

"Come now Mr. Decker, we both know better. Our world is still primitive, ugly, and shameful. People neglect, destroy, and are intentionally reckless. They need order. The kind of order that will come from the progression of an integrated consciousness."

"You're suggesting a new brand of holocaust," Josh spoke as if his teeth were clenched. "Your psychotic vision will not take away things like genocide or atrocities. It will impose them by taking away free-will. Humanity."

"A very limited view. The dawn of our new age will not be a displacement of humanity. Merely the subjugation of it's flawed, less desirable nature."

"Less desirable nature?" Josh questioned. "It is human nature to resist subjugation. Tell me, what will happen when the future generations you speak of no longer have such flaws? No longer have a purpose to grow. What happens when you rob humanity of its very soul?"

"Sacrifice is necessary Mr. Decker. When they built the Brooklyn Bridge, twenty seven men lost their lives. Over a hundred building the Trans-Continental railroad. The dawn of the atomic age came at a cost of millions! Progress comes at a cost! And my cost, for such a momentous societal transformation, is comparatively negligible."

"Well then tell me, doctor, how many victims are you willing to go through in order to perpetuate this menacing utopia?" There was no immediate answer. "I know of two but surely there must be more. Or is that all you were able to finish off? How sloppy."

"Only eight," Sullivan interrupted. "An extremely acceptable figure that I am quite proud of."

"It won't stop with eight. Your dream of power, the power to dictate morality, to administer the 'general will,' and to stamp out every trace of humanity will mean no purpose, no art, no flaws, no reason to go on. Nothing. You convince yourself of the cost of progress, but ignore the reality of destroying the hopes and dreams of thousands, millions of people whose humanity you'd 'subjugate' and destroy. But to me, one life is too great a cost, 'Doctor.' You snuffed out the life potential of these young girls, each no less worthy than your own. You took it from them you arrogant prick! You're nothing more than a monster praying on innocent life.

"I will *save* humanity!" Sullivan shouted over the phone. "It is ruinous, hideous, deceitful! And I can set it right! Wouldn't you want to read the mind of a terrorist to uncover the plots of other fanatics and stop them before they happen, without any torture? Wouldn't you like to be able to prevent violent behavior all together? Isn't that our human purpose, Mr. Decker? To stop death? To live forever?" He finished having to catch his breath from being over excited. "You have to stay ahead of the wave in order to come out on the right side of history."

"The right side? It is right that in order to destroy the evil tendencies of humans, you must destroy what makes human beings human in the first place. No struggle. No meaning. No purpose. Just your own glory. But then there won't even be people human enough to recognize that glory and honor you for it. You'll be a meaningless fragment of data, imprinted on the brain. Worth nothing."

"I suppose, Mr. Decker," Sullivan responded having composed himself, "We shall soon find out."

"You played judge, jury, and executioner," Josh added, "Suppose I do the same with you?"

"Forgive me," Sullivan answered, "I have so enjoyed our little chat that I neglected the reason for my call in the first place. You see, I am leaving the country soon and I wanted to make sure I didn't leave you with any concerns. Young Abby was a wonderful specimen. I was happy to learn from the physicians that she will be fine."

Josh struggled to control his anger at the thought of what Abby had been through. It made it personal, but the information confirmed all his suspicions.

"A beautiful young girl," Sullivan continued. "Far more intellectual than the others. She was to embark on a mission with me to change the world. How sad she must now pay the price of being not a martyr, but a tragic waste of life."

"If you come near her..."

"I am near her!" Sullivan interrupted. "And I know where you are."

Just then the driver side window smashed and Josh was struck on the head by shards of glass and the end of a crowbar. He was thrusted down to his right. A second swing into the car landed a blow onto his left shoulder. Josh groaned in pain, then looked out the window to see the man readying for another swing. He recognized him, Gordon Chase. He managed to release the door latch with his left hand and plunge down into the passenger seat just as the third blow was coming, avoiding most of its impact, a portion hitting his left arm a second time. Just then, he kicked the driver's door open with all his strength. The door hit the man in the knee, elbow, and face, taking him aback.

Josh pulled out his gun, but not before Gordie had done the same. Both saw the other with a weapon and opened fire prematurely.

BANG-BANG! The first two shots came almost simultaneously. Gordie's struck the steering column of the car, less than an inch away from Josh's right arm in which he held his gun. Josh's shot ended up in the ceiling of the parking garage – not having turned far enough in time to hit his target.

Gordie stumbled backward toward the rear of the car, then stood up and fired into the back of the car three more times shattering the rear window.

"Stop! Police!" shouted Officer Balogh who had bolted from the hospital door upon hearing the shots. She aimed her weapon at Gordie. He turned and fired, hitting her in the chest. The impact resulted in the discharge of her weapon in Gordie's direction, but it missed him by several feet. Officer Balogh fell to the ground as additional officers began rushing out of the hospital.

Gordie took to his heels and ran off. He escaped in a waiting car which drove him a block away where he exited and hailed a cab. There was no movement from Josh's car.

58 – Chicago

"What is going on?" Molly asked as Anita started her car, seemingly in a hurry.

"What did he tell you?" Anita asked.

"He busted in and woke me up to tell me to get dressed, that we're going to a party," Molly said, her English accent taking on a more disgusted tone.

"Hm," Anita thought for a moment. "A party indeed? Well, I suppose that's one way to put it."

"What do you mean?"

"Don't worry dear. The doctor will be here very soon. We had to get you over there, right?

"We? What do you mean?"

"Nothing, don't worry. Just that the doctor has been urgently called out of town tomorrow, but he agreed to meet with you tonight. He's attending a party, that's all he meant. Still, I would have come up with a better excuse than a party!"

"I'm not so sure. Gordie doesn't pass up such things." Molly said as she looked out the window at the Chicago skyline. "It's beautiful at night."

"You know, I am really going to miss our little chats," Anita said. The subtle nature of her comment stuck with Molly. She then added almost sarcastically, "It has been such a treat to take you all around the city for the past few days." She then forced a fake smile to Molly, who started to take note of where exactly they were and where they were going.

"Well, I hope that someday I'll have the chance to return your kindness. Should you ever pay a visit to London."

"Oh yes," Anita feigned interest, "that does sound wonderful doesn't it."

The car pulled into the Essex parking garage. Anita parked on the top level and the two exited the vehicle.

"Now, stay close and follow me." Anita instructed. "Don't look anxious! Remember, you're a guest and about to have a great time."

Molly forced a quick smile and as soon as Anita's back was turned she also rolled her eyes. The two entered the hotel and proceeded to the elevator. The doors closed and Anita swiped a key card through a card reader on the control panel enabling her to press the button for access to the 8th floor. The car moved upward rapidly. Molly tried to hold still, but her eyes were darting around the car: a dinner menu, an advertisement for the Field Museum, and Anita's face. She looked different than every other time they were together. She seemed nervous. The more she tried to conceal her nerves, the more obviously fake she became. Molly began to notice very subtle things now, like how Anita was perspiring, and her upper lip so neatly painted a dark, saucy red, was quivering ever so slightly. She was swallowing frequently, and her fingers were twitching.

The elevator doors opened on the 8th floor. Two large men in business suits were sitting on chairs opposite the bank of elevators, a small round table between them. As they stood up, Molly noticed the man on the left had a gun concealed in a holster under his jacket.

"Good evening gentlemen," Anita began, putting out all her charm. "I had no idea we were going to be welcomed by two, amazingly handsome men!" she smiled and extended her left hand to one, her right one to the other.

"Madam," the one of the left said. His tone and demeanor was extremely serious. Anita's flirtatious powers were seemingly having no effect whatsoever. "This floor is restricted," he added.

"Lew, is it?" Anita asked.

"Mam," he responded.

"This is a special guest of Mr. Zhukov. I'm sure he's told you."

"No mam, he hasn't. Who is she?"

Anita turned to Molly as if it was clearly now her turn to speak. "My name is Molly Wheeler." The two men just stared as if there was supposed to be more. After an uncomfortable moment Molly added, "I'm visiting from London with my boyfriend." Still no response. "His name is Gordie Chase."

"He sent you?" the man asked.

"Yes. He did," Molly answered sweetly.

The man looked back at Anita who resumed her smile. The man nodded to his left indicating that he would allow them to continue.

"If there's ever a way I could repay you, all you have to do... is just say so." She reached up and stroked his right cheek as they began walking away down the hall.

They reached room 804. Anita pulled out a stack of card keys and began trying them one at a time. Finally, after three failures, the fourth card unlocked the door and they went inside. Anita immediately walked over to the phone and picked it up. She checked for messages, listened for a moment, then hung up the phone. She then turned to Molly and said, "Everything is fine. You're safe here. Just wait until I come back for you." She walked to the bathroom and quickly checked her hair and make-up. As she headed toward the door to leave she stopped in front of Molly and looked at her gravely. "Do not leave."

Anita opened the door and left the room. Molly walked slowly toward the door and attached the chain lock. As she did so she noticed her hand was trembling. Nothing about this situation felt right. She slowly made her way across the room toward the window and looked out into the darkness of the lake beyond. She noticed her reflection and began to wonder how she had gotten there. How had it all come to this.

59 – Chicago

The door handle clicked and slowly began to turn. It seemed like slow motion. The door was heavy and took a little effort to push open. A blast of cold air from the room hit his face as he scanned it. A recliner sat ready, facing out toward the window and opposite the door. An I.V. bag hung and an instrument tray was laid out on a table next to the chair. A single lamp in the corner was illuminated. And finally, on the bed he could see a pair of sensuous legs resting comfortably. He walked in and shut the door behind him.

"You should never keep a woman waiting darling." Anita said, then took a sip of the drink she had made to steady her nerves.

Dr. Sullivan looked around the room and into the dark empty bathroom. "Where is she?"

"We have a problem," Anita said calmly, then took a large sip. She looked as if all was lost.

"What? The girl?"

"They got to her before I did. Said they wanted some collateral to be sure it all worked. They still think you have the other girl, Abby." Anita stated.

"What? Collateral?" Dr. Sullivan stood in amazement. "Damn Russians! That was never part of the deal. Why the hell do they think she matters to me anyway?"

"She is Gordie's girl. Perhaps this is more about him than you."

"But I need her! Here! Now! For this to even work!" Dr. Sullivan began to panic. "We must complete the implantation by dawn in order to catch the flight out and get to Moscow on time. How do they expect me to finish this?"

"They expected we would be using the other girl!" Anita slammed her glass down on the nightstand, spilling much of what was left of its contents. "What are we going to do?" There was a long silence. Sullivan paced a few times slowly, then sat on the end of the bed.

"There is one thing…" Anita began. "The only thing I can think of to do," she said. "You can use me."

"What?" Dr. Sullivan said in astonishment.

He turned around slowly and looked at her from the corners of his eyes. He looked pained at the thought. Anita's eyes widened, her face turned pale and she wore an expression of despair at the idea of being subjected to the Sapphire drug and mechanism. He pondered it for a moment.

"Oh no, my darling," Sullivan quickly reassured her after seeing her dreadful expression. "I wouldn't dream of asking you to do such a thing."

Anita sat up straight and took a deep breath. She then crawled over to Sully and wrapped her arms around him.

"Oh my dear! You know I would do anything for you, absolutely anything! But thank you. Thank you for not putting me through such an ordeal." He patted and squeezed her hand which was over his chest, reassuring her as she kissed his neck and ear.

"You have given so much of your life to this cause, Sully. I'm so sorry. I just don't know…" she began a pitiful sob on his shoulder. "You just don't deserve this. You are such a brilliant man, so close to greatness and immortality! Just so close!"

"So close," he repeated.

"I know there must be something. Destiny will not do this to us… to you! But we're leaving for Moscow in a matter of hours… I just don't…" she continued her caressing, kissing, and whining.

Dr. Sullivan pushed his thin glasses further up onto his nose and turned away from her saying, "I will do it myself."

"What? No Sully!" Anita scantly protested.

"Yes. It is the only way now. They wrote the encryption sequence that must be extracted in Moscow. If we don't deliver it they will kill us anyway. I won't let that happen to you, my dear. As for the code, I couldn't have seen much less memorized it. No human could. Yes, it will still work."

"But you're the doctor! You can't perform this process on yourself! How do you plan on…" Anita paused. After a moment she continued, "I could do it," she said confidently.

"Yes. You could!" Sullivan echoed. "You've seen it done a few times now and I will arrange for the sedative to be a bit milder so I can talk you through the initial steps." He stood up and removed his coat and dress shirt. "My brain may not be the optimum physical specimen, but since it is a willing one, I believe it will work."

"Oh Sully, your mind is the most insatiable part of you! But are you sure?" Anita asked in a concerned tone.

"Yes," he answered confidently. "I was able to confirm at the hospital that the girl suffered no adverse effects whatsoever. The formula was perfect! And the process is not difficult." He stopped and turned toward Anita, taking her by the shoulders and pulling her close to him. "Are you sure you're okay to do this?" He looked at her with great concern for her well-being.

"I will do anything for you Sully," she glowed in return and kissed him passionately.

"You are an amazing woman." He smiled, then walked over and powered up the computer. "And Mr. Decker is no longer a concern."

"What happened?" she asked.

"He's been... incapacitated, if not worse." He answered with a somewhat depraved smirk. He then prepped the sensor pads and conduits, the I.V. solution and anesthesia. Anita watched carefully throughout the entire process. Finally he looked up at her and said, "I'm ready."

He took the Sapphire blue oval flash drive from his pocket. The key to accessing the Sapphire program and the Russian encryption code. It had never been out of his possession. He handed to Anita saying, "The first step toward my destiny and immortality."

"Your dream, my love," she said taking the Sapphire key from him. She then put on a pair of latex gloves, as Sullivan took his seat in the recliner. He reached over and inserted the I.V. himself. The narcotic began to drip from the I.V. into his system and he became sleepy.

"Sterilize the area before you insert the probe needle," he instructed.

Anita sat beside him and picked up the long, thick needle that would be inserted just behind his jaw, upward and just far enough to touch the cerebral cortex.

"Once this is in, you must hold very still," she instructed.

"I will not flinch, my dear," he said, looking up into her eyes. He could feel the drug had begun having a greater effect. "Put in the key now," he instructed.

Anita complied, reaching over him and inserting the flash drive into the computer. A tone indicating that the device had been recognized sounded and the command menu appeared on the screen. She placed the sensors onto his head and clicked on the button which ran an initial test. A few seconds later another tone sounded, indicating that the sensors were functioning perfectly.

"Excellent," Sullivan said. "Let destiny be fulfilled. In the name of progress," he said nobly.

Anita wiped an alcohol pad over his skin and slowly began to insert the probe. Sullivan perceived an incredible sensation once the probe touched its destination. It was as if there were electrical fireworks shooting throughout his brain, and a sensation of light, sound, and sensual feelings flooded his awareness simultaneously. He gave out a moan and lifted slightly from the back of the chair. Then all receded and he returned to a state of rest.

"That's…. it…" he said slowly.

"Yes, my dear. I'm afraid that is it." Anita leaned over top of him so that his eyes would be trained onto her breasts. He slowly looked up from there and saw her necklace, a string of sapphires he had given to her, sparkling in the light. Then he heard her voice.

"Sully dear…" she said. Fighting the sedative he looked up and into her eyes. They were different now. Cold, blue eyes staring down at him like icicles.

"Did I ever tell you about the first time I ever saw a sapphire?" she asked. He was unable to answer. His eyes flinched his response. "My father held me on his knee and showed me all sorts of gemstones. He explained their power. What they really mean when one would give them to another. Like you gave these sapphires to me. The stone itself is just a rock. But those whom they adorn are granted power over others. The giver becomes submissive in the end. Never knowing what a fool they've been to give it away in the first place. And for what? A little tenderness?" she stroked his hair. "A cheap hooker can do that. But the precious stones, they are a symbol of strength, influence... and power. The power to win in life. To be the favored and the chosen. The power to force others to kiss your ass!"

Confused and concerned, Dr. Sullivan tried to lift his arm but it was as if a hundred pound weight was resting on top of it.

She leaned closer to him and whispered, "I have always had the power. I get what I want, my dear. I always have. And I always will. By whatever means necessary."

She reached over to the I.V. and began to squeeze it forcing additional sedative into his bloodstream. He reached up with all his might in an effort to stop her. His right hand grasped her left arm tightly. Anita's lips tightened with stern resistance and her eyes narrowed with the upmost of tenacity. His face convulsed in terror, his eyes pleading with her, begging her to stop.

"Goodbye my dear Sully," she said as she squeezed harder on the I.V. bag. The sorrow in his eyes was unmistakable. "Don't be like that sweetie," she said. "I'm giving you what you always desired." Then she leaned over and kissed him on the edge of his lip and his cheek. "Your immortality." She squeezed the bag again and Sullivan convulsed in pain. She looked straight and deep into his dying eyes as if to glimpse the moment when death eclipses life.

Sully's grip on Anita's arm languished and gave way, falling back down to his side. He made no further movements. Anita turned and picked up a second syringe and filled it from the small bottle of the sedative. She then injected the entire lethal amount into Sullivan's right arm, just to be sure. She waited a minute, then took his pulse. It was over.

She stood up and closed the laptop computer. She pulled out the sapphire blue oval flash drive and placed it securely in her bra, then turned toward the window overlooking the lake. She took a moment to admire her reflection, touching up her hair a bit. The sunrise was just beginning to overtake the clear horizon with a mixture of magenta and violet.

She took up her phone, texted a message: 'it is done,' and waited for a reply. The notification sounded and it read, 'Meet me as planned.' She packed the computer into its carrying case, swung it over her shoulder, put on her heels, and departed the room leaving the 'Do Not Disturb' sign on the door handle.

60 – Chicago

His phone rang. He had been waiting for the call.

"Yeah," he answered.

"Where is Decker?" Zhukov's thick Russian accent poured through the speaker.

"He's in the hospital," Gordie answered.

"Did you finish him?"

"Yeah, I don't think he's gonna make it."

"I hope not. Our deal with the Doctor is over."

"What?" Gordie asked.

"He's dead."

"I didn't off him," Gordie said defensively.

"We found two of our guards dead and the Doctor. Someone talked to the Americans, or British. Do you know who?"

"Not me, Zuk. I've been tracking this Decker bastard all night."

"Well, we have invested hundreds of thousands of dollars and now the whole damn thing is missing! That means I will have to face the creditors myself. So I want answers!" Zhukov shouted losing his calm demeanor on the phone. "Get me the laptop and the Sapphire encryption key. Clean things up. I meet you in Moscow! You can start with your girl."

"Was it her? Did she fucking talk?"

"Doesn't matter. She knows enough. She must have had contact with someone for them to track you there! We know British Intelligence is in Chicago now. She could've brought them."

"Don't worry. I'll rip her fucking tongue out!"

"No. Bring her to Moscow. We will find out everything she knows and then begin our own experiments with whatever's left of her."

"I still get paid, right? I did my job."

"You're job isn't finished," Zhukov said. "If she won't go quietly, then kill her. And the doctor's blonde lover. Kill them both, get me the 'Sapphire,' and then get to Moscow." Zhukov hung up the phone.

61 – Chicago

Dawn had broken and Molly found herself awakened by the bright sunlight peering into her room. She was still dressed for the evening in her black strapped dress, but had fallen asleep waiting for Anita or Hawks to retrieve her.

'Maybe they've forgotten about me? Or something has happened,' she wondered. The room had been cleared of virtually any identifying items. There was no television, no complimentary soaps with the hotel name embossed on them, nothing except a short menu of food items listed on a plain white sheet of paper.

Molly was hungry, looked at the menu and decided to call the number listed. The line rang several times until it was forwarded to a voicemail box that had no outgoing message. She hung up the phone. She went to her bag and removed her purse. She put on her heels and slowly opened the door. It was then that she realized that she didn't have a key to get back inside. She turned the security slide on the inside of the door and used it to prop it open so she could return. She walked down the hall.

As she turned the corner toward the elevators she saw the two men from the prior night, slouched over in the cushioned lobby chairs, covered in dark red blood. They were dead, blood having ran from their chests down onto the floor.

Molly's face turned white. She wanted to scream but she had no voice. She covered her mouth with her hands and frantically ran back toward her room. She barged in and ran to the bathroom, vomiting into the toilet. She soon recovered, trying hard to keep calm. She reached into her purse for her phone and dialed for Hawks.

The phone rang and rang, but there was no answer. Suddenly she heard loud men's voices in the hallway. They were coming from far down the hall and were soon gone. She tried Hawks again. Still, no answer. Then she began to rummage through her purse, looking for the white card Josh had given her. Even though she didn't know him, he was now her only hope.

"No, no, no..." she whispered out loud to herself. "I didn't throw it away!" she worried. Finally, she dumped the contents of the entire purse out onto the floor. The card fell in front of her knee. She picked it up and dialed.

62 – Chicago

He groaned from the stinging of iodine on his temple as the nurse prepared the sight for a small suture.

"There, there…" she said. "That wasn't so bad."

Josh found the words less than comforting, reminding him instead of his reoccurring dream. A dream in which he felt helpless, not unlike his present situation.

"Okay Josh, I have something for you," Marty announced as he entered the room.

"Is the officer ok?" Josh asked.

"Yes. It was close, but she was wearing her vest and should be ok."

"Good."

"Not bad for a rookie only a few months on the job, wouldn't you say?"

"Yeah, I guess so." Josh responded wanting to get past the small talk. Marty stared at him for a moment. "I'll be sure to stop in and thank her." He added.

"Good. She just saved your life and all, you know."

"I do know" said Josh.

"The man who shot at you, you say was this Gordon Chase?" Marty asked to confirm.

"Right."

"Well, he's a resident of Croydon, suburb of London. We have Scotland Yard checking into him more, but our friend over at the CIA believes he's working for a man named Valery Zhukov, a practitioner of human trafficking."

"Okay," Josh acknowledged.

"He hasn't been on the scene long though, there doesn't seem to be much more about him except the obvious that he's dangerous."

"Well, I let my guard down," Josh admitted.

"There you go." The nurse finished dressing the cut on the left side of Josh's forehead, proceeded to excuse herself and left the room.

"I was on the phone with him Marty. The good doctor himself."

"Must have been an interesting conversation."

"He's a mad man. But the kind with just enough power and influence to be extremely dangerous."

"What is this all about?" Marty asked.

"He's used the victims as guinea pigs for a mind reading machine. And the crazy things is, apparently it works."

"No shit?" Marty exclaimed.

"Well, it works well enough to get some basics apparently. But his victims have all died on him as a result of the procedure. From here I'm only speculating, but with the international connections popping up, I'm sure the technology has a much more practical use than his desire to preserve himself into a computer program and live forever. I'm thinking they all want it for interrogations and a sort of covert mind control. The ability to control a person through some sort of brain conduit eventually."

"Really? Sounds ridiculous to me. The guy has more than a few screws loose," Marty chuckled.

"They laughed at Edison and Columbus too, didn't they?" Josh pointed out.

"Well..." Marty was interrupted by the door opening. Josh leaned back to see around Marty.

"Good morning," said a fine English voice. "I'm not interrupting I hope?"

Josh took a long breath and said, "Marty, this is Hawks."

"Mr. Bowen," Hawks stated.

"Mr. Hawks," Marty replied.

"Could we have a moment?" Hawks asked, wanting to be alone with Josh.

Marty looked at Josh.

"It's fine," he said. Marty nodded and left.

"I heard about your run-in with our friend Gordie Chase. Don't say I didn't warn you."

"I like to think I was keeping him occupied so he couldn't get to his real target," said Josh.

"How is she by the way?" Hawks asked, referring to Abby.

"She's fine." Josh answered stoically. He didn't trust Hawks and was not buying into his sincerity.

"I don't believe there is any more reason to be concerned." Hawks paused and Josh looked at him intrigued. "Dr. Sullivan is dead."

"You?" Josh asked.

"No. But I have assurances."

Josh thought for a moment. "And you wanted to make the trip down here in person just to let me know?"

"You may find it hard to believe, but yes. I would also like to meet with you in a couple of days to... compare notes?" Hawks said. Josh gave no reply or indication of cooperation.

As Hawks turned to leave, Josh stopped him saying, "What about the girl?"

"The girl? She's here. She's fine," Hawks reminded.

"No, I mean the other girl. Molly. What about her?" Josh asked.

"With Sullivan dead she's in no danger," Hawks said.

"No danger? You don't really believe that."

"I'll make sure she returns to London."

"Oh will you now?" Josh began to stand up, the pain biting at his arm. He stumbled a bit, dizzy from the blow to the head. "Or are you still using her?"

"After that, she's on her own. As if none of this ever happened."

"But it did happen. The Russians know it and so does her boyfriend." Josh said in a condescending tone.

"Careful Josh," Hawks warned, feigning concern over his stumble.

"Does she even know why she's here? That you were using her?" Hawks offered no reply as Josh inched closer to him. "How much *does* she know? How far was she supposed to go? Did she know she was going to be hooked up to a mind-reading machine, injected with chemicals, subjected to a brand of torture? Used to transport information and be a sacrificial lamb for the cause of 'intelligence'?" Josh stopped inches away from

Hawks. They stood eye to eye, staring at each other like duelers in the old west.

"You really should not get so attached, Josh. It gets in the way of business." Hawks spoke calm yet sternly.

"That's why I'm not in your fucking business!" Josh snarled with contempt.

The two stood there for a moment, then Hawks raised an eyebrow and turned back toward the door.

"I came here to let you know. It is no longer your concern," he said sternly. Then, he opened the door and left.

Josh's phone began to vibrate. He removed it from his pocket and answered,

"Hello."

"Is this Mr. Decker?" an English voice said on the other end. The voice sounded terrified.

63 – Highland

"Well, I know he told me not to talk to anyone. But I thought I could tell you." Johnny said as he sat at the bar with a soda Charlie had served him.

"You can, don't worry." Charlie said.

"Do you think she's going to be okay?"

"I don't know. I'm not gonna make it sound like it ain't. Things look pretty bad son and you have some blame in that."

"I know." Johnny sighed and looked upset. "I've always been a wimp. I never meant to hurt her. I didn't know what they were going to do to her, I swear it."

"Maybe so. But you were there, you went along with it. You'll have to answer for it." Johnny began to tear up, his lips contorted downward as he tried desperately to hold back his emotions and keep up a tough front. "But remember Johnny, you can't change what's done. What counts now is what you do from this point on."

"They're gonna kill me." Johnny added as he sniffled. Charlie didn't know how to respond because he thought the kid might actually be right. Still, the act of contrition was sincere and Charlie felt badly for him. "So, what can I do then?" he asked.

"Right now? Just wait, like he told you to. When everything's settled down, we'll all have a talk."

Johnny nodded his head in agreement, then he noticed Charlie had a packed bag sitting behind the bar. He took a sip of his 7-Up and asked, "Are you going somewhere?"

"Ah... yeah. My brother is flying in and I'm off to pick him up in a few hours." Charlie was careful not to say too much, knowing Johnny's tendency to give up information under pressure.

"Where at?" the kid asked.

"Oh, ah... Detroit. In fact, I need to get going if I'm going to make it in time." He smiled and took out his keys preparing to lock up the bar.

"What am I going to do Mr. Webber? What if Derrick comes back again looking for me? I was just lucky this time. What if..." his strength trailed off.

"Listen, I'll have Dino keep an eye out on you. Maybe he'll even let you stay with him a couple nights, huh?"

"Really?" Johnny sniffled again. "You think he would?"

"I'll ask him on my way out."

"Thanks."

"Listen Johnny, coming here took guts. If you mean what you say, you'll have a friend in Josh Decker."

The kid looked up, still trying to project his tough exterior, but a glimmer of hope shot through his eyes.

64 - Chicago

"Is this Mr. Decker?" her voice trembled with fear.

"Molly?" Josh recognized her voice and accent immediately.

"Yes. I don't know what to do. I called him but he didn't answer and then Gordie called me and is looking for me, and I tried to leave but these men in the lobby are dead, and I'm trapped and they told me I should never call the police or I'd be in danger..." she rambled in the process of growing hysterical.

"Easy Molly, stop," Josh spoke firmly but calm. "Slowly now, tell me where you are."

"I'm not sure. We drove in from the back last night and I don't remember seeing a sign. I'm in a hotel, on the eighth floor near downtown. I can see the lake."

"Who were you trying to call?"

"A man named Peter Hawks. But there's no answer. He was helping to set things up. I was helping him I guess."

"Okay, relax," Josh said. "I know him. Look, you're going to have to trust me now, okay?"

"That is why I'm calling you, Mr. Decker. I have no one else." She covered the phone and allowed herself to break down for a moment in paniced tears. She quickly recovered.

"Now Molly, look on the phone in the room. Is there a directory that tells the name of the hotel?"

Molly looked. "No."

"Okay, what is the phone number listed on the phone?"

She read the phone number.

"And you're in what room?"

"803"

"Okay, good. I'm on my way to get you. Just stay there and let no one in your room, understand?" Josh did not hang up as he hurriedly left the examination room and headed down the hallway toward the hospital exit.

"Yes. How long will you be?" she asked, as calmly as she could.

"Not long." There was silence on the other end of the phone. "Molly?" Josh asked.

"Yes," she sobbed.

"I promise, I'm coming over right now."

"Thank you, Mr. Decker."

"Call me Josh."

"Thank you, Josh."

He ended the call. He was still feeling dizzy and there was a great deal of pain in his left arm from the blow with the tire iron. But he managed to whip past the police, who were still on sight, out into the ramp where he found Marty, obtained his car keys and, despite the damage, jumped into his car. He drove off and stopped just outside the parking garage. He called the phone number Molly had given him.

"Essex Properties, how may I direct your call," a pleasant voice answered.

"Where are you located?" he asked. She proceeded to offer directions. Josh made a couple of notes and ended the call. He reached under the passenger seat of his car and pulled out his second pistol. He dropped open the magazine to make sure it was full, then snapped it back into place, pulled back the slide and cocked the weapon. He then drove off in the direction of the Essex.

65 – Chicago

She set her coffee cup onto the saucer adding to the general sound of dishes clinking throughout the Yacht Club's dining room. Of course she realized the attention she was drawing, especially from the older male members of the club. The glances, the 'I sure wouldn't mind a bit of that' whispers, and even a few stares waiting for the inevitable eye contact when they would throw her a wink and a nod. And while Anita would typically return them with a sly smile and perhaps a raised eyebrow, this morning she paid them no attention at all.

"Sorry I'm a bit late," the gentleman said as he approached and sat down next to her. "A few business matters to attend to."

"That's fine. As long as everything has been arranged, Mr. Hawks," Anita said firmly.

"You do have it?" Hawks asked.

"I had a bit of trouble. The two guards securing the floor. You should know, in case there're any questions, that I had to... deal with them," Anita said, choosing her words carefully.

"I see. Any other surprises?"

Anita smiled and innocently said, "I don't think so."

"You are efficient."

"Now, I believe you have something for me?" she asked.

He retrieved an envelope from his suit jacket and slid it across the table to her. "Here is your new identity and bank account. You can check the balance of your account, the remainder will be there after you arrive. The rest of your backstory I'm sure you'll have no problem creating on your own."

Anita inspected the papers which included a birth certificate, passport, debit card, and a few other necessities. "You've been kind to me with regard to my age."

"Have I?" Hawks smiled. "And I believe you have something for me?"

Anita replaced the papers into the envelope and reached down into her blouse, between her breasts. She removed the

Sapphire blue oval shaped flash drive. She looked at it for a moment.

"I've worked all my life for power, Mr. Hawks. Thanks to this little 'Sapphire' and your government, I now have a great deal of wealth and independence. It is only the beginning of what I expect to be a long and illustrious career. My family has many important connections in Eastern Europe. I do hope we will have the opportunity to do business again in the future." She smiled seductively at him.

"Time is precious, Ms. Reynolds."

"As promised," she said handing the blue crystal drive over to him.

"Very good," he said as he stood up. "Your plane leaves at noon. I wouldn't miss it if I were you."

Hawks walked out of the dining room and into the foyer where Tina was waiting.

"Everything fine with the girl?" Hawks asked her.

"She's not there, Hawks," Tina answered in her Irish accent.

"What do you mean? I had her take the girl to our room at the Carlton."

"That's the one I checked. The clerk hasn't seen her, or Anita."

Hawks turned around to look for her in the dining room, but the table was empty.

"We need to find her, fast."

No sooner was Anita out of the club than she was into a private car and being driven to the airport. Along the way she took out her phone and texted: 'The girl is at the Essex, #803'.

'That will secure my departure' she thought to herself. She then opened the phone, removed the battery, and tossed the phone out of the window into the street where it was smashed almost instantly beneath the tires of the morning rush hour traffic.

66 - Chicago

Abby stirred from what seemed like an incredibly long and deep sleep. Still a bit unaware of her surroundings, she couldn't help but smile as she woke to a familiar face.

"Where's Josh?" she asked.

"He was here not long ago to check on you. He had some things to do," Charlie said.

"I need to see him."

"I know kiddo, he'll be back. How are you feeling?"

"I have a terrible headache," she said. "And I'm thirsty."

"Have some water." Charlie handed her a foam cup with a straw.

"Where am I?" she asked.

"Hospital. Chicago," Charlie answered. "Do you remember what happened?"

"No, not really. Everything's kind of a blur."

"It'll get better. You've been through a lot."

"Chicago?" Abby said to herself. "You came all the way here?" she asked.

"Josh asked me to come and keep an eye you. I guess he thinks you might run away again!" Charlie smiled.

Abby smiled and thought for a moment. "Am I in danger? Is Josh? He is isn't he? That's why you're here and he's not." She became anxious.

"No, no. You're safe. I promise," Charlie assured.

"And Josh?"

Charlie hesitated.

"Tell me the truth," Abby said calmly.

"I'm not sure. He's trying to get to the bottom of all this," Charlie said. "But listen, I know of no one better…" he wasn't able to finish. His affection for his friend was clearly evident. He smiled and squeezed Abby's hand. "I do know he wants you to get better in a hurry."

"I saw him. He was there. I heard his voice and he told me I was safe. I remember that," she said.

"Yes. Apparently they wanted to use you in some experiment. But Josh found you, and they had done nothing but keep you sedated. You are going to be fine."

"You sure?"

"Yes. Do you think Josh would've left your side if he thought otherwise?"

Abby finally cracked a smile. "I should hope not."

Charles laughed.

"I'm going to miss him," she said sadly.

"Where are you going?" Charles asked.

"I don't know. I've been thinking a lot though. I'm tired of running away. I want to be running toward something. I want to go back to school. There's no future for me in Highland that's for sure."

Charlie chuckled, "For a bright young woman like yourself, no way."

"There isn't much there I'd miss. No family, no friends," she paused. "I'd miss Josh, but I think I need to go. Look at the trouble I've brought him."

"You haven't brought him this trouble. You've been a bright spot in his life, Abby. He may never admit it, but you have."

"So have you," she returned the compliment. "You know, it's funny how things work out. When I ran away I hoped to catch a ride to Chicago, or St. Louis. Some decent size city where I could get a job and go back to school. I'd love to be a pediatrician. Caring for kids, you know?" Charlie smiled. "I could see that," she finished with a gentle smile. "And I have dreams of someday reaching Paris. I figured I could just get lost there for a while."

"That sounds wonderful, Abby."

"Yeah, but I don't know where to begin."

Charlie thought for a moment then said, "Well, I know someone who might be able to help."

"Who?" she asked.

Charlie shrugged, "Let me see what I can do."

67 – Chicago

'The girl is at the Essex, #803.' As soon as he read the text Gordie turned the car around and headed there. He arrived through the back service entrance and proceeded into the elevator. The button for the eighth floor would not answer, having been secured by the hotel management for their select guests. Gordie settled for the seventh floor and proceeded up. He exited the elevator and made for the stairway up the additional flight where he found the door to the eighth floor locked. He was calm, determined, and kept his sunglasses on as he partially jimmied the lock and then forced it open by thrusting himself against the door. As he walked onto the floor he immediately noticed the two guards who had been shot slumped in their chairs. Gordie looked around carefully, then walked down the empty hallway to room 803.

Molly heard a gentle knock and her head turned instantly toward the door. 'Who?' she thought, but did not speak. The knock came again, a little harder now. 'Mr. Decker?,' 'the maid?' she wondered. She took up her phone planning to call Josh when without warning the door blasted open as a result of a swift and violent kick! The noise seemed deafening and she cried out in fear, dropping the phone!

Gordie stood towering in the doorway. His face like an angry stone statue.

"You can scream. No one will hear you on this floor," Gordie said calmly. Molly was shaking with fear, her hands covering her mouth as if to hold in her anguish and to try to be strong.

"Why didn't you answer my calls, love?" he continued. "You knew it was me calling. What, don't you trust me?"

"I.. I.. didn't know... it was..." Molly stammered.

"They tell me it was you. You were the little snitch. They warned me, but I thought for sure the blond bitch was the one. But no, it was YOU!" he smashed his fist on the top of the empty television council and then whipped a set of four glasses across the room, shattering them against the back wall. Molly let out another shriek.

"Gordie no... I didn't do anything..." she begged.

"Oh no? The ol' man is dead. The guards are dead. And yet, you're still alive and well. How'd all that happen, eh?" With his right hand he pulled out a razor sharp six inch blade, it glistened in the light. She began to shake uncontrollably and fell to her knees.

"No, please! No..." she murmured. He stopped and stood right above her.

"I think I'm gonna enjoy watching you beg! You worthless little bitch!" With his left hand he grabbed her hair and pulled her to her feet. She let out a painful scream. He shoved her head down onto the desk, let go of her hair, and held her down by the neck with his left hand. Molly was openly sobbing, unable to contain herself.

"I tried to teach you!" he said. She suddenly struggled to free herself from his grip. He shoved his knee into her left side and placed her head back securely onto the desktop. "Like I did your friend! She got it. She behaved. But no, not you! You had to be a hero? Is that it? You want to be a fucking hero? Huh!!" he pounded the desktop hard, Molly shrieked loudly.

"Leave me alone you stupid son of a bitch!" she yelled at the top of her lungs in what she was sure would be her final act of defiance. He didn't react. He was through talking. He placed the blade under her throat as she faced the open doorway. It was at that moment she saw him.

"*I wouldn't do that...*" Josh stood in the doorway, gun drawn and aimed.

Gordie immediately pulled Molly up from the desk and wrapped his arm around her neck with the blade virtually piercing her throat, using her as a shield.

The moment that had haunted him for over two years now suddenly flashed through his mind all over again. It was as if time had frozen and before him stood that seventeen-year-old girl he had shot and killed as she too was being held at knifepoint. It was that moment of doubt playing over in his mind like a flash of lightning. Her face crystal clear again and she, like Molly, was calling for help.

'I didn't know...' the kaleidoscope of voices echoed simultaneously through his head.

'I want answers!' accompanied by screams...

'BANG!' the shot was deafening...

'He's under the gun...'

'What have I done? My God, what have I done...' It was my job to know.

'Gun? My gun... where is it?' the warm sloshing of blood flooding the floor again, his hands were soaked and warm...

'That didn't hurt much, did it?' she was so kind... innocent...

'That didn't just happen...' 'I want answers!' 'I didn't mean to...' 'I can't feel it! My gun, where...' 'hopeless... hopeless...'

'tis a fearful thing to love...' with this last voice, the entire vision that had lasted only a split second, suddenly collapsed like a wormhole in his mind. He felt his gun, securely in his hands. The room was clear. It was Molly, with her hands clutched against her attacker's arm, fighting for her life with the fear of death in her eyes, standing before him. It did cross his mind, 'should I take the shot?' But Josh did not tremble.

The moment seemed to crawl through time. Molly was struggling, Gordie wavering back and forth slightly to firm up his grip. A moving target, just like before.

After a moment of struggle, Gordie began to speak, "I'll kill her if you..."

Before he finished, Josh lined him up and, without hesitation, squeezed the trigger. The bullet struck Gordie instantly in the forehead, it was a perfect shot. He never had the chance to react. His head convulsed and he instantly fell backward to the ground, the knife falling out of his hand as he landed. Molly had been struggling and was also pulled down with him. As they hit the ground she sprung forward as Gordie's weight was suddenly released from her. At the same moment, she had let out another scream of terror.

Josh took in a deep breath and held it. Suddenly, he let it out again. Then he gasped for his next breath, before he began to start to feel normal. For a moment he wondered if he had hit his mark. The doubt flew into him like a sickly feeling, only to be flushed out as he heard Molly's cries. He moved into the room and using his left foot he slid the knife out of Gordie's lifeless hand, all the time his gun trained on him.

He slowly lowered his weapon and then quickly knelt down and embraced Molly. Still shaking, as if by reflex she wrapped her arms around him and clung tightly. Josh lifted her just enough to back up toward the doorway and away from Gordie's body. He stopped short of the door and remained kneeling with his arms around her securely.

"I'm here. I have you now," Josh repeated, stroking her hair. He could feel her entire body tremble as she slowly began to compose herself.

After a few minutes, she managed, in a horse and broken voice, to ask, "Is.. he... Is he dead?"

Josh paused and placed his hand on the back of her head. "Yes. It's over."

Molly began to cry, releasing all the fear and tension from her soul. It was a long, hard cry. 'Well deserved' Josh thought to himself. She buried her wet face into his neck and chest. Josh looked back across the room at the dead man and wondered if the beautiful life he now held in his arms had not just also saved his own.

68 – Chicago

"Abby's doing great," Charlie smiled as he held the phone. "How are you?"

"I'm okay," Josh said on the other end, with some thought and hesitation.

"She wants to see you... when you're done there."

"Marty has me tied up for a while longer. I'll stop in later this evening."

"Do you remember Al and Jenny?"

"Yeah, didn't he move his business to Milwaukee?"

"Yup. And she's a school teacher."

"Yeah?" Josh was wondering what he was getting at.

"Well, I think they're going to be her guardians. They're coming down to meet her and the social worker here at the hospital in a couple of days."

"Okay," he said in an unreceptive manner, still processing the news.

"You know, she has to finish school..."

"I know." Josh thought about it for a moment then added, "Thanks for looking out for her, Charlie. I appreciate it."

Although he was sincere, Charlie could tell he would miss her. He decided to change the subject.

"You learn anything new?" Charlie asked.

"Molly told me they wanted her to undergo a 'harmless' medical procedure."

"Harmless my ass," Charlie reacted.

"She was advised on the basics. A mind reading device, the idea of electrical waves and a sort of mind control experiment. Her boyfriend Gordie was getting paid to transport victims, dispose of them, and so on. Molly was MI6's way into their inner circle," Josh said with disgust.

"Good god, they are a dirty bunch. Both sides really," Charlie grimaced.

"She did mention that Hawks was after an oval flash drive that was blue and resembled a large sapphire gem. It contains the key for the Doctor's technology I'd imagine."

"What kind of technology?"

"Not sure. Software to interpret the brain waves perhaps. It seems the plan was to essentially implant and retrieve information on brain tissue as if it were a hard drive. And without the perfect combination of chemicals and this software, it would be completely undetectable. No one would be the wiser."

"Unbelievable!" Charlie was astonished.

"Anyway, they are finishing up here now. She'll need to stay here for a week or so until they're sure they have everything they need and that she'll be safe back home. CIA is involved now. Finally."

"Yeah."

"You know Sullivan told me it was all about progress. That you have to stay ahead of the wave in order to come out on the right side of history. But I don't know Charlie. Sometimes I think this whole world is madness and we're just in a struggle to stay sane for as long as we can."

"You could just be getting old!" Charlie broke the tension with his smart remark.

"Maybe. But I would love to get my hands on that flash drive," Josh finished.

"Another time perhaps. How is the girl holding up?" Charlie asked.

"Molly?"

"Yeah."

"Charlie..." Josh took a breath, "She is incredible. I've never met someone with so much strength. Having gone through what she just went through, I think she's going to be just fine. There's a lot of hope in her eyes." The phrase resonated with Charlie who smiled like a proud father. It was gratifying to hear it spoken by his friend. There was hope.

"Did you get a chance to talk much with her?" Charlie asked.

"A little." He paused and as if he was thinking out loud he added, "But I can just tell."

69 – Chicago

"You see how the light almost sparkles and dances as you move? It's less about the colours and the paintings themselves and more about how it manipulates the light." Molly explained as she and Josh observed the Chagall windows at the Chicago Art Institute. "I always felt like the art was in perpetual motion. That it moved with the sunlight, or the weather. If you focus on the light, it's never the same way twice." She chuckled, "I must be boring you."

"No," Josh answered. "Not in the least." She turned briefly to him and they smiled at each other. He noticed how the blue hues were occasionally interrupted by delicate rays of white and yellow light that flashed gently across her face and eyes. More impressive were the depth of her thoughts regarding the works of art. She saw things in them that others failed to see, including himself. A similar gift with which he was often credited as a detective.

"I've been amazed by stained glass windows since I was a child. My auntie would take me to different churches and point them out, telling me their stories. I don't know why I was drawn to them. They just seemed so alive, and hopeful, I suppose." Josh stood silently contemplating what she had said in the context of his own life. Always in motion, a motion designed to keep him from dealing with things. Finally she broke the spell, "Are you sure? I mean, I could be here all day!" Molly joked.

Josh turned to her. "Absolutely. You're wonderful company," he smiled.

She turned and paced a little back and forth, altering the shape and intensity of the illuminated glass. A moment later she turned to see if he was actually enjoying the windows. He had been. But every time she looked at him, a moment later he returned the glance with a sincere half smile, as if it was her attention he truly appreciated. They looked at each other for a moment, then she took his hand and led him to the next display.

A while later the two ended up talking over a cup of coffee at a café down the road, sitting inside due to the cold.

"I wanted to thank you, Josh." Molly began. "Not just for... but for this week as well."

"Well, I thought that while you were still here I should at least show you around," he answered.

"You're certainly a much better tour guide than Anita. She made it known how much of a burden I was to her," Molly chuckled.

"I'll still take that as a compliment," Josh grinned.

"Oh please do!" she added with a laugh.

A moment later Josh asked with concern, "So. How are you?"

She didn't immediately answer. He noticed how a few strands of Molly's hair were slightly blowing across her eyes as she stared downward toward her coffee. After a moment she took a short but deep breath and looked up at him. "I'm okay," she said. "At least..." she paused and looked over his shoulder at the café. People were standing in line, carrying on a friendly conversation. There was an old woman sitting nearby with her dog at her feet. The world seemed quite normal, but she was still not a part of it. She looked back into his eyes and said with confidence, "I will be."

"I know you will," he said. They both took a moment to sip their coffee.

"Did I show you?" she asked suddenly.

"Show me what?"

"The photo of my latest creation? A project I've been working on." she began going through her purse looking for the photo. "Here it is." She handed it to Josh.

He took the photo and looked at it deeply.

"It's not finished. Actually, it's in about a hundred pieces now. But I'm going to restart and finish it eventually."

"What happened to it?" Josh asked.

"He smashed it." He could see the disappointment in her face.

"It's beautiful, Molly." He nodded his head and continued to study the photograph.

"It came to me in a dream. I usually don't remember dreams, but this one was so vivid. The butterfly is a symbol of hope, bright and beautiful, trying to fly high and far away. But she's tied down by a string and doesn't understand why, or how. The world is like that really, placing you where it wants you to be. As free as we think we are, it can box you in without realizing it. I've felt like that a lot. Like I was just someone else's entertainment. But she continues to struggle. Maybe she's just naïve."

"Or she just has faith," Josh added. "The struggle to be free, to be who we are and nothing more. No matter what the world thinks of us. To be individuals with flaws and mistakes, but always sincere." Molly listened carefully as Josh described her sentiments and intentions with incredible accuracy. "You're right. The magic of this is in the light. She'll be in constant motion, never giving up. Strong, yet gentle. Determined." He put the photograph down and looked across at her. "Beautiful."

Molly's eyes moistened. She smiled and wiped them with a napkin.

"I'm sorry," Josh offered.

"No. No really, it's not..." she struggled. "It's exactly..."

There was a pause in the conversation before he continued, "So where are you going to have it displayed?"

"You're going to laugh." She rolled her eyes saying, "In a tavern."

"A tavern?"

"Yes!"

"Seriously? A British pub?" he smiled.

"Yeah, well, the owner is my friend's husband and she's making him do it!" They both laughed for a bit then silently sipped their coffee and looked out the window. It was cloudy, and a light rain was falling.

"I have nightmares," Molly said breaking the silence. "About him... about... things."

"I know," Josh answered.

"I scream but have no voice. I try to run, but I can't seem to move." Her lip began to quiver. Josh took her hand and placed it into his.

"You don't have to run anymore. You don't have to scream," he assured. "Now that nightmare is just a dream. An echo that will fade away in time."

"It's not hopeless," she said.

"No. Not at all. Actually, it's a good sign. Means you're human," he smiled.

"I'm so happy you're not a cynic."

The irony was not lost on him. "Some might disagree."

"I haven't seen it. Maybe you're just good at hiding it. No matter how dark things look, you find a way to help me be positive. All the questions they've asked me. "What did I know and when did I know it?'" She stopped for a sip of coffee then continued, "I've always believed that people are basically good. There is so much good in the world, but people hide it... like you do Joshua," For the first time in years he felt the touch of happiness again as Molly smiled and squeezed his hand. "How long are you staying?" her question had a hint of sadness at the pending answer.

"Marty tells me you'll be on your way in a couple of days. I'll see you off," he said. Molly nodded and sipped her coffee.

"Then what will you do?" she asked.

"Go home for a while. Charlie is set on making me Police Chief. I don't know."

"Well, I hope you get what you want," she said.

"Sometimes we tie ourselves down," Josh said, looking again at the photograph.

"More often then we realize," she answered. "Are you okay?" she asked.

After a moment he looked back up at her and answered, "I will be."

70 – Chicago

The theater was dark and the first act of *Rigoletto* had begun. Hawks sat patiently in the upper tier looking down onto the stage. He was near the back row and fairly isolated. He never turned his head as Decker approached from his right and sat down with one seat between them.

"I didn't know you enjoyed the opera," Hawks said.

"I don't. It gives me a fucking headache."

"Well, not my fault. This time, you called me," Hawks said, getting down to business. "I was just about to leave for England and I don't want to miss my flight."

"I don't want you to miss it either," Josh said. "I know you have the encryption key to the Sapphire program."

"I'm sure your American authorities have that good fellow," Hawks replied haughtily.

"Oh, I think we both know better than that," Josh said, looking straight at him. "Beautiful blonde, with a fondness for sapphires. How long was she working for you?"

Hawks finally turned his head to face Josh saying, "Well, I'm afraid you've wasted your money on these tickets, old friend."

"You left her to be used as a guinea pig you son of a bitch." Josh leaned over and spoke to him intensely with his teeth clenched. "You and your M.I. shit-for-brains set her up. An innocent girl to be used in order to test and then steal the technology. And if she survived you'd really be on to something. You'd even beat the Russians to the dance. And the beauty of it all is that if by some twist of fate the girl died, well, then you and your M.I. shit-for-brains colleagues could hold up your delicate, pasty white hands – clean as a whistle."

"I had an eye on her, Josh. I was lied to about her last whereabouts. But I was on my way." Hawks defended himself.

"You were late. Too late."

"Still, I never intended for her to be harmed," he said firmly.

"All you ever wanted was the technology for yourself, no matter the collateral damage. Then maybe someday, you all might share the precious 'discovery' with the hapless Yanks." Josh went on, "What was it, a little Cold War jealousy? Needed to have a little leverage in the EU? What?" Hawks continued to watch the entertainment on stage, then looked at his watch. "The funny thing is, despite all your clever cloak and dagger antics, you made it so easy."

"Well bravo to you," Hawks calmly replied in his dignified British accent. "You know Josh, despite what you may think, I've never underestimated you. In fact, of all the men I've ever met, you are the one who is the most true to his principles and himself. I trusted you tonight. You got me here, all's fair. But I don't have what you want."

"I think you do. And since the information on that little sapphire flash drive was written here in the United States, I don't think the British government would want to violate U.S. copyright laws now would they?" Josh said sarcastically.

"The key is no good without the computer program, Josh."

"I know that. I guess that just doesn't bother me."

"In the hands of the British government, an ally Josh, I assure you the technology can be learned and better motives applied to its use – if it is used at all."

"How comforting."

"You could always join us, you know."

Josh scoffed.

"I know your answer," Hawks continued, "So then you'll just have to trust me. Trust, Josh, is an important thing. Something in our business that doesn't come easy."

"Do you trust your new friend, Anita?" Josh asked. The question gave him pause. "I know she gave it to you."

"I do not trust anyone who will double cross another." Then he turned to Josh and added, "Don't you see? That is why I know I can trust you Josh. Because you will never join me." Hawks moved his hand slowly toward his coat pocket.

"Don't," Josh said, his eyes piercing into Hawks as the stage lights shifted from a bright white to a red-orange hue.

Hawks paused, trying to gage Decker's next possible move. "Do you know how Abraham Lincoln was killed?" Josh asked.

"I believe, he was shot," Hawks answered.

"In a theater," Josh added. Just then Hawks heard a click from over his left ear. It was very distinctive: the sound of a small Derringer pistol only inches from the back of his head. He slowly returned his hand to his lap, and smiled.

"I don't believe I've had the pleasure," Hawks spoke to the person holding the weapon.

"My name is Abby," she answered. "Copyright enforcement."

Hawks chuckled, "I see."

"Trust is a two-way street, Hawks."

"You're walking a very thin line my friend," Hawks warned. He opened his coat so Josh could see into the left side pocket. Josh nodded. Hawks then slowly took out a small manila envelope and handed it to him.

Josh opened it and removed the blue oval shaped flash drive. It was the original. He replaced it into the envelope and put it in his coat pocket.

"I'm sure I'll be hearing from your government on a proper, mutual use of the technology, since you don't have the computer program. All this effort is futile, Josh."

"We'll see. You know Hawks, you never would have been able to pull it off."

"What's that?" Hawks asked, playing along.

"The last time we were here. Your umbrella trick, the miniature silencer in your pocket, the red head and the ticket vender. I had you marked the whole time. If you ever come after me, it won't be so easy."

"If I ever come after you, Josh, you'll never know it," Hawks warned.

"I'll know. *Trust* me," Josh assured.

"Someday ol' chap. Perhaps we'll find out."

"One more thing. I want you to enjoy the show. The *entire* show." Josh insisted. "You'll like it. It's about a girl who sacrifices for someone she loves. Something refreshing for you to consider. Then, get the fuck out of my country."

Josh stood up and left.

"And will you be joining me for the duration my dear Abby?" Hawks asked, still facing the stage.

There was no answer. Hawks turned his head around, then stood up and looked about the entire back few rows of the house. He saw nothing. She had come and gone so stealthily that even he was thoroughly impressed. He sat back down and remained through the first act.

It was raining outside the theater. Josh said goodbye to Abby as Charlie picked her up for the drive to Milwaukee. They managed a long embrace.

"I love you Josh." She said.

"I love you too, Abby." He managed to finally say it.

With that she got in the car. He watched as they drove off. He thought about all she had been through and about all the other victims who were less fortunate. Standing alone in the rain he grew more and more angry. He removed the oval sapphire flash drive from his pocket, looked at it, and then dropped it onto the wet concrete. Then, in a burst of anger, he stomped on the 'Sapphire' with all his might, shattering it into pieces.

71 – Highland

"The job is yours," Charlie said as he handed Josh the badge of the Highland Police Chief.

"I didn't know I wanted it," Josh replied. "You put my name in anyway?"

"No. Dino did," Charlie answered with a smile. "I had nothing to do with it, I swear."

The two old friends spoke on the front deck of Charlie's second cottage, the one he'd occupied and had now turned over to Josh.

"Sure," Josh said suspiciously.

"It's true. Once Kel sent word he wasn't coming back in the spring, Dino asked about you. Hell, you know how he idolizes you. He wants to be the chief someday and he wants you to train him."

"He is a good kid," Josh sighed. "But I'm not really..."

"Josh," Charlie interrupted. "You need this. You need a purpose. When you retire from your calling, it's like losing an essential part of who you are. It's dangerous. And helping someone else along the way is meaningful." Charlie held out the badge once again.

Josh looked at Charlie and took the badge, "Ok."

"Good!" Charlie said and slapped him on the arm. "I'll let the town council know you accepted."

"When is your seat on the council up? I'm going to campaign hard for your opponent."

Charles laughed. "You'll have to wait another season I'm afraid."

"Thank you again for the cottage."

"No problem. I'm getting tired of the hike up here every day. I'd been thinking about converting the room over the bar for a while now anyway. It's just fine for me. And this is more suitable for you. I know how you like to be on your own."

The two sat in silence for a while. Charlie finished his drink and got up to leave.

"See you tomorrow chief?"

Josh looked at the badge he was still holding in his hand, shook his head and answered, "Yeah. See you tomorrow."

Charlie patted his shoulder and walked off to town.

The view from Charlie's second cottage seemed darker, even more secluded. The lake was not visible and he'd have to walk even further to get to his car. But the red orange glow of the sunset over the lake still shown through the woods as an evening breeze kicked up and rustled through the trees. Josh poured himself another drink and took his place on the deck dressed in a thick coat.

As he gazed off toward the sunset he was left wondering about many things, but mainly he noticed a distinct feeling slowly coming back over him, something he hadn't felt in quite a while. He took a few sips and it finally dawned on him. The feeling was loneliness. He had grown accustomed to having Abby around. He wondered how she was making out with her foster family in Milwaukee. He took a gulp of whiskey. Charlie was right. He was not the role model she needed to get her life on track. A moment later, he said out loud to no one, "We got him."

A couple of weeks passed and Josh's winter routine saw him grow more and more isolated. The new job would really not begin until springtime and he declined any additional consulting work that might keep him occupied elsewhere. He wanted to be alone.

He came across Charlie's old six string guitar. While Charlie had played for years, Josh knew only a few chords. Still, he would often sit on the front deck or in the living room by the fire and fumble around on the nylon strings. It seemed soothing if nothing else.

Often, he imagined Abby sitting next to him complaining about something she'd heard or asking him questions. Questions he never felt comfortable answering, until now. Now, he found himself answering these phantom questions out loud to no one. Even carrying on imagined conversations with her. He found it comforting, recalling echoes of their many conversations, as if she was still there speaking with him…

'It's not as nice as your cottage was,' she'd say.

"No. But it's not bad," he answered.

'What do they say? If you can't beat 'em, you might as well join 'em?'

"Join who?" he replied. His tone suggested that he was at yet another cross roads, a dead end in his life. The events in Chicago had changed him, but he was still sitting in the woods, drinking whiskey, and more or less right back where he had started.

'Change,' she said. 'You can't stop it. Everyone tries to fight it, you know? But no matter what we do, it just keeps going. Like waves on the lake.'

"It destroys." he responded after a moment.

'It creates.' she countered. 'Don't be a cynic. You deserve to see more than just this moment. Just this sky. Isn't it a shame that someone with so much more to give would rather leave the prophecy unexplored simply because he's afraid to learn that the story may not end happily ever after? But sitting here ensures only the world that might have been.'

He thought about it for a long time. He could hear her voice so clearly reciting, *"a fearful thing to love, to hope, to dream, to be… your laugh once lifted me… your word was gift to me… To remember this brings painful joy…. 'Tis a human thing, love, a holy thing…"* He missed her.

Then one evening, Josh walked into The Chance and took a seat at the end of the bar. Charlie was finishing up with a customer at the opposite end and soon walked over to greet his friend.

"How are you tonight, Josh?" Charlie bellowed in his usual manner. But as he drew closer he saw that he looked somber and pale. "You okay?" he asked.

"Charlie, have you ever… I mean…" he struggled for words.

"Hang on," Charlie stopped him and prepared him a drink. He had seen Josh in various states of emotion, but no matter how passionate or angry he was, he was always composed. But this night he seemed different. He seemed nervous. A flash of concern ran through Charlie's body like a static shock. "You look like you could use this." Josh took a gulp of whiskey and a deep breath.

"Have you ever had a hallucination?" Josh asked bluntly, looking downward toward the bar. Then he raised his eyes to gage Charlie's expression.

"Hallucination?" Charlie thought about it then added, "No. Dreams, nightmares, that sort of thing. Flashbacks." He paused and repeated himself as a question, "Flashbacks?"

Josh quickly shook his head and looked back down.

"But those aren't real," Charlie said.

"Neither are hallucinations," Josh added.

"What's going on?" Charlie asked, trying to get right to the point as usual.

"I've been talking to myself."

"That's not a bad thing."

"I've been talking to myself, but the voice I hear in my head that answers is Abby's. I can hear her as clearly as I hear yours," Josh told him somewhat anxiously. "We were talking. Like we always do. Or did." Charlie just waited and a long moment passed. Josh took another drink and sighed. He then looked up at Charlie as if needing a bit of reassurance.

Charlie gave a half-grin and answered, "You've just been through a lot, Josh."

"Yeah, a lot," he added. "People come into your life and then they go. Nothing changes." He kept his composure but looked back down at his drink again before adding, "She's okay?"

"She's doing fine. Al and Jenny tell me she's doing just fine." Charlie quickly reassured.

"For a moment, I ah... for a moment I thought I was really going crazy," Josh said.

"You care a lot about her," Charlie said with a smile as he leaned down resting his arms on the bar moving a little closer to Josh. "She's a good kid."

"You know Charlie," Josh said as he slowly raised his drink toward his lips, "We don't have a lot of time. Before you know it..." He didn't have to finish, he just took a long sip of whiskey. After another quiet moment passed, Josh looked up again at his friend and said, "I'm leaving for a while. There's something I have to do."

Charlie picked up the bottle and said, "One more for the road?" Josh smiled and nodded his reply. Charlie poured Josh a shot of whiskey, then one for himself. They toasted and drank together. The two friends had always had a bond of understanding to the point that more was said by their expressions than by their words.

Josh stood up, reached into his pocket and took out the badge. He placed it on the bar and slid it over to Charlie.

"Sorry," he said.

"I think I understand," Charlie smirked. "So, what's her name?"

He offered no answer and began to walk back toward the front door.

"Where you going?" Charlie asked. Josh paused, looked out the window for a moment, then back toward his friend.

"London."

Made in the USA
Columbia, SC
25 March 2018